Julia Justiss wrote her own ideas for Nancy Drew stories in her third-grade notebook, and has been writing ever since. After publishing poetry in college she turned to novels. Her Regency historical romances have won or been placed in contests by the Romance Writers of America, RT Book Reviews, National Readers' Choice and the Daphne du Maurier Award. She lives with her husband in Texas. For news and contests visit juliajustiss.com.

THE AWAKENING
OF MISS HENLEY

Julia Justiss

MILLS & BOON

First Published in Great Britain 2019
by Mills & Boon, an imprint of HarperCollins*Publishers*
1 London Bridge Street, London, SE1 9GF

© 2019 Janet Justiss

ISBN: 978-0-263-26935-2

MIX
Paper from
responsible sources
FSC™ C007454

This book is produced from independently certified FSC™ paper
to ensure responsible forest management.
For more information visit www.harpercollins.co.uk/green.

Printed and bound in Spain
by CPI, Barcelona

To the tireless Regency experts
of RWA's Beau Monde Chapter,
whose wealth of knowledge helps me avoid making
(most) historical mistakes. I appreciate you all!

Chapter One

'Who did you say was calling?' Emma Henley asked, looking up at the maid who'd interrupted her avid study of the new travel journal recently lent to her by her friend Temperance Lattimar, now the Countess of Fensworth.

'I didn't catch the name, miss,' the maid said. 'Someone important, which was why Lady Henley sent me to fetch you.'

For a moment, Emma considered refusing, then closed the volume with regret. 'Someone *"important"*?' she repeated under her breath. Why her mama continued to insist she receive visitors with her, Emma couldn't imagine. As she was now embarked on her fifth Season, it wasn't as if all the society doyennes hadn't had ample opportunity to look her over. And who of *importance* would call this early in the morning?

'Very well, Marie,' she said with a sigh, 'tell her I will be down in a moment.'

'You look right fetching in that new turquoise gown with your hair up in that twist of curls,' the maid said. 'I should think you'd want to be showing off to important visitors.'

'I do appreciate your efforts,' Emma said, smiling at the girl as she curtsied. Sweet Marie, she thought, watching the maid walk out, who in the face of all indications to the contrary, seemed to remain as optimistic about her charge's chances of marrying as Emma's ever-hopeful mama, despite the fact that Emma had gone through five years on the Marriage Mart still unwed.

Not that she hadn't had opportunities, she thought as she checked herself in the glass, tucking an errant pin back into her curls. But a lifetime of witnessing her parents' union, in which each spouse went their own way, had left her with little enthusiasm for the married state. Papa contented himself with his clubs and his mistresses, Mama with her admirers and her circle of friends. Added to that disinclination was the sad fact that her older sister had received all her mama's famous beauty, leaving Emma tall, plain and unremarkable, and the *happy* fact that an aunt had given her a competence that would allow her to remain independent without having to marry. Those two factors meant she was able to be as choosy about her prospects as a well-dowered Incomparable.

Confident she could avoid penury even if she didn't marry, she had not once been tempted to accept any of the several offers made to a girl her own mother described as 'not pretty enough to tempt a rake and not rich enough to tempt a fortune hunter.' Her sister, Cecilia, might have dazzled the son of a duke, but Emma knew well her tall, lanky figure, long, pale face and drab brown hair were unlikely to inspire a man with ardour. She simply refused to succumb to the traditional fate of a plain wife, contenting herself with home and children and looking the other way while her husband pursued prettier women.

No, she thought, smoothing the lace at her sleeves as she proceeded to the stairs, she wanted a much more interesting life than managing a household and keeping track of servants, nursery maids and a pack of squalling brats. Or filling her days with calls and shopping and her evenings with endless, and endlessly repetitive, balls, musicales and soirées attended by the same people doing the same things, year after year.

When her friend Temperance introduced her last Season to Lady Lyndlington and her Ladies' Committee, whose purpose was to write letters in support of the reforms introduced by her husband's group in Parliament, Emma felt she'd finally found her calling. Women might not yet be able to vote or sit in Parliament, but as a member

of the Ladies' Committee, she could do her part
for the betterment of her country.

Now, she wouldn't consider taking on the
burdens of marriage and motherhood unless her
spouse were a man of purpose like Lord Lyndlington, who believed a wife his equal and supported her involvement in the reform movement.

A rather unlikely prospect, she conceded with
another sigh. If only she could convince Mama to
give up her useless husband-hunting! But by the
end of *this* Season, if not before, she told herself
firmly as she reached the main floor and turned
towards the front parlour, she would dig in her
heels and simply refuse to go through another.
She would finally secure a home for herself and
her friends to share, where they could eschew society and devote their time to the political causes
they believed in so passionately.

'Not in there, miss.' Haines, their butler,
stepped forward from his post to arrest her progress. 'Lady Henley wanted you in the Green
Salon.'

'The Green Salon?' she echoed. 'Are you sure?'

'Yes, miss. She was quite insistent.'

Puzzled, Emma shook her head. Her mama
normally received 'important' visitors in the large
front parlour, the smaller Green Salon at the back
of the house, overlooking the garden, being reserved for calls by friends or for family gath-

erings. Wondering who might have arrived that would induce her mother to choose that more intimate space, Emma walked past the front parlour and entered the Green Salon.

Where she found, not Lady Henley and some bosom friend, but Mr Paxton Nullford, pacing nervously before the hearth.

Alarmed and irritated in equal measures, she whirled about, intending to immediately quit the room. Mr Nullford hurried over to seize her arm and prevent her escape.

'Please, Miss Henley, won't you allow me to speak?'

'That is entirely unnecessary, Mr Nullford,' she replied. 'I expect my mother must have encouraged you, but surely you remember that I have made it quite clear on several occasions that—'

'I know, I know,' he interrupted. 'But won't you hear me out? You may be…mistaken in what you think I intend to say.'

She wanted to snap back that there was nothing he could say that would be remotely of interest to her. But the earnest expression on his broad face and the pleading look in his watery blue eyes made her hold her tongue.

He might be stocky and stodgy, and not very intelligent—certainly, he seemed not to have taken to heart any of the repeated, quite definite indications she'd given him that she was not interested in his pursuit—but he was also inoffensive and well meaning. She couldn't quite bring herself to rudely dismiss him.

Maybe it would be better to let him come out with the declaration she'd been trying to avoid for the last month, turn him down with a finality even he must understand and be done with it.

'Very well, Mr Nullford,' she capitulated. Avoiding the sofa, where he might try to sit beside her, she took instead one of the wing chairs by the hearth. 'Say what you must. But please—' she held out a hand as he seemed prepared to lower his thick body to one knee '—say it standing or seated.'

He gave her a brief smile. 'Seated, then, like the sensible individuals we are.'

Please, Heaven, be sensible enough to depart quickly, she thought, not wishing to drag out what was certain to be an uncomfortable interview.

After choosing the wing chair opposite, he began, 'I know you have not...actively encouraged my suit.'

'Without wishing to be unkind, Mr Nullford, it would be more accurate to say I have actively *dis*couraged it.'

'True,' he admitted. 'Lady Henley explained to me that you have this...unusual aversion to marriage. But she and I both believe that, sooner or later, you will realise that, as a gently bred lady, marriage is the only option that will secure for you a comfortable future. Surely you don't intend to…to take up a *trade*? Hire yourself out as a governess or companion, or some such?'

'No,' she said shortly, irritated anew that her mother had discussed her future with a man to whom she'd given not a particle of encouragement. 'As my mother evidently did *not* inform you, I have funds from an aunt that will allow me to maintain a household of my own, without having to seek the sort of employment available to a genteel lady.'

'You are mistaken; she did tell me of your intentions. But you cannot have seriously thought through the consequences of such a choice. A single woman living alone, even with a companion? You would be thought such an oddity! I expect your family would continue to receive you, but over time, most of society would stop including you. She and I both fear that, as you grow older, you would find yourself increasingly isolated and, as your family passed, virtually friendless.'

Though Emma was reasonably confident she could build a full, satisfying life on her own, the niggle of doubt in the back of her mind made her hesitate.

And thereby missed the chance to interrupt before Nullford continued, 'I know you don't have any great enthusiasm for my company, but I don't think you...*dislike* me, do you?'

'No, Mr Nullford. In fact, if you cease to be a suitor, I think I could like you quite well,' she replied with a smile.

'That's a start. I think we could live...comfortably together. I know I'm not handsome, or witty, or clever, but unlike most of the unmarried girls I've met, especially the pretty ones, you've always been...too kind to show that you hold that opinion. Though you are far more clever than I am, you've disparaged marriage, but not the man,' he added with a slight smile.

Emma squirmed, feeling somewhat guilty. Though she might never, by word or implication, have *expressed* derogatory sentiments to him, she'd certainly thought them. Even as far as to mentally refer to him as 'Mr Null', devoid of looks, personality and wit.

However, having been disparaged herself by a society that prized beauty more than kindness or character, she felt an unwanted swell of sympathy for the earnest man before her.

And so she remained silent as Nullford continued, 'Society wouldn't consider me rich, but I have sufficient funds to maintain you in style, with Seasons in London and summers at my country estate. I can offer you respect, fidelity and the certainty that you can live out your life surrounded by the friends, family and society in which you've grown up.'

Despite her entreaty, at this point he came over, dropped down on one knee and seized her hand. 'Miss Henley, we are both sensible enough to recognise that neither of us are the sort to inspire… an all-consuming passion. But we could build a quiet, satisfying life together.'

Her sympathy evaporating, Emma wasn't sure whether she was more dispirited—or furious. A 'comfortable' life married to man who inspired in her nothing but a tepid respect wasn't any more attractive a prospect than becoming the neglected wife of a handsome man she desired. And though she'd always known in her heart that she wasn't pretty enough to inspire passion, it still stung to have him point that out.

'So you propose a marriage *devoid* of passion?' she flung back.

'Well, not exactly,' he tempered. 'Of course, I'd be prepared to offer you…' His words trailed off and his face went scarlet. 'The, ah, prospect of conceiving children.'

She might be an unmarried lady around whom no one discussed the details of the marital embrace, but having grown up in the country, she had a good notion of what it involved. The idea of submitting to such intimacy with a man for whom she felt…nothing seemed unendurable.

Especially since, if her thoughts strayed towards passion, a very clear image came to mind.

Struggling to banish the memory of Lord Theo Collington's handsome face and control the volatile emotions that made her want to scratch Nullford's eyes out, she pulled her hand free.

'While I appreciate the kindness of your offer—' *to this plain, unfortunate female who will never inspire passion* '—I cannot accept it. My helpful mother should also have informed you that I aspire to something different than the normal female role of running a household and raising children. I wish to be involved in political causes—indeed, I have already begun to involve myself. I doubt you would appreciate having a wife who abandons the domestic realm to go about speaking in public, or who writes letters to Members of Parliament urging passage of legislation restricting child labour and extending the vote. Activities for which, unlike marriage, I feel a *great* deal of enthusiasm. As I am already two-and-twenty, and well on the shelf, that enthusiasm is unlikely to dissipate at the prospect of remaining a spinster.'

'Political activities?' he echoed, a look of horror dispelling his expression of entreaty. 'Writing letters to *Members of Parliament*?'

'Yes. So you see, despite your and my mother's kind efforts to push me towards more traditional feminine pursuits, I am absolutely committed to a path of which you could never approve. Now,' she said, rising briskly and holding up a palm to forestall a response, 'I don't think any more needs to be said. Except,' she added as she gestured him to the door, 'that I am certain, with a little perseverance, you will discover another plain female much more amenable than I to settling for respect and a conventional future. Goodbye, Mr Nullford.'

Looking shocked and a little bewildered, her rejected suitor gave her a shaky bow and walked out.

Once the door closed behind him, a still-furious Emma blew out an exasperated breath. Mama had encouraged, prodded and harangued her towards marriage before, but to have prompted Nullford into a proposal—and so insulting a proposal—was outside of enough!

Too angry to want to confront her mother at the moment and too unsettled to return to her book, once she heard the close of the door announcing that her unwelcome caller had departed, Emma hurried down the hall and up to her room.

With Nullford's words having stirred up too many raw emotions, she needed to get away until she felt calmer. Since it was still early enough that Hyde Park should be devoid of society, she'd have Marie help her into her habit and go for a ride.

Marie, she recalled suddenly, halting in midstride, who had coaxed her to wear the new gown and let her hair be styled in a different manner.

Then there was Haines, who had known very well that it wasn't her mother awaiting her in the Green Salon.

Apparently the whole household had been complicit in luring her to that fiasco of a proposal.

Her anger deepening, she stomped up the remaining stairs. Her groom had better bring his best horse, because she needed to indulge in a tearing gallop.

Chapter Two

Running a hand over the stubble on his chin, Lord Theo Collington turned his horse down one of the pathways bordering Rotten Row. Despite not returning home until morning, he'd been too restless and out of sorts to seek his bed, deciding instead to order his gelding and head to Hyde Park for a ride while the park was still thin of company. He needed to think and he didn't want to encounter anyone who would require him to play the increasingly wearying role of the devil-may-care man-about-town.

Not that he had any viable alternative to evenings of gaming with his friends or nights spent visiting the opera, the theatre, or whatever select society entertainment he expected to be amusing. But of late, a vague discomfort had begun to shadow his pleasure in those activities. A long-suppressed sense that there should have been something more to his life.

Not the 'something more' his mama continually urged on him—which was marriage and the setting up of his nursery. Though he very much enjoyed the female form and figure, he hadn't yet encountered a woman *out* of bed who didn't, after a time, grow tedious.

Well, perhaps one, he thought, smiling as he recalled the sharp verbal fencing that occurred whenever he encountered Miss Emma Henley. Fortunately, however, that lady was as little interested in marriage as he was, so he might indulge in the delight of her company without raising expectations in either her or society that he had matrimonial leanings in her direction.

When it came to ladies, though, one thing he did know for certain. After the contretemps at the opera last night, his liaison with Lady Belinda Ballister was definitely over.

That resolution was the easiest of the conclusions he'd needed the crisp morning air to clear his head enough to make. Still, forcing himself to give up the admittedly exceptional pleasure the skilfully inventive Belinda had given him the last few months was a sacrifice heroic enough to deserve a reward. He'd allow himself a gallop before returning home.

Gathering the reins back in both hands, he signalled his mount to start.

Ah, now *this* pleasure truly never would pale,

he thought as the gelding reached full stride. His heart exulted with the rapid tattoo of the hoof-beats, the thrill of speeding over the ground, while the rush of wind blew the last of the brandy fumes out of his head.

This pleasure of another sort was, in its own way, nearly as satisfying as a rendezvous with the tireless Belinda. Maybe he ought to take up racing horses.

That nonsensical idea had him smiling as he rounded a corner—and almost collided with a rider galloping straight at him.

Both horses shied, fortunately to opposite sides of the path. It took him a moment to control his startled mount and bring him to a halt before he could turn to check on the other horseman.

Or rather, horsewoman, he corrected, noting the trailing riding habit. Noting also the expertise of the rider, who had quickly brought her own plunging, panicked horse back under control.

Straightening the shako on her head—the only damage she seemed to have suffered—the lady turned towards him. 'Lord Theo,' she said, the tone of her musical voice sardonic. 'I should have known. Who else could I have expected to almost run me down in the park?'

His spirits immediately brightening, he felt his lips curving back into a smile. 'Thank you, Miss Henley, for your solicitude in enquiring whether my mount and I sustained any harm in the shock of our near-collision. But then, what other lady might I expect to find galloping through the park like a steeplechaser?'

'Temperance Lattimar,' she tossed back. 'Although now that she's wed, she's generally too occupied with the business of being an earl's wife to have time to gallop in the park. One more good reason to remain single.'

'I agree with you there. But isn't it a bit late for your ride? You usually come earlier if you intend to race like a Newmarket jockey.'

He waited in anticipation, but she didn't rise to the bait, merely replying, 'True. Whereas you, Lord Theo—' she gave him a quick inspection '—appear to have not yet found your bed. Carousing late again?'

'As would be expected of the *ton*'s leading bachelor,' he replied, his smile deepening.

What a singular female she was, he thought, captured anew by the force of the intense hazel-eyed gaze she'd fixed on him. She was the only woman of his acquaintance who, rather than angling her face to give him a flirtatious look or a seductive batting of her eyes, looked straight at him, her fierce, no-nonsense gaze devoid of flattery.

'If I rode close enough, I suppose I would catch

the scent, not just of horse, but of your latest lover's perfume.'

Grinning, he shook a reproving finger. 'You know a gentleman never gossips.'

As she tilted her head, studying him, he felt it again—the primitive surge of attraction of a male for a desirable female. He'd been startled at first to have the plain woman society dismissively referred to as 'the Homely Miss Henley' evoke such a reaction. But though she possessed none of the dazzling beauty that had made her elder sister, 'the Handsome Miss Henley' a diamond of the *ton*, there was something about her—some restless, passionate, driving force he sensed just beneath her surface calm—that called out to him, as compelling as physical beauty.

Unfortunately, he reminded himself with a suppressed sigh, it was also an attraction quite impossible to pursue. A gentleman might dally with willing married ladies, but never with an innocent.

He'd have to content himself with indulging in intellectual intercourse. A delight in which Miss Henley was as skilled as his former lover was in dalliance.

'Then I shall not *press* you for details, but send you off to your bed,' she said after a moment, the trace of heat in her gaze sending another wave of awareness through him.

Did he only imagine it, or did that comment imply that she, too—virginal maiden though she was—envisaged beds and a pressing together of flesh when she focused so intently upon him?

'I shall resume my interrupted gallop,' she continued as he sat speechless, distracted by that titillating speculation.

'This late in the morning?' Dragging his mind from its lecherous thoughts, Theo turned his attention back to the lady—and frowned.

Miss Henley's face, normally a long, pale, unremarkable blank, was flushed. Her jaw was set and those exceptional hazel eyes glittered with more than usual fire.

Even more unusually, he realised, she was completely alone. Though Miss Henley often scoffed at society, she usually followed its conventions, which forbade an unmarried lady of quality from going anywhere unaccompanied.

'Something *happened* this morning, didn't it?'

Though she shook her head in denial, her quick huff of frustration and a clenching of her teeth belied that response.

'Come now, give, give! Your groom is nowhere in sight, which means you must have outridden him, and no one attends you—not even the *very* attentive Mr Null.'

Her flush heightened. 'It wasn't well done of

me to have dubbed him that. And I should never have let you trick that name out of me!'

'Ah, but the description is so apt, I would have tumbled to it myself, had you not beaten me to it.'

To his surprise, she lifted her chin and glared at him. 'You shouldn't mock him, just because he is not handsome and clever and irresistible to women, like you are,' she cried, her tone as angry as her expression.

'I don't mean to mock,' he protested, surprised by her vehemence. 'But even you admit he has the personality of a rock.'

'Even a dull, ordinary rock has feelings.'

'I imagine it does—and has as much difficulty expressing them verbally as Mr Nu-Nullford. Why this sudden concern? I thought you'd been trying to *avoid* the man! Surely you haven't suddenly conceived a *tendre* for him!'

'No, of course not.' The fire in her eyes died, leaving her expression bleak. Breaking their gaze, she turned her horse and set it to a walk—away from him.

'You should know you can't be rid of me that easily,' Theo said, urging his mount to catch up with hers. 'Come now, finish the conversation. If you haven't inexplicably become enamoured of Mr Nullford, why this sudden concern for his feelings?'

As she remained silent, her face averted, an

awful thought struck, sending a bolt of dismay to his belly.

'Has your mama been after you again to marry? Surely you don't intend to give in and *encourage* his suit!' When she made no reply, he prodded again. 'Do you?'

'No, of course not,' she snapped, looking goaded. 'If you must know, he made me an offer this morning. I refused it.'

'Ah,' he said, inexplicably relieved. 'That's the reason for the ride. Avoiding what will doubtless be your mama's attack of the vapours once she learns you've turned down another offer. How many will that make?'

'Far fewer than the number of women you have seduced,' she retorted.

He laughed. 'Probably. Although, I should point out, I've never seduced a lady who didn't wish to be seduced.'

'Why do I let you trick out of me things I should never admit? And cajole me into me saying things I shouldn't?'

'Probably because you know I will never reveal the truths you—and I—see about society to anyone else.'

She sighed. As if that exhale of breath took with it the last of her inner turmoil, she turned back to him with a saucy look. 'You deserve the things I say that I shouldn't, you know. Like the very first time you deigned to speak with me.'

He groaned, recalling it. 'Very well, I admit, you showed me up on that occasion—which was most unkind of you!'

'You shouldn't have pretended to remember me when clearly you didn't.'

'One could hardly admit to a lady that one doesn't remember her. I was trying to play the Polite Society Gentleman.'

'No, you were playing Ardent Gentleman Trying to Impress a Dazzling Beauty by Pretending to Know her Plain Friend,' Miss Henley shot back.

'Well, even so, it wasn't nice of you to embarrass me in front of the dazzling Miss Lattimar.'

She chuckled—a warm, intimate sound that always invited him to share in her amusement, even when it was at his expense. 'It did serve you right.'

'Perhaps. But it was a most unhandsome response to my attempt to be chivalrous.'

'If I am so troublesome, I wonder that you continue to seek me out and harass me. Why not just cut the connection?'

'Don't tempt me! But every time I contemplate giving you the cut direct you so richly deserve, I recall how singular you are—the only woman in society who doesn't try to attract my attention. Who says the most outrageous things, one never knows about what or whom, except that the remarks will not adhere to society's polite conventions—and will be absolute truth. A lady who, most inexplicably, appears impervious to my famous charm. I'm always compelled to approach you again and see if you've yet come to your senses.'

'Why, so you may add me to your harem of admirers?' she scoffed. 'I shall never be any man's property. But all this begs the question of why, if you were merely returning from a night of pleasure, *you* felt the need for a gallop.'

He hesitated, knowing it would be better to say nothing. Yet he was drawn to reveal the whole to perhaps the one person with whom, over the last few months, he'd inexplicably come to feel he could forgo the façade and be honest.

'Come, come, bashful silence isn't in character! You bullied me into revealing *my* secret. You know I won't stop until I bully you into revealing yours.'

'You are a bully, you know.'

'And now who is being unkind?' she tossed back, grinning. 'So, what is it? Have the Beauteous Belinda's charms begun to fade?'

He gave her a severe look. 'You know far too much about discreet society affairs about which an innocent maiden should be completely unaware.'

'Oh, balderdash! Even innocents in their first Season gossip about your exploits. Besides, I'd hardly call the liaison "discreet". The Beauteous Belinda was boasting at Lady Ingraham's ball just two nights ago about what a skilled and *devoted* paramour you are.'

'Was she now?' he asked, feeling his jaw clench as fury smouldered hotter. He should have broken with the wretched woman weeks ago. 'Then you haven't yet heard about the most recent incident. Last night, at the opera.'

Her teasing expression fading, she looked at him with genuine concern. 'That sounds ominous. Did she finally try to demonstrate her supposed control over you *too* outrageously?'

He envisaged the scene again, struck as much on the raw by the succession of disbelief, then discomfort and then rage as he'd been when the episode unfolded. 'All right, I concede that I probably should have reined in Lady Belinda long ago. It…amused me when she boasted of having me "captivated". I thought, apparently erroneously, it was a mutual jest, both of us knowing the connection was as convenient as it was pleasurable, with no serious commitment on either side. But for her, on one of Lord Ballister's rare forays into society, to desert her husband, track me down in the box I was sharing with friends and remain there, hanging on my arm, trying to kiss and fondle me in full view of the audience—and her husband! It was outside of enough!'

'Oh, dear,' Miss Henley said, her gaze surprisingly sympathetic. 'That was not at all well done of her.'

'I can appreciate that she wasn't enthused about wedding a man thirty years her senior. A discreet affair, quietly conducted, is understood by all concerned. But though he may be elderly and often ill, Lord Ballister is an honourable gentleman of excellent character. He didn't deserve to be made to look the cuckolded fool so blatantly and in so public a forum.'

'No, he did not. But honestly, I'm surprised it took you this long to notice how flagrant she has become. She's been singing the aria of your enslavement at full voice for months now.'

'Have I truly been that blind?' At her roll of the eyes, he sighed. 'I shall have to be much more observant in future.'

She gave him a thin smile. 'In my experience, the acuteness of a gentleman's observation varies in inverse proportion to the beauty of the lady.'

'And a lady's observation is so much more acute?'

'It is—and it isn't. A lady always, always has much more to lose than a gentleman. And having few options, with marriage normally the only way to secure her future, she may…overlook quite obvious deficiencies.' She sighed. 'I just don't think that anyone should be judged solely on the basis of their looks—or lack of them. Character should count for something, shouldn't it?'

Picturing Lady Belinda, he said acidly, 'I'm afraid society is usually more impressed by flash and dash.'

'Which is why I'd rather eschew marriage and devote my life to good works.'

'What sort of good works? You're not going to become one of those dreary Calvinists, warning sinners of fire, brimstone and destruction?'

'No, I prefer building to destroying. I should like to do something useful. Unlike *some* I could mention, who seem to think all that's necessary for a satisfying life is to seduce silly women, drink other men under the table and win at cards.'

'I can't imagine to whom you refer,' he said with a grin. 'I do ride horses rather well, though.'

'Perhaps your only noteworthy skill.'

'Oh, no! I drive quite well, too. You've seen me handle a high-perch phaeton.'

'Excellent. You can look forward to life as a Royal Mail coachman when you run through all your money.'

Laughing, he said, 'I'd still have my charm. Isn't charm useful?'

'For cozening the unwary, perhaps. I'm too downy to fall for that.'

Their teasing gazes collided—and once again held, something undeniable, and undeniably sensual, sparking between them.

'Ah, that you were not,' he murmured, regretting her innocent, unmarried state more keenly than ever.

Her pale face colouring, she looked away. 'Well, enough banter. Thank you for helping me restore my equilibrium so I may return and face down Mama. I've half a mind to tell her I am done, absolutely done, with society. No more Season. I've had enough!'

He shook his head doubtfully. 'A noble resolve! We'll see how long it takes for your mama to squash it.'

'Thank you so much for the encouragement,' she said drily. 'Good day to you, Lord Theo.'

'And to you, Miss Henley,' he said, watching her ride off to meet her belatedly approaching groom. Remembering the unwelcome proposal that had prompted the gallop that had left her servant eating dust, he had to smile again. Thank heavens Miss Henley was so resistant to being forced into the usual female role.

Thank heavens, too, that most men were too dull-witted and dazzled by bright and shiny society beauties to recognise the quiet gem among them. Meaning Miss Henley was unlikely to be pursued by a man she might actually want to accept.

Although…if she were married, especially to someone she couldn't possibly admire, like Mr Null, he might actually be able to indulge this annoyingly strong urge to pursue her.

Damn, but she was unusual! The woman drew him far too strongly, on too many levels. More and more frequently, he found himself struggling between two polar opposite desires: to throw caution to the wind and see if she truly possessed the passion of which he caught tantalising glimpses. Or the much more prudent course of avoiding her completely.

Chapter Three

As it happened, after returning from the park, Emma did not gird her loins and confront her mama.

Instead, she found herself having to soothe Marie, who sobbed as she helped Emma change from her habit into an afternoon gown and then fell before her, apologising for having kept Mr Nullford's presence a secret and begging Emma's forgiveness for the deception. In between hiccups, she explained that she only wanted her dear, sweet mistress to find a kind man who would take care of her and give her a happy life, like Lady Henley was always saying Emma needed.

Not until Emma had reassured the maid over and over that she was not angry and would never turn Marie off without a character, that she understood Marie just wanted the best for her, was the girl finally able to dry her tears.

By the time the maid bobbed a final curtsy

and headed back to the servants' quarters, Emma had had enough of sobbing and confrontation. Although it was likely her mama would be sobbing, too, when *she* confronted Emma, rather than apologise for her part in the deception, she was more likely to heap recrimination on Emma's head for having turned down a perfectly unexceptional suitor.

And then lament, with another bout of tears, what was to become of her poor, plain, maiden daughter if she kept throwing away every chance to become respectably settled when, at her age, Emma could not hope to receive many more offers—perhaps not any!

It would not be the first time Emma had endured such a scene, though she devoutly hoped it would be the last. But after suffering Marie's outburst, it made her head hurt just to think about meeting her mother, who seemed as oblivious as the maid to what Emma really wanted.

Which sealed it. She would grab a footman to escort her and slip away to Hatchards before her mama found out she'd returned home. There, she could dash off quick notes asking her two best friends from school to meet her at Gunter's for some ices, after which, although it wasn't the day for their normal weekly meeting, they might call on Lady Lyndlington.

Being able to write a few strongly worded appeals to various Members of Parliament decrying the continuing miseries of child labour should be just the thing to put today's events in perspective and calm her for the coming showdown with her mother.

A little more than an hour later, Emma arrived at Berkeley Square and took a table inside Gunter's, where she awaited the arrival of the two people dearest to her in the world: Olivia Overton and Sara Standish.

Olivia was first to arrive. Smiling as she waved over to her table the tall, angular girl who had a long, plain face and dull brown hair just as she did, Emma felt again the surge of gladness that Olivia had taken the lead and turned three shy outsiders at Mrs Axminster's Academy for Young Ladies into the dearest of friends.

Inviting them to share her table for dinner one night, Olivia had observed that Emma and Sara also seemed to enjoy books and seemed as uninterested as she was in the conversations about Seasons and husband-hunting that occupied most of their classmates. She then suggested that the three of them would have a better chance of surviving the miseries of school if they banded together.

They soon become inseparable. After discovering the feminist writings of Mary Wollstonecraft and the calls for democracy and social reform of Thomas Paine, they'd decided that, for them, the future would involve working for noble causes, rather than competing for suitors or devoting themselves to securing—and measuring their worth by—the brilliance of the marriage proposals they received.

She and Olivia had just exchanged hugs and greetings when Sara Standish walked in, her plump face wreathed in a smile that magnified the sweetness of her expression. Petite, blonde and curvaceous, she provided a sharp contrast to her friends' tall angularity.

As Emma settled in beside them at the table, the doubt and turmoil in her heart eased. With her friends to stand by her, she knew she could face anything.

'I'm so glad you could come on such short notice,' Emma told them after they'd given the waiter their order. 'I was afraid you might both be occupied with calls this afternoon.'

'Your note did take me away from perusal of a quite fascinating book,' Olivia said.

'I bargained with my aunt that, if I agreed to attend without protest whatever society events she chooses, I would only have to make calls with her twice a week,' Sara said. 'Luckily, today was not one of the designated calling afternoons. But what has transpired that you needed to summon us so precipitously?'

In a few terse sentences, Emma told them about Nullford's proposal, her refusal and the scene with her maid that had sent her scurrying from the house before it could be repeated, in more ominous tones, with her mama. Though she mentioned in passing her ride in the park, she omitted describing her encounter with Lord Theo.

Not that her friends would tease her about him, or press for more details of the meeting than she chose to relate. In truth, she was a bit embarrassed to find herself so attracted to a man who was exactly the sort of too-handsome, too-charming, too-faithless and too-purposeless gentleman she's always scorned.

Even thinking about Lord Theo made Emma feel edgy and unsettled. So she would just *stop* thinking about him, she told herself.

'You escaped before your mama could take you to task for refusing Mr Nullford?' Olivia asked, pulling Emma from her thoughts.

'Yes. I scuttled off to Hatchards, where I bought some paper and was kindly lent a pen and some space on their counter to write my notes.'

'But given that the suitor was *Nullford*,' Sara said, 'are you so sure your mama will be disappointed?'

'Since she put him up to it, yes. After the episode with my maid, I couldn't bear the prospect of sitting still while she scolded me for my foolishness, then wondered for the millionth time why I fail to see the necessity of marrying so apparent to every other female, and then worked herself into a deep despondency, worrying over what will become of me. I hope later to use this incident to persuade her to finally accept that my vision for my future is quite different from hers and get her to agree to release me from the social obligations of the Season. But I've no hope of doing so before we go through the ritual of outrage, puzzlement and despair.'

'At least you know she does care about you—even if she cannot understand you,' Sara said.

Olivia reached over to press their friend's hand. After her daughter's birth, Sara's mama had taken to her sofa, claiming her health prevented her taking any further part in society. There, she received calls from select gossipy friends and the various physicians and apothecaries summoned to treat her latest ailment, while delegating all responsibility for managing her daughter's future to her sister, Sara's aunt, Lady Patterson.

'Yes, and I do appreciate that she's sincerely concerned about me,' Emma replied, 'which is why I have so far tolerated yet another Season, when I would much prefer to be done with it and set up my own establishment. Oh, to be able to come and go when and where I please, without dragging along a maid or a footman!'

'I know,' Olivia said, sighing as well. 'Though we are all more than one-and-twenty and could legally access the funds to establish the household together we planned at school, it's turned out to be not nearly as easy as we envisaged. Merely mentioning the possibility of our hiring a house is enough to set Mama off in a swoon.'

'Even we must recognise that our families will suffer a good deal of scorn and pity for producing daughters with such odd, unfeminine aims,' Sara said. 'I'm sure your mama genuinely believes that choosing not to marry and giving up your place in society would mean not just censure for her, but ruin and heartache for you, too.'

'Another point on which Mama harps,' Emma agreed. *And one Mr Nullford had stressed.* 'Sadly, none of us can escape the burden of appreciating our families' sensibilities, no matter how much their expectations conflict with our own wishes.'

'I have no intention of "appreciating" my family's sensibilities to the point of marrying, just to spare them distress,' Olivia replied acidly. 'Bound to a husband for whom I feel at best a tepid respect? Ending up a wife either neglected in favour of prettier, mindless females like the ones we knew at school, or scorned for having the temerity to display my intelligence and work towards political goals? Never!'

'I'm not suggesting we give in to society's pressure and marry,' Emma replied. 'Only that withdrawing from society to live and work together, as we envisaged at Mrs Axminster's, will have to be deferred a while longer.'

'How much longer?' Olivia asked, frustration in her tone. 'Until all family members likely to be embarrassed by us have passed on?'

'Certainly not that long!' Emma said, giving her friend a rueful smile. 'I remain hopeful that I may escape by the end of the Season, perhaps even before. Especially after the contretemps over Mr Nullford, which Mama is sure to bewail as perhaps my last chance to wed.'

Inwardly wincing again, she refrained from disclosing Mr Nullford's hurtful remark about her desirability.

'Nullford!' Olivia said scornfully, shaking her head. 'Only a female who believes *any* husband is better than none could seriously consider wedding that blockhead. And for someone as intelligent and perceptive as you to marry such a man… it would be a travesty!'

'Certainly a waste of intellect,' Sara agreed.

'Thank you, kind friends. Unfortunately, Mama is just the sort of female who would think Nullford better than no one. Enough about that dispiriting offer! Though I did need to vent my ire over that event, my other purpose in bringing you here was to suggest that we call upon Lady Lyndlington. Perhaps she will have some letter writing for us, to help redeem what has so far been a most trying day.'

Except for the interval with Lord Theo. That exchange had been as stimulating as it was disturbing.

Truly, she ought to try harder to avoid the man, though he had a disconcerting habit of occasionally turning up at the social engagements to which her mama insisted on dragging her. She should avoid him especially since some foolish feminine part of her seemed to respond intensely whenever he was near. The man represented a clear danger to her good sense—and self-control.

And now she was thinking of him again, after telling herself she wouldn't.

Shaking her head with irritation, Emma said, 'Shall we finish our tea and call on Lady Lyndlington?'

'Yes, let's,' Olivia said. 'All this talk of marriage makes me want to write angry letters, too.'

'Indeed!' Sara agreed with a smile. 'Let's hear it for a limit to child labour, votes for all—and a wider role in society for women!'

Though Emma and her schoolmates were fortunate enough to find Lady Lyndlington at home, they did not end up writing letters. The head of the Ladies' Committee, the butler informed them, was already entertaining a guest—Mrs Christopher Lattimar, wife to the brother of Emma's good friend Temperance.

Since that lady also happened to be the former Ellie Parmenter, who before her marriage had for years been the mistress of an older peer and was thus, despite her gentle birth, not accepted in society, the three had heard about, but never met, her.

'Would you ladies like to join them, or would you prefer to call again later?' the butler asked.

The *ton* might shun his wife, but Christopher Lattimar's close circle of political friends and associates in Parliament had quietly welcomed her. Lady Maggie, wife of his good friend Giles Hadley, Viscount Lyndlington, had become something of a champion for her and one of the leading supporters of her school for girls.

It took only a moment for the three to exchange glances and a mutual nod. 'We would be pleased to join them,' Emma replied.

'Ladies, so kind of you to stop by,' Lady Maggie said, she and her guest rising as the butler ushered them in. 'May I present you to my good friend, Mrs Christopher Lattimar.'

'Only if they feel…comfortable meeting me,' Mrs Lattimar said to Lady Lyndlington before turning to Emma and her friends. 'I shouldn't wish to cause you—or your families—any distress.'

Even if Emma had not already known the circumstances beyond her control that had thrust this lovely, dark-haired woman into a position of shame, the fact that she had Lady Lyndlington's support would have influenced Emma towards her. Anyone who'd earned the respect and affection of Lady Maggie, daughter of an earl and wife of one of Parliament's leading reform politicians, would have to be intelligent and interesting.

In addition to which, her friend Temperance also held her brother's disgraced wife in high esteem.

'On the contrary! We would be honoured,' Olivia said, expressing the friends' feelings exactly.

'Excellent!' Lady Lyndlington said. 'Mrs Lattimar, may I present Miss Emma Henley, Miss Sara Standish and Miss Olivia Overton, all three hard workers—and enthusiastic letter writers—for my Committee. Ladies, my dear friend, Mrs Ellie Lattimar.'

'I'm so pleased to meet you,' Emma said as the ladies exchanged curtsies. 'I've heard so much about you from Temperance. She admires you tremendously.'

'As do we all,' Lady Lyndlington said, pressing Mrs Lattimar's hand.

'You are sure we are not intruding?' Sara asked. 'We don't mean to interrupt.'

'Not at all,' Lady Lyndlington assured her. 'In fact, given the enthusiasm you have all displayed for our committee's aims, I've been hoping to persuade you to work for another of our projects. As you may remember, Mrs Lattimar runs a school that provides education and training to indigent girls. It's an endeavour I think you might also like to support.'

'You rescue girls from the streets or from houses of ill repute, do you not, Mrs Lattimar?' asked Olivia.

Though Lady Maggie's eyes widened and Emma felt a pang of dismay at Olivia's customary bluntness, Mrs Lattimar merely smiled. 'Not to dress it up in fine linen, yes. Now, if we are to be friends who speak the truth plainly, shall we dispense with formality, as Lady Maggie tells me she prefers among members of her Committee? Please, call me "Ellie".'

'We'd be delighted to—Ellie,' Emma replied. 'How do you find the girls?'

'Some find me, having heard murmurs about the school on the streets. I also maintain contacts with various houses, whose proprietresses I knew in my former…position. Sometimes, the girls I take in are daughters of working girls who don't want to follow that life. More often, they are orphans with nowhere to go but the streets.'

'There are few enough choices for girls, even honest ones who wish to go into service,' Olivia said. 'I imagine it's almost impossible to escape a life on the streets—and eventual prostitution—when you have no resources at all.'

'Very difficult,' Ellie agreed.

'What sort of training do you provide?' Sara asked.

'All the girls are taught basic reading, writing and simple maths. The rest of their day is devoted to mastering practical skills that will lead to future employment—needlework, cleaning tasks, cooking. Our goal is enable them to become honest, hard-working members of society, protected by their skills and experience from the threat of ending up back on the streets—or in the brothels.'

'What inspiring work! How can we help?' Emma asked.

'Monetary contributions are always welcome. But if you wished to become personally involved, I would be happy to have you visit the school itself. Having genteel ladies describe to the students the duties domestic servants perform in an aristocratic household, stressing the skills that would impress a housekeeper interviewing them for a position, or make them valuable to their mistress after they are hired, would be very helpful.'

The three friends exchanged another look and a mutual nod. 'We can certainly pledge to do that,' Emma said. 'Perhaps during our visits, we can find other ways to be useful.'

'I would very much appreciate it,' Ellie said. 'But now, I must return to the school.'

'I'm afraid I am due elsewhere soon as well,' Lady Maggie said as the ladies all rose. 'No time for letter writing today! But I will see you Tuesday morning, as usual?'

'Of course,' Olivia said. 'We look forward to it.'

After bidding the others goodbye, the friends descended the front steps to await the hackney a footman had summoned.

'What obstacles Ellie Lattimar has overcome,' Olivia said.

'Temperance told me her father virtually sold her to an older lord to pay off his debts,' Emma confided.

'Much as I sometimes feel…unappreciated, at least Mama cared enough to delegate my aunt to look after me,' Sara said.

'Imagine, being cast out at sixteen all alone, with nothing to protect you or secure your future but your own wits and determination,' Olivia said, shaking her head in awe.

Emma seized both her friends' hands and

pressed them. 'Thank heavens, whatever happens, we will always have each other, no matter how scandalously unconventional we become.'

The hackney arrived and they set off, planning where they would meet at the various upcoming social engagements as they dropped off first Sara in Upper Brook Street and then Olivia at Hanover Square.

After seeing her last friend to her door, Emma descended the stairs back to the street. No reason now to delay returning home—and facing the inevitable, and inevitably unpleasant, encounter with her mother.

Halting in mid-step, Emma surveyed the position of the sun. It was still mid-afternoon, she calculated. Her mother would only now be rising from her bed to drink her morning chocolate—and learn of her exasperating daughter's latest folly. She probably had another hour or so before she would add tardiness to the tally of faults her mother would bring against her.

Deciding on the moment, she waved away the hackney and set off walking.

Chapter Four

⁕

A short distance away, having consumed a restorative beefsteak and ale at his club and won a few guineas at cards, Lord Theo descended the steps to St James's Street in a contemplative mood. The afternoon being mild and sunny, he elected to walk while he thought about the best way to end the liaison with Lady Belinda without having to endure an explosion of tears, pleading, excuses and recriminations.

Dismissing the lady face-to-face might be kinder, but was almost guaranteed to set off the unpleasant encounter he wished to avoid. After his pointed escort of her, unwilling, back to her husband's box, his coldly furious demeanour sufficient to convince even that volatile lady that he would not tolerate protest, she must know he was at least considering ending their association. Hopefully she wasn't so confident of her beauty and allure that a bland note and a handsome parting gift would come as a shock.

Resolved to follow that course, he halted his perambulations around Mayfair and walked northwards up Bond Street, intending to get a hackney and go to Rundell and Bridges. He'd just turned on to Oxford Street when, to his surprise, he spotted a well-dressed female walking at a brisk pace in front of him. From her speed and determined gait, he was able even at a distance to identify the lady as Miss Emma Henley.

The happy chance of meeting her twice in one day set him smiling. But even as he picked up his pace to close the distance between them, caution warned that, despite his own and the lady's disinclination towards marriage, it probably would not be prudent to be seen walking with her outside the park or shopping areas where he might reasonably have encountered her by chance.

He'd halted to heed the voice of self-preservation when he suddenly realised that, once again, Miss Henley appeared to be quite alone. She was on foot, so there couldn't be a groom trotting somewhere behind her. Concerned, he surreptitiously began walking after her.

After a few more minutes spent trailing her, he had to conclude that there wasn't a slower-paced maid or a dawdling footman following her, either.

For another few minutes, he debated the wisdom of approaching her. But concern for her safety soon outweighed the possible complication of having to come up with some glib excuse to explain away his presence to any member of society who might chance to spy him escorting her, unchaperoned, so far from her home.

The scene he observed as he drew closer justified that concern. A fat, red-faced fellow in a bulging waistcoat was loitering some distance ahead of Miss Henley, openly gawking as she approached. The man's blatant scrutiny was definitely making her uneasy, for her pace had slowed and she was darting occasional, surreptitious glances at the man.

Indeed, so preoccupied was she with Greasy Waistcoat that Theo was able to draw quite near with her still unaware of his presence.

'What, escaped your traces again, Miss Henley?'

Gasping, she whirled to face him. 'Lord Theo!' she cried, the alarm in her voice fading as she recognised him. 'You gave me such a start!'

'As you did me. I've followed for a few streets, enough to confirm, to my astonishment, that you are, in fact, walking without any escort at all. Outriding your groom in the park is one thing. Whatever are you doing in this part of town, bereft of footmen or even a maid to attend you?'

'Shop girls and housemaids walk everywhere

in London without anyone to attend them,' she responded, aggravation and a touch of defiance in her tone.

'Shop girls and housemaids are not dressed in a gown of fine silk topped by a fur-trimmed pelisse. In some streets in London, you could be robbed for the clothes you stand in—if not worse.'

Her eyes widening in alarm, she glanced towards still-loitering Greasy Waistcoat. Who, after Theo caught his gaze with a look of unmistakable warning, hastily turned and scurried off in the opposite direction. 'Surely not here!' she protested.

'No, probably not here,' Theo allowed. 'But where are you going? Stray a few streets to the east and you could find yourself in trouble in short order.'

'In my defence, I hadn't *intended* to walk alone. After visiting Lady Lyndlington with some friends, I shared a hackney home with them. I'd just bade Miss Overton goodbye in Hanover Square when the idea struck me to make…one more visit before returning home. The day being fair, I decided to proceed on foot.'

'Visiting Lady Lyndlington, were you? Attempting to avoid the confrontation with your mother a while longer?' he guessed. 'Or delaying your return home to put off having to deal with the consequences of that interview?'

She grimaced. 'If you must know, I haven't

spoken with her yet. It's a discussion I freely admit I'm not looking forward to. But it must take place, for I am determined to assert my independence, sooner rather than later. I suppose I could have returned to the Overtons and borrowed a maid from Olivia—but why should I? If I'm soon to be on my own, able to come and go freely as I please, why not begin now? It's not as if Mrs Lattimar's school on Dean Street is a dive in St Giles.'

'Ah, so that's where you are headed. Is supporting her endeavour to be part of the good works you mentioned?'

'I certainly hope so. It's a worthy cause.'

'I applaud your intentions, but even an independent lady takes a care for her safety. Shop girls and maids often walk in pairs and few women wander about London entirely on their own.'

She sighed. 'Much as it pains me to admit it, you may be right. This is the first time I've ever walked in the city entirely on *my* own. Perhaps I just never noticed before, while accompanied by a maid or footman, how men…stare at a woman. Which is so unfair! Men can walk unmolested wherever they please!'

'Gentlemen walking alone are still cautious and generally carry a potentially lethal walking stick. A well-dressed female going about unattended is remarkable enough to invite scrutiny from a number of quarters, some of which are bound to be unsavoury.'

'Perhaps it would be more prudent to take an escort,' she conceded. 'But admitting that doesn't mean that I intend to waylay *you*! Surely I can get from here to Dean Street without incident. I promise I will send for a footman to accompany me home.'

'I'm sure Mrs Lattimar would not allow you to leave the premises without an escort. But I can delay my task long enough to see you safely to her school.'

Somewhat to his surprise, she didn't protest further. If the scrutiny of Greasy Waistcoat had shaken her enough to eliminate further argument, he could only be grateful.

But, being Emma Henley, the chastened mood didn't last long. A moment later, she peeped back up at him, her unsettled look replaced by one of curious scrutiny. 'A "task", you said? The word implies a burden. I thought you adept at wriggling out of doing anything truly onerous.'

'This task isn't precisely "onerous". Completing it does get me out of something that has become…annoying.'

The lingering anger beneath that innocuous word must have coloured his voice, for she raised her eyebrows and chuckled. 'Headed to Rundell and Bridges to find just the right bijou to inform Lady Ballister of her congé?'

Both impressed and exasperated by her perspicacity, he said loftily, 'A necessary task is best done as swiftly as possible.'

'Putting you in quite a dilemma! What, exactly, to select? It must be something fine enough not to insult the lady, but not so opulent as to give her any hope that the gesture isn't a final one.'

'Does your lack of sensibility have no bounds?' he shot back, surprised once again. 'A gently bred virgin should know nothing about such matters!'

'Oh, pish-tosh. Just because—alas—I am never likely to be in such a situation doesn't mean I can't imagine it.'

Meaning she never intended to take a lover— or would never behave badly enough to lose one? He found his gaze lingering on the full, sensual lips that so often uttered such unexpected comments…and heat built again within him. Would she make as unconventional and surprising a lover as she did a conversationalist?

Noticing the gaze he'd fixed on her mouth, she felt her fair skin colour. Self-consciously, she licked her lips.

The intensity of desire fired by that simple gesture sounded a warning in his distracted brain. This would never do! The longing she inspired could go nowhere.

Reining himself back in, he managed to summon an amused tone. 'So, using your ever-active imagination, I suppose you have suggestions for a suitable gift?'

'Ah, let me see.' She put a finger to her chin in an exaggerated gesture of concentration. 'Might I propose…a jewelled chatelaine?'

Though her comments were often unusual, that suggestion was so outrageous he burst out laughing. 'An exquisitely worked piece on which she can hang the keys to her husband's manse? Implying that she would do better to devote her talents to tending *him*?'

She grinned. 'Do you think the recommendation might work?'

'It might work to make her furious! So furious, I'm halfway tempted to try it. Though I'd risk having her come after me some time in the night, attempting to strangle me with it.'

'A noble death, trying to lead a wayward lady back to the straight and moral path. But obviously too daring an undertaking for such a timid soul as you. I suppose it shall have to be a ring or necklace, then.'

He was trying to come up with a suitable reply to that jibe as she led him around the corner. 'Well, here we are. The school is just down this street. You've delivered me safely and may proceed to discharge your dangerous task.'

'A gentleman always sees a lady inside the front door of her destination,' he replied, reluctant to leave her energising presence, as he seemed to be so often of late. No other female dared talk to him as she did, offering taunts instead of flattery. And few individuals of his acquaintance came up with as many startling, out-of-the-ordinary observations.

'The school already boasts several influential patrons to assist in its good work, does it not?' he asked, compelled to draw out their time together a bit longer.

'Yes. In addition to Lady Lyndlington, it's supported by her father, the Marquess of Witlow, and her aunt, the Dowager Countess Lady Sayleford, as well as Mrs Lattimar's mother-in-law.'

'Lady Vraux?' He gave a derisive chuckle. 'All upstanding members of society—save the last one.'

'May I remind you, Lady Vraux is the mother of my dear friend Temperance. That dazzling Beauty whom you were once so eager to impress.'

'And the mother is as dazzling as daughter.'

'No doubt you dangled after her yourself, once upon a time. I understand doing so is almost a rite of passage for rich, cocksure, indolent young men just out of university. Given how confident you are of your "charm", you must have been foremost in the pack.'

'Not of *that* pack. I never pursue ladies who are unlikely to be caught and Lady Vraux, for all her reputation, was determinedly unattainable. But it's probably not wise for *you* to advertise an acquaintance that would do the reputation of an innocent young maiden no good.'

'Fortunately, Temperance was able to escape its taint.' Miss Henley shook her head, a militant light in her eyes. 'How ridiculous, to hold the daughter responsible for the sins of her mother! Or to imply that Temper would be equally promiscuous, simply because she so closely resembles that lady? To say nothing of the…mitigating circumstances behind the mother's behaviour, or the fact that, had her sins been committed by a man, the consequences wouldn't have been nearly as severe.'

Theo held up a hand. 'I'm not about to debate society's unequal treatment of men and women.'

'Wise of you. In any event, I'm so weary of all the silly rules and conventions. I'm not sure how much longer I can put up with them.'

'That will depend on the outcome of that oh-so-important discussion with your mama, won't it? Do you really think you can win her over?'

Looking away from him, she flicked an invisible speck of lint from her sleeve. 'Haven't you got an errand to dispatch?'

Smiling at her attempt to rid herself of him rather than address a problem she clearly didn't wish to think about, he said, 'It's not only my duty as a gentleman to see you come to no harm—at least, from anyone else—but I'm curious to see this school.'

She stopped short, her gaze scanning his face. He forced himself not to expand on that ill-advised parenthetical remark.

Fortunately for them both, after a moment, she turned away without questioning his meaning. Relieved, he took a ragged breath. Prudence dictated that, had she pressed him about it, he must make light of it—and he wasn't sure he could make himself lie to her.

Ah, the wicked things he would like to do with her, were it ever possible!

'At her school, girls are given a better chance in life,' she said, following up on his previous remark. 'Lucky them. When they finish their training, they will be able to do something useful.'

'I wouldn't be too envious. They may end up with respectable occupations, but their lives will be full of toil.'

'At least they will own themselves.'

He shrugged. 'Perhaps. If they marry, they will become as subject to their husband's authority as any gently born woman.'

'They just don't bring a dowry for that husband to spend.'

'True. Which means they may not be treated as kindly.'

Miss Henley fixed him with a derisive gaze. 'I never heard of girl being treated more kindly because she brought her husband a handsome dowry. At least, not *after* the wedding.'

She had a point there. 'Very well. I concede that there are disadvantages to marriage.'

'Especially for a female.'

Shaking his head at her persistence, he said wryly, 'You are the most bizarre woman. Most females think marriage confers protection, as well as status, upon them!'

'Only if a woman is lucky enough to wed a superior man.'

'There are a *few* such men in society, you know.'

She gave him a saucy look. 'Unfortunately, I don't think I've ever met any.'

He put a hand to his chest dramatically. 'What, you would lump me in with Mr Null?'

'Oh, no. *You* could find work as a coachman. If poor Mr Null ever lost his fortune, he'd be lucky to get a job mucking out stables. Well, I mustn't keep you any longer.' Stopping before the door to the school, she rapped on it, then turned to make him a curtsy. 'Thank you for your kind escort, Lord Theo, and good day.'

Leaving him smiling as he bowed in response, she turned to walk in the door the porter opened for her.

Chapter Five

After dispatching Miss Henley to her destination, Theo found a hackney and went on to the jeweller's, chuckling inwardly as he reviewed the assortment of glittering bijoux the clerk brought for his inspection. Though almost tempted to ask about a chatelaine, he chose instead a handsome pair of sapphire and diamond earrings which, he thought, fit the irrepressible Miss Henley's description of being 'fine enough not to insult the lady, but not so opulent as to inspire hope'.

That purchase made and enclosed in a velvet box, he found another hackney and proceeded to the reading room at his club. Requesting pen and paper, he spent some time choosing just the right words to accompany the gift, then summoned a footman to deliver it. Envisaging the detonation of hysterics likely to result once the gift had been opened, he decided it would be wiser to remain at the club for the evening, rather than risk encountering Lady Belinda at some society entertainment while her volatile emotions would likely still be unsettled. And chuckled again as he recalled Miss Henley's jibe about him being a 'timid soul'.

Not timid, just prudent, he silently answered her, and then shook his head again at how he tolerated from her remarks that would earn anyone else who dared utter them a steely-eyed gaze, if not an outright challenge. Not that a gentleman could invite a female to a round of fisticuffs or clashing blades.

But then, he couldn't imagine any other woman making such nearly insulting remarks. As the rich younger son of an ancient aristocratic family, he was accustomed to having females, be they young or old, married or single, treat him with courteous attention and deference, if not outright flattery. Miss Henley alone tossed out remarks that confounded, even rebuked him, her keen gaze focused on him, her raised chin almost challenging him to cut her or give her a sharp set-down.

But then, she'd done that from the start, he thought, recalling that now infamous first meeting—or rather second meeting.

He'd been riding in Hyde Park when he'd spied last Season's Incomparable, Miss Temperance Lattimar, riding ahead of him, accompanied by another lady. Though he had no serious intentions

towards the Beauty, she was an amusing companion and, as no gentleman was currently claiming
her, he decided to approach.

'Lord Theo, good afternoon,' Miss Lattimar
said, nodding as he rode up and doffed his hat.
Turning to her companion, a tall, plain girl of
no particular distinction, she said, 'Miss Henley, I believe you already know this gentlemen,
do you not?'

Her eyes examined him with a disconcerting
directness before she nodded as well. 'Yes, we are
acquainted, though I doubt Lord Theo remem-
bers me.'

In truth, he had no recollection whatsoever of
having met her, but it would be most unchival-
rous to say, so—especially as she appeared to be
a friend of the divine Miss Lattimar. 'You are
mistaken, Miss Henley,' he protested smoothly.
'How could I forget so charming a lady?'

'We were partners for a waltz.' After a short
pause, giving him a strangely speculative glance,
she'd added, 'At Lady Mansfield's ball last Season.'

Theo didn't recall it, but then, he'd danced
countless waltzes over the last year and could
hardly expect to remember every one. So he nodded and smiled, and said, 'A most enjoyable occasion. You danced delightfully.'

Miss Henley gave him a falsely sweet smile.

'Except, we were in fact introduced at Mrs Dalworthy's soirée, where we were partnered for a country dance.'

He must have looked as shocked as he felt, for Miss Lattimar burst out laughing. 'Shame on you, Emma, you naughty thing! Lord Theo, I'm afraid Miss Henley is a most singular female. She says exactly what she thinks and does not tolerate idle flattery.'

Embarrassment flooding his face, he'd been at first incredulous, then angry that she'd had the gall to expose his white lie so blatantly. He'd been about to return some blighting reply when he met her fierce gaze and noted that confrontational tilt of chin.

She *expected* him to blast her, he realised. And unlike any single female he'd ever met, she didn't care a jot if he did.

It hadn't been, as she later accused, his desire not to appear churlish in front of Miss Lattimar that had induced him to choose a milder reply—but rather the urge to confound her expectations as neatly as she'd confounded his.

'So I see,' he said drily, giving her his most charming smile. 'How unkind of you to trick me, Miss Henley.'

'I expect it was, Lord Theo,' she allowed, looking a bit surprised that he hadn't dealt her the set-down she deserved. 'However, I would prefer you to admit you didn't recall meeting me, rather than offer me the polite lie. Although I do dance delightfully.'

She'd laughed then, the charming sound of her merriment defusing the rest of his irritation. 'I expect you *will* remember this meeting! But I shall certainly understand if you do *not* ask me to dance when next we meet.'

She really *didn't* care whether or not he wanted to associate with her. Surprised anew, and intrigued, he said, 'An honest female who disdains flattery and says exactly what she thinks? On the contrary! I shall add you with Miss Lattimar to the very short list of eligible females with whom I dance or converse.'

'You generally preferring, of course, *in*eligible females,' she'd tossed back.

Laughing in spite of himself, he nodded. 'And now you are trying to make me blush at my scandalous reputation.'

'Not at all. I hope to be scandalous myself, some day. Ah, Miss Lattimar, I believe we're about to be overtaken by a host of your admirers. Sadly, I fear you will have to cede your place, Lord Theo.'

'Until the next time, then, ladies,' he said, tipping his hat and riding off as the group of gentlemen Miss Henley had spied approaching arrived to surround Miss Lattimar.

His interest piqued by a female who dared treat him in such a radically unconventional manner, he'd been drawn to seek her out each time they'd chanced to meet at various entertainments. And once he knew to expect a different sort of commentary from her, he soon recognised the humour that softened the edge of her sharp remarks, as well as the keen intelligence that prompted her pointed, unconventional but absolutely accurate observations on all manner of things. He was led ever further down the garden path, curious to hear what new, startling, unacceptable-to-society remarks she might put forth—and what new, blighting comments about his character she might utter.

And then there was that unexpected but unmistakable sensual attraction. The intensity of her hazel-eyed gaze, the sense of barely controlled energy beneath the outward guise of a demure, properly behaved young female, and full lips that were an invitation to sin... She called to him on a physical level as powerfully as a fêted beauty like Lady Belinda.

Recalling her recommendation that he take up a career as a Royal Mail coachman, he laughed softly. That humour faded as he went on to wonder just how loud a peal her mama would ring over her for dismissing Mr Null. Fortunately, he was reasonably certain that no matter how roundly she was abused, the pressure applied by her mama would be more likely to push her into finally declaring that independence she kept telling him she meant to seek than to capitulation and acceptance of the numbing sterility of an arranged marriage.

It really was a shame that society offered so few options for intelligent, clever women. He could easily see Emma Henley taking a seat in Parliament, arguing for the causes about which she'd told him she'd been writing letters.

He shifted uncomfortably. Recalling her desire to do something important, to make a difference, touched too closely on the festering sore deep within which, though covered over by a dressing of busyness and society's acclaim, had never completely healed.

Although they were not nearly as hemmed in by rules and conventions as females, the opportunities for well-born young men to 'do something important' were also limited.

As a younger son, he would never inherit the responsibility for managing his family's various estates or providing for the welfare of their tenants. Though he enjoyed books, he felt no call to retreat into scholarship, and though he dabbled in investments, a gentleman never dirtied his hands dealing with money. Nor had he any taste for engaging in the push and pull of politics that so fascinated Miss Henley.

Only one thing fired in him the sort of enthusiasm he glimpsed in that lady and it was as impossible a career for a gentleman as standing for Parliament was for a woman.

Sighing, he glanced down at the writing paper on the desk before him. Almost of their own accord, his hands set aside the pen and inkwell and rummaged in the drawer for a pencil.

Quickly he sketched the silhouette of a lady bent over her side saddle, urging on her galloping horse. He added hash marking and shading, the bend of the delicate feather in her riding hat against the rush of wind. The stance, and the hat, obscured her face, but he had no trouble envisaging it: the long, pale oval, rather prominent, determined chin, the unexpected sensual lips. And those eyes! What a transformation they underwent, when she escaped from the conventional trivialities of social conversation!

He ought to do a sketch just of her face, to portray the fire that illumined those eyes once she began to speak about something that truly interested her. How they lit up her face, changing it from forgettable to arresting! Better still, he should do a study in oils, to be able to capture their mesmerising gold-green hue.

Adding a few more quick pencil strokes, he

finished his equestrienne sketch and studied it, nodding his satisfaction.

One more useless skill I possess, about which you don't yet know, he told her silently. *Else you might recommend that, should I lose my fortune, I take up work as a portrait painter.*

Restoring the pencil, quill and unused paper to its place in the drawer, he rose, sketch in hand, and walked towards the door. He'd enjoy a fine dinner and then, 'timid soul' that he was, avoid the society entertainments he'd meant to attend in favour of a few pleasant rounds of cards and brandy.

Pausing before the fireplace, he gave the sketch one more glance, smiling again at the vibrant energy that was Emma Henley. But it wouldn't be wise to subject himself to the enquiry and abuse that would result, should any of the other members discover him carrying around a sketch of a society lady.

With regret, he tossed the paper into the fire and strode out of the room.

Pausing in the doorway to the card room, Theo surveyed the occupants, looking for a group that would provide both stimulating play and agreeable company. Spotting a friend from his Oxford days, Theo strolled over.

'Ready for a game, Kensworth?' he asked.

'Ah, Lord Theo, just the man I hoped to see,' Kensworth said, gesturing him to a seat. 'I'm about to head out, but I did want a quiet word with you.'

Theo felt a flicker of concern. 'Is something wrong? An illness in your family?'

'No, nothing of that sort. It's…something else entirely.' Looking suddenly uncomfortable, Kensworth hesitated, sipping from the glass of port beside him.

'Well, out with it,' Theo said, both amused and curious. 'Have I flirted too blatantly with a lady you covet? Bought a horse you had your eye on?'

'No, this is about…your welfare. I saw you this morning, galloping in Hyde Park with Miss Henley. Just the two of you, no groom anywhere in sight. Now, I'll grant you that she appears to be a fine horsewoman, but I do wonder what else you see in her. Plain as a doorpost, with a tongue caustic enough to strip the varnish off your carriage.'

Theo managed to choke down a heated defence of Emma Henley's looks and wit. Forcing himself back into the role of careless courtier, he said in a bored tone, 'She is clever for all that. One never knows what she will say. I find her amusing.'

'You'd better watch that you don't "amuse" yourself right to the altar! Riding alone in the park with her? You run a terrible risk!'

'It might be, were she interested in marriage,

which fortunately she is not. And she did bring her groom.' He chuckled. 'She'd just out-galloped him.'

'I'd be careful in any event. *Miss Henley* may claim not to be interested in marriage, although—' Kensworth gave a derisive sniff '—I never believe any female who utters such rubbish! But you can be sure that mother of hers is. Been pushing the chit at every remotely eligible gentleman these last five years!'

Theo didn't need Kensworth's warning to know he must be very circumspect about how and when he met Emma Henley. 'I appreciate your concern, but I'm well aware of the need for caution.'

'I should hope so. Wouldn't want to see you start down a slippery slope! Enough about the depressing topic of wedlock. How do you intend to "slip out of" this latest contretemps with Lady Belinda? Granted, she's beautiful and has most luscious bosom I've ever ogled, but her behaviour...'

If it diverted Kensworth's attention from Miss Henley, Theo was happy to talk about his latest scandal. 'Her conduct, this time, is truly beyond the pale. Indeed...' he made a show of consulting his pocket watch '...she should by now have received a bouquet and a pair of fine sapphire and diamond earrings.'

Kensworth's eyes widened in surprise. 'You've given her her congé, then! So the field is open.'

'All yours,' Theo replied, gesturing towards him.

'Not mine!' Kensworth replied, holding out a hand palm-up. 'I'll stick with demi-mondaines who know their place! Sapphire and diamonds, you say? In the end, I'd wager the muslin company is less expensive. But you've always had a preference for the exclusive. So, who will be next?'

The image of Emma Henley's fierce, challenging gaze flashed into his head. Firmly he suppressed it. 'I think I shall allow the bad taste left in my mouth after the incident with Lady Belinda to dissipate before I contemplate any new liaisons.'

'Well, you can't wait too long. A man has needs, after all! Let me add one more recommendation for the professionals. A high-flyer knows which side her bread is buttered on and will never turn up in some public place, embarrassing you in full view of society.'

'Thank you, but, no. I shall console myself with cards and brandy, and call it a good night.'

A good night. Identical to so many others. At that observation, he felt again that vague stirring of ennui. 'Did you ever think there might be…

something more?' he asked abruptly, dropping for the moment his usual irreverent mask.

Kensworth blinked at him in confusion. Which Theo should have expected—Lord Theo Collington was not known for uttering serious remarks. 'Something more than cards, drinking—and ladies? Possessed of time and blunt enough to enjoy them, what more could a man want? Especially you—with pockets deep enough you'll never have to worry about finances and no onerous duties to keep you from your pleasures? Best of all, as a younger son, you don't have your family nattering on about you finding a wife. Now truly, what more *could* any gentleman want?'

'Onerous duties' recalling Miss Henley's phrase, Theo almost replied, 'To do something important.' But that remark would be guaranteed to increase the puzzlement on his friend's face. Theo knew a few men who possessed burning political ambitions, or were committed to acquiring property and improving their estates, but what Kensworth described—a life devoted to cards, drink and chasing women—was indeed considered the ultimate to be desired by the majority of the gentlemen with whom he had come down from Oxford.

Certainly it was the life his father had urged on him and the brilliance with which he'd mastered the charming rake's persona had garnered him the few compliments he'd ever received from the Marquess.

Suppressing an inward sigh, he slipped back into his expected role. 'Yes, what higher calling than to be a rich, handsome, charming bachelor, an incomparable horseman, excellent shot and prime *parti*, regarded with longing eyes by every chaste single lady and with desire by every naughty married one?'

Apparently he wasn't able to keep all the sarcasm from his tone, for Kensworth frowned and shook his head at him. 'Can't imagine what brought on this green melancholy. The irritation of breaking with the Beauteous Lady Belinda?'

'After the sobering experience at the opera, perhaps I will repent of my licentious ways. Put on sackcloth and ashes. Vow a denial of the flesh and—'

'I envisage the picture!' Kensworth held up a hand, laughing. 'I shall leave you to your melancholy, laughing as I go at the impossibly amusing idea of Lord Theo Collington denying himself *anything* he truly desires.'

Pushing away the image of Emma Henley's enticing mouth, Theo waved his friend off. *If you only knew*, he thought, motioning to a waiter to bring him a bottle.

But Kensworth had given him cause for thought. If seeing Theo riding with Miss Henley in Hyde Park was apt to raise speculation, he was all the more relieved that apparently no one had spied him walking with her to Dean Street.

He probably ought to be more circumspect—for he knew better than Kensworth how determined Lady Henley was to marry Emma off. If she could refashion some action of his to make the *ton* believe he'd compromised her daughter, he'd have no choice but to wed Emma, no matter how much the lady herself protested. He might have perfected the guise of a careless rogue, but he *was* a gentleman, and such an accusation would touch his honour as well as Emma's.

Maybe it was time to heed that voice of prudence and avoid her.

So what do you intend? another voice replied sardonically. To give her the cut direct after you nearly collide while riding in the park? Allow her to walk alone down a city street, disregarding her safety in order to safeguard your unwed status?

Wise as avoiding her might be, the choice didn't set well.

Rejecting the offer from two newcomers to join them in a round of cards in a tone only a hair removed from churlish, he poured himself a generous drink from the bottle the waiter brought him.

He'd downed half a glass in one swallow, savouring the burn that matched the heat of his disgruntlement, when another, more appealing possibility occurred. True, sooner or later, he would have to break with Emma Henley, lest their friendship grow too marked to be concealed. Or when, as was more likely, their interaction went from energising to insipid.

As different as she was, no lady who attracted him had ever held his interest for long. When the unique became expected and the unusual commonplace, he *would* end the association.

But before then, with a few simple changes to his social schedule, he could enjoy her company a while longer. And, he thought, grinning, confound some of society's expectations, and perhaps the lady's, while he did so.

Pleased with the plan, he poured another glass, saluted himself for his cleverness and rose to join the group he'd just rebuffed.

Chapter Six

Needing to create order out of the chaos of questions and alternatives racing through her head, Emma set out for the park the next morning at her usual early hour, despite a chilly mist. The session with her mother had shaken all her expectations and, as that meeting had not taken place until just before they left for Lady Mansfield's ball last night, she'd had no time yet to sort them out.

Unfortunately, this being a day on which both Olivia and Sara would be preparing to make calls with their respective chaperons, there could be no luring them away for a consultation at Gunter's.

She was silently bemoaning how much she missed having her friends' counsel when, from out of the swirling mist, she spied Lord Theo on his gelding. Her spirits soared as a little voice whispered, *You could talk to him.*

Or you could exhibit a modicum of dignity

and discretion, and ride the other way, a sardonic voice answered back.

Before she could take that wiser course, Lord Theo happened to glance in her direction. When he recognised her and smiled, she couldn't help smiling back. Nor could she make herself give him only a wave and ride off.

Instead, summoning just enough restraint to keep herself from trotting over to meet him, she pulled up her horse and waited.

Though she would never admit it to him, he having enough admirers already to sing his praises and inflate his already high opinion of himself, he *was* charming, she thought as he approached. He was also undeniably handsome, sitting astride his horse with ease, impeccably turned out in sober riding gear, a stray lock of dark hair that made one's fingers itch to comb through it shadowing his forehead under the fashionable beaver hat.

An image guaranteed to fill a maiden with longing—even a rational, realistic one like her, she acknowledged ruefully as every foolish, feminine part of her tingled with anticipation.

But slavish admiration wasn't what he expected from her—or what she would ever be prepared to offer him. Damping down the tingling as much as she was able, she gave him a cool nod as he halted beside her.

'Clearing your head of brandy fumes again?'

He grinned. 'And cigar smoke, after a successful night at cards. A pleasant good morning to you, Miss Henley. How fresh you look on this misty day.'

'Trying to shame me by giving me a polite and complimentary greeting after my abrupt and unflattering one?'

'My, my, we are sensitive this morning! What have I done this time to incur your disapproval?' he asked, a wry expression replacing the smile.

'Incur my disapproval? Nothing more than the usual.'

'Are you sure? Because I got the distinct impression that, rather than ride with me, you were prepared to gallop off in the opposite direction. I must have offended you deeply if you almost preferred avoiding me to blistering my ears.'

Her distress must be deeper than she'd thought if her face had mirrored her feelings that transparently, she thought, dismayed. Before she could pull herself together and find a flippant reply, he continued, 'Or is it that you've had that little talk with Lady Henley?'

Her feelings still raw, she fumbled to come up with an answer. Her gaze rising to meet his, she saw real sympathy there, which only increased her inner turmoil. While she hesitated, he said quietly, 'Was it as bad as you feared?'

The memory of her surprise, chagrin and uncertainty tightened her chest, until the swelling need to give it voice made her feel she might explode. Her intention to remain dignified and distant struggled to resist it and was knocked flat.

'Worse,' she capitulated on a sigh.

'Then you must tell me what happened. Shall we walk the horses?'

Her surrender complete, she nodded as he guided his mount to fall in step beside hers, her groom dropping back to follow at a discreet distance.

'So, how worse? More sobbing recriminations? Did she wash her hands of you?'

'No, quite the contrary, which is what was so confounding! Nothing followed the usual pattern; there were no tears, no maid waving a vinaigrette, no bewailing her undutiful and incomprehensible daughter.'

After pausing a moment, frowning as she recalled the scene, she continued, 'When I finally went in to see her, she simply motioned me to a seat. Before I could gird myself to Confess All, she said in the calmest voice that she knew I'd refused another offer of marriage. Then, instead of the explosion of tears and recriminations I expected, she…*apologised*!'

'Apologised?' Lord Theo echoed, looking as surprised as she had been. 'For what?'

'Pushing Mr Null—Nullford to propose. She said she actually *agreed* with me that he was a poor match for an intelligent woman. That she knew I thought her silly and flighty for devoting her life to society's trivia, ignoring the great political issues I find so compelling. She then went on, in the softest, saddest tones I've ever heard her utter, to tell me how much she loves me, how the one last, great desire of her life is to see me safe and happy. That she understands I have the funds to secure my future and support a household on my own and an important purpose that drives me, but that she fears a life without companionship, passion and children would end up being so cold and sterile that she'd wanted to do everything she could to prevent it—even grasp at a straw as flimsy as Nullford.'

Emma shook her head, the shock and guilt of her mother's confession roiling in her stomach again. 'I hardly knew what to say. Because I *have* secretly thought her frivolous, shallow and selfish. I felt…terrible.'

'It is hard to be angry with someone who declares her last wish is for one to be happy.'

Emma nodded. 'She left me with all my usual arguments thwarted. What could I do but apologise back, for being so undutiful and unappreciative a daughter?'

'You didn't, I hope, feel so terrible that you were tempted to recall Mr Null.'

Trust Lord Theo to come up with something that would make her smile. 'Nothing could make me feel *that* terrible,' she assured him. 'Mama even admitted that, save for the children it gave her and much as she'd been urging me to it, she herself had not found marriage very…fulfilling. That it didn't fire her with the enthusiasm she sees in me when I talk about my work for the Ladies' Committee.'

'A handsome concession!'

'Oh, there's more.'

'More?' Lord Theo clapped a hand to his chest theatrically. 'I'm not sure my heart can withstand the shock.'

Emma laughed ruefully. 'I wasn't sure mine could, either. I would never have believed such words could issue from the mouth of my beautiful, fashionable, oh-so-*conventional* mother. But she said she thinks me *brave* to want to stand on my own, without the status and protection of a husband, whereas she has never been strong enough to manage without her circle of admirers. That she is *proud* that I want to step outside the normal female role and do something to better the world.'

'She approves of you eschewing marriage?' Lord Theo shook his head sceptically. 'You truly think she believes that? Or is *she* the clever one, playing devil's advocate to lure you into being more compliant?'

'Since Mama so seldom speaks of what is in her heart, there's no way I can be certain,' Emma allowed. 'She seemed sincere enough, but she did ask if I'd agree to a bargain.'

'Ah, now the trap is baited!'

'How cynical you are!' she exclaimed.

'Perhaps,' he said, his voice turning serious. 'But I find that cynicism has protected me far better than innocence or gullibility would.'

'I hope I am never so jaded!' she said loftily— before ruining the effect by admitting, 'However, Mama being Mama, I am a trifle suspicious as well.'

'So, what did this bargain entail?'

'She said if I would agree to finish out the Season, she would support my efforts to look about for a house of my own—as long as I go about the business discreetly. She also promised she would not try to manoeuvre any other gentleman into making me an offer. If, by the Season's end, I haven't found a suitor I truly want to marry, she will release me to live the life I want, and wish me happy with all her heart. Now, can you find a "trap" in that?'

Lord Theo gazed into the distance, his expression considering. 'Very well,' he said after a moment. 'I don't immediately see one. Do you intend to accept her bargain?'

'Despite my own suspicions that she may simply want more time to devise some new scheme to dissuade me from abandoning society, I'm inclined to. There isn't much chance of my winning my independence before the end of the Season anyway. And if Mama does allow, rather than hinder, my search for a house, I will be that much further along when the Season does end. Perhaps I'll even be ready to move out and begin my new life!'

'So why the distress? I would think you'd be shouting for joy.'

'I know,' she said on a sigh. 'I suppose it's like the adage says: when the gods wish to punish you, they grant your request. I've expended so much effort pushing and pushing to be allowed to fashion the life I've long dreamed of, having those barriers suddenly removed makes me feel like I am…falling headlong into the unknown. It's thrilling, but also…'

'Frightening?' he supplied.

'Yes! Much as I hate to admit being such a poor honey. What if—' she continued in a low voice, not sure she wanted to express the alarming possibility even to herself '—what if Mama and all the others are right, and a life on my own *is*…lonely and unfulfilling?'

'I don't think you'll need to worry about being alone.'

Emma looked up to find Lord Theo's intense gaze fixed on her, a strange little smile on his lips. Her anxiety and confusion faded as a wave of sensual awareness washed through her.

Was it truly desire she saw in his eyes, or did she just want him so much, she only imagined it? Could a handsome man like Lord Theo truly want *her*?

And if he did… His romantic entanglements had all been brief, no matter how lovely the lady. Such a man would make a poor husband for a woman who valued fidelity and involvement in some higher purpose, if he could in fact be induced to marry her.

But if she were living in her own establishment, on her own terms, no longer subject to the rules and restrictions society imposed on a gently bred maiden… Could she dare explore passion for its own sake…outside the bonds of marriage?

Every nerve humming in response to his molten gaze promised the pleasure he could give would be incomparable.

A rider suddenly emerged from the mist, making her mount shy. Feeling her cheeks heat, she bent to control her horse, turning away from Lord Theo's perceptive gaze.

Forcing her thoughts from the carnal, she said

bracingly, 'I expect my life will be as fulfilling and happy as I make it. If I do accept Mama's bargain, as I am inclined to, I intend to begin immediately to investigate how one leases a house—a subject about which I know nothing. And to consider seriously what good works will occupy my time.'

'Letter writing for Lady Lyndlington and supporting Mrs Lattimar's school being foremost among those efforts?'

'Yes. Although,' she added with a laugh, remembering, 'after I told Mama I intended to assist the school, she asked what, besides financial support, I thought I had to offer the students. As she reminded me, I'm an indifferent needlewoman, know nothing of cookery and have never cleaned anything in my life.'

'Perhaps you could improve your stitchery, or take up polishing brass.' He grinned. 'Now, that's an appealing image: Emma Henley, a rag in hand, rubbing down some precious object.'

Her thoughts mustn't have wandered too far from the physical, for his words immediately conjured up the image of her rubbing down... Lord Theo's bare torso. *A precious object, indeed.*

Her mouth going dry and her pulse rate speeding, she wondered what it would be like to skim her fingers over his bare throat. To trace the curve of his strong shoulders, the outline of his ribs and the tight, flat skin of his stomach.

A disturbing warmth shot to her belly. Feeling her face grow even hotter, Emma struggled to banish that beguiling image as she replied disjointedly, 'I'm sure I might—I could be— competent enough to perform…whatever task was needed.'

'I'm sure you would. Ah, that I might participate in that process,' he murmured, his words confirming that he knew precisely why her face was flushed.

For a long moment their gazes held, the air between them crackling with connection. This time, with a shuddering breath, *he* looked away.

'Let's put aside the imaginary and focus on the practical,' he said, his voice shaking a little before he recaptured his usual light tone. 'You told me, didn't you, that Mrs Lattimar asked all your friends to talk to the students about the behaviours and attitudes that would best help them secure their position in a noble house?'

'Yes. And I warned Mama that, if I remain in society for the rest of the Season, I also intended to *discreetly* sound out ladies about their staffs, hoping to discover positions for Mrs Lattimar's students.'

'I'm sure Lady Henley was delighted to learn

of her daughter's intention to set up a hiring bureau.'

Emma laughed. 'Believe it or not, she said as long as I went about *that* matter discreetly, she thought my intentions admirable! I plan to stop by the school today and get started. That is, if I can find an escort. My good friends will be occupied making calls, and my maid is laid down with a putrid cold.'

Her spirits lifted by his sympathy…and emboldened by the physical undercurrent she sensed between them—impulsively she said, 'You…you wouldn't consider driving me there and speaking with the students as well, would you? A maid or cook must please the housekeeper and her mistress, but she must also please the master. You could describe to them the behaviour you expect of your servants, or the particular meals you prefer to serve your guests.'

'As I keep a bachelor establishment, I don't do much entertaining,' he replied, dashing her hopes. 'However…' He hesitated, looking thoughtful. 'I suppose I could offer such experience as I've gained, growing up in a noble household.'

'Excellent!' she cried, delighted more than she should be to have his company on this new endeavour. 'If anyone should question your acting as my escort, I shall tell them that…that you are considering becoming a patron of the school yourself, like the Marquess of Witlow and the Earl of Lyndlington. You're accompanying me to look at the school and decide whether or not to support it.'

'Lord Theo Collington, sponsor of a school for respectable females,' Lord Theo said with a laugh. 'Who would believe that?'

'I think, below that frivolous surface, you may be more serious than society imagines,' she replied, for once giving him her frank opinion. 'Besides, even the dimmest member of society would soon realise that the elegant Lord Theo, who with a crook of his finger might have any lady of the demi-monde and half the matrons of the *ton*, would hardly stoop to seducing *housemaids*. They'd be forced to conclude you were considering supporting the school.'

'Unless they thought I was trying to seduce you.'

She whipped her eyes to his, trying to assess whether he was serious or teasing, but could read nothing from his enigmatic smile. Trying to squelch a silly surge of hope, she looked away and shook her head. 'Lord Theo, with the Homely Miss Henley? No one would be foolish enough to believe that.'

'Then more fools, they,' he murmured.

Taken aback again, before she could decide whether she dared ask him to explain, he uttered an exaggerated sigh. 'Oh, very well, I agree to play the "school mistress's escort". At what time should I call for you, Madame Instructrice?'

Still rattled, not sure whether to place any credence in the undercurrents she thought she felt or heard in his remarks, Emma named a time. And then, before she could recover her composure, with a tip of his hat and a goodbye, Lord Theo rode off, soon disappearing into the mist.

Though her groom, who trotted closer as Lord Theo departed and halted at a respectful distance, was clearly ready to head back to Henley House and escape the chilly damp, for a few minutes, Emma held her mount motionless, her thoughts still whirling.

Over and over in her mind, she replayed the remarks full of double entendres, reviewed the image of his heated gaze. Could she believe the desire she was almost certain she'd seen and heard?

Handsome as he was, he was definitely every maiden's dream of the romantic hero one hoped would rush in and sweep one off one's feet. But then, given the verbal abuse to which she so often subjected him, he was more likely to plant her a facer for embarrassing or challenging him than try to sweep her up in his arms.

Shaking her head, she sighed. She ought to squelch such ridiculous imaginings and be thank-

ful for the amusing, uncomplicated sort-of friendship they now shared.

And yet…

What if he truly was drawn to her? *Desired*
her, as his oblique comments seemed to hint?

If he felt for her as strong an attraction as she
felt for him, was it wise for her to see more of
him? Or would it be better to avoid him and content herself with the safety of imagining? She
might be uncertain of his true feelings, but she
was very sure that any dalliance with Lord Theo
Collington would not end in marriage. Not that
he was the sort of man she'd choose to marry
anyway.

But passion…that might be another matter indeed.

As she'd already noted, when the gods wish to
punish you, they grant your request. Acting on
her desire for Lord Theo Collington would almost certainly open a Pandora's box of unfore-
seeable consequences no sensible female should
want to risk.

Chapter Seven

Later that afternoon, Emma was seated on a bench at the school table in Dean Street, a bevy of students around her, while Lord Theo lounged next to Ellie Lattimar on an armchair brought from her office. Though the girls were paying fairly close attention as Emma described the routine duties her housekeeper performed every morning, she couldn't help noticing that, from time to time, their eyes strayed to Lord Theo.

Not that she could blame them. He was probably one of the handsomest men they'd ever seen. He was most certainly the most dashing, with his elegant, perfectly tailored clothing, shining boots and gleaming white cravat. And though he was far above their touch, a cat could look at a king.

Or, she thought, suppressing a sigh, a plain, foolish girl. Who, unlike the schoolgirls, should know better to gaze upon the unattainable.

If it were truly unattainable.

He'd done little on the drive over to support her hopes that he might not be, devoting most of his attention to the horses drawing his high-perch phaeton at a brisk pace through the busy, crowded streets.

Except for one instance, she recalled, her heart beating faster as she remembered. He'd been so unusually silent during the drive, she'd expressed her fear that he was regretting his offer to escort her.

He'd looked away from his horses to flash her a quick glance that lingered on her lips. 'With you beside me, that's not what I'm regretting,' he tossed back before returning his attention to the street. 'Sorry if I seem distracted, but we would both regret it if I overturned us!'

She'd been quite impressed by his behaviour at the school. Though he couldn't help but be aware of the girls' awed admiration when Ellie introduced them, he'd greeted them with perfect correctness, neither as top-lofty as his superior status might have entitled him to be, nor overly familiar. Though he didn't flirt—as some of the older girls seemed to hope he would—neither did he treat them as children, or as unfortunate lesser beings of little understanding.

'Those are the principal things Mrs Wren sees to every morning,' she said, dragging her attention back to the girls who sat expectantly waiting for her to conclude her remarks. 'Lord Theo, would you care to add any comments about the housekeeper's duties at the home of your father, the Marquess, whose establishment is quite a bit grander than Windmore Place, the manor in Kent where I grew up?'

'In London, Mrs Culpepper's duties are much as you describe. Similar also when the family returns to Wynchgrove Hall, my father's estate in Wiltshire, except that there are more rooms and servants to oversee.' Lord Theo smiled. 'Though Mrs Culpepper has a large staff, she always demanded that every one of them complete their tasks before the family rises. Once, I almost reduced a housemaid to tears as I surprised her early one morning when I came into the library before she'd finished dusting—a lapse that could have earned her quite a scold.'

'Poor girl!' Emma said as the girls murmured sympathetically.

'Did you get her punished, then?' piped up a girl in the far corner, surprising Emma. Since she'd sat throughout Emma's talk with her head lowered, gazing at her lap, Emma thought she'd been paying little attention—except when she looked up occasionally to admire their handsome visitor.

'No,' Lord Theo replied. 'I promised her I wouldn't say a word. I even hid behind the curtains until she finished, in case Mrs Culpepper chanced to come in.'

'You, hiding behind a curtain?' the girl exclaimed as the others giggled. 'Well, that were right handsome of you, sir.'

'I thought so,' Lord Theo said. 'She must have, too. I never asked her about it, for fear of really getting her into trouble, but for several weeks after the incident, when I went up to my chamber at night, I'd find on the table by my bed two of the custard tarts I particularly liked.'

'Thank you both so much for coming,' Ellie said. 'I know hearing first-hand about the duties they must be prepared to perform will spur the girls to renewed efforts. Now, Miss Wendell is here to take you for your maths lesson. Bring your slates, please, girls.'

The others hopped up obediently, but the girl who'd spoken out hesitated, looking around anxiously before catching up the edge of her skirt.

'What's the matter, Arabella?' Ellie asked.

'I... I forgot the cloth to erase my board,' the girl confessed. 'I must have left it in the dormitory. I'll run upstairs and fetch it.'

'Doodling again?' Ellie asked with an indulgent smile. 'No matter, give your slate here. I'll erase it and lend you my cloth. You fetch yours later.' She held out her hand.

For a moment, the girl clutched the slate before

handing it over with marked reluctance. Frowning, Ellie looked at it, only to chuckle.

'Arabella, you naughty girl! Although I have to admit, this is quite good!'

Smiling, she offered the slate to Emma and Lord Theo, while Arabella, her face reddening, stood mute.

After glancing at it, Emma understood why. While the other girls had been listening intently, Arabella had been surreptitiously sketching a portrait of Lord Theo.

'It is a good likeness,' Emma said, impressed at how well the girl had caught Theo's handsome face and smiling eyes with just a few strokes of chalk.

'I was puzzled why you were crouched in the corner so inattentively,' Ellie said. 'Arabella wants one day to become a housekeeper,' she turned to explain to them. 'I'd expected her to be one of your most avid listeners.'

Pleating her fingers in her skirt, the girl looked up at Lord Theo. 'I didn't mean no disrespect, sir! But, begging your pardon, I just had to get down your likeness, you being so handsome and all.'

'Isn't he?' Emma said with a grin. 'No wonder you were reluctant to have the slate erased.'

Having been the subject of such intent scrutiny, Emma expected Lord Theo to be a bit embarrassed—or more likely, to preen a little and tease the girl. Instead, he studied her drawing with unusual intensity.

'This *is* quite good, Arabella. Have you had any drawing lessons?'

'Oh, no, sir. Never done much drawing at all afore Miss Ellie found me. Nothin' to draw on 'cept dirt, living on the streets like we was, though I did that sometimes. Didn't really take to sketching until Miss Ellie gave us these slates. Paper would be nicer, but it's too dear to waste.'

Still studying the board, Lord Theo said, 'You have a great deal of natural talent, then. The way you've caught the angle of my chin? And the soft highlights you added here. Very fine!'

Blushing, Arabella dipped a curtsy. 'Thank you, sir.'

Ellie patted the girl's arm. 'Arabella is one of my best students. She learned to read in record time, is an absolute whiz at sums and has a wonderful memory. I have no doubt she will advance rapidly and eventually achieve her goal of becoming a housekeeper. Valued by her employer, living in a good home, with excellent prospects for the future!'

'But you like to draw?' Lord Theo asked the girl.

'Oh, ever so much, sir. But only when all my work's done,' she added hastily after a quick glance towards Ellie. 'I wouldn't neglect my studies or my chores for it, Miss Ellie.'

'Well, when you do sketch, if you want to create shadow, add a few hash marks, like this,' Lord Theo said, taking up the chalk and making several quick strokes. 'You can blend them in with your finger, like this, to soften the effect.'

Arabella studied the slate and nodded. 'Yes, I see, sir. Thank you! That's ever so much better.' With obvious reluctance, she said, 'I guess I should erase the board and get ready for lessons.'

As he watched the girl's woebegone face, some emotion flitted across Lord Theo's face, so swiftly Emma hadn't time to identify it. 'I suppose you must. Before you do though, a few more pointers. If you really want to make me as handsome as I deserve, you need to change the angle of the nose and its shape.' Smiling, he rubbed out the line Arabella had drawn and drew an exaggerated beak. 'And the eyebrows. They're not quite in the right place.'

As the girl began to giggle, with a few deft strokes, he created a shaggy brow, pointy ears sticking out from an elaborate upsweep of hair and an enormous cravat that dwarfed the face. 'Now, that's a more accurate likeness, wouldn't you agree, Miss Henley?'

The drawing he'd made was such a cleverly exaggerated caricature of his real features that

Emma burst out laughing. 'Yes, Lord Theo, much better! Especially the nose.'

'Yes, we all know what a timid, retiring soul I am, with a tiny proboscis that so accurately reflects my character.'

'You're a complete hand, sir!' Arabella said, still giggling. 'Thank you for the lesson. I guess I can erase this now!'

'I certainly hope so,' Theo muttered. 'Perhaps another day, we could have another lesson.'

'I would love that, sir!' Beaming, the girl scampered off to join the others.

Shaking her head, Ellie turned back to them. 'That Arabella! So full of life, always so busy! I suppose I haven't paid much attention, but she does seem to always be doodling on her slate. And you think she has real talent, Lord Theo?'

'I do. It's hard to put that much expression into a sketch drawn with chalk, the drawing tool being so wide and blunt.'

'If she were gently born, she'd have had instruction in drawing and watercolours, her talent encouraged,' Ellie said. 'But given her birth, it might not be…kind to encourage her artistic bent. She would do better to concentrate all her efforts into preparing for a position in service. As I mentioned, she possesses the energy and intelligence to rise to the highest level, thereby obtaining a position of respect and security. I don't see that sketching will help her achieve that goal. And there's no career to be made from sketching alone.'

'There's no career in art for gently born ladies, either,' Emma pointed out. 'Filling a sketchbook with lovely drawings, or creating pretty watercolour scenes of spring flowers to hang on your dressing table, is quite acceptable. But trying to actually sell a painting or drawing? That would be unthinkably vulgar!'

'Absolutely,' Lord Theo agreed in a dry tone. 'Although you always lament that men have so much more freedom than ladies, in this instance, Miss Henley, I think you must admit that gentleman suffer from the same restrictions.'

'True,' Emma admitted. 'For a gentlemen to perform as a professional musician or to paint portraits for hire would be as scandalous as him opening a shop.'

'Still, it was very kind of you to compliment Arabella's talent,' Ellie said. 'I suppose it wouldn't do any harm to indulge her with another lesson, should you chance to visit again. After your encouragement today, if you do come, I'm afraid she will almost certainly ask you for one!'

'I would enjoy encouraging her. Drawing is a wonderful outlet, even if she can only practise it in her infrequent leisure moments. Perhaps I'll bring her some pencils and charcoal next time.'

Ellie looked sceptical, as if she believed Lord Theo was unlikely to darken the door of the school again, much less come armed with gifts, but was too polite to say so. 'She would love them,' she said at last. 'Now, can I offer you tea in my office?'

'No, thank you, I must be getting back,' Emma said, rising. 'I did so enjoy spending time with the girls. I have a much clearer idea now of how they are trained, which ones should complete that training soon and the positions they will be seeking. I shall begin looking around immediately to discover what posts might be available.'

'That would be wonderful!' Ellie said, rising as well, her face lighting in a smile. 'The dearest wish of my heart is to see their hard work culminate in their being hired for positions that will provide them a secure and honest future. Bless you for wanting to help make that happen.'

'It's I who feel blessed, to finally see some real benefit to be gained from trudging through yet another endless Season! One last thing, though. I'm of no use, helping them master most of the skills they study here, but you mentioned earlier that they enjoy listening to you read aloud. Not to boast, but I'm a very good reader. My older sister used to say that having me narrate a story was almost as good as watching a play.'

'Good at voices and impersonations, are you?' Lord Theo asked. 'Why am I not surprised?'

'I suppose all of us have roles we must play,' Ellie said.

'With varying degrees of success,' Emma said ruefully.

Lord Theo looked as if he would speak, but remained silent. Though his face resumed its usual genial expression, once again, Emma sensed some glimmer of deeper emotion behind the pleasant mask.

Perhaps even Lord Theo had his private pain. Emma felt a niggle of shame that she too often dismissed him as an aimless social wastrel. Had he not proven on several occasions that he was perceptive and discerning as well?

She, of all people, ought to know to look deeper than a person's surface charms. Though she wasn't sure it would be wise to discover the already beguiling Lord Theo possessed even more compelling virtues.

'Indeed, the girls love having me read aloud and increasingly I have less and less time to do so. If you would enjoy that, I'm sure you would be a welcome addition to their day.'

'It would be a welcome addition to mine, too.'

'Reminding you of your innocent youth, when play-acting a story was the most complicated part of your day?' Lord Theo asked.

'Something like that,' Emma replied. If only, she thought, ever conscious of the temptation posed by the man seated beside Ellie, it would be that straightforward to figure out the future direction of her relationship with Lord Theo.

'You will be welcome whenever you have time to visit,' Ellie said as she walked them to the door. 'Both of you.'

As Lord Theo directed the phaeton back towards Henley House, recalling the excellence of his sketch, Emma said, 'I was very impressed by how you altered Arabella's drawing. She is not the only one possessed of real talent. What a masterful caricature you created!' She shook her head, remembering. 'I almost wish I could have kept it.'

'Ah, so that's the way you think of me? Massive nose, prominent ears, unruly hair, outrageous raiment? No wonder you are able to resist my charms.'

'Actually, to make the sketch truly accurate, I would have to suggest adding horns and a forked tail,' she shot back.

'You are merciless,' he said mournfully. 'One might even say "cruel". And poor me, only trying to amuse the young lass.'

'You did do that successfully. You seem to have as a deft hand as a teacher as you do with a stick of chalk.' Suddenly recalling his remark about the restrictions placed on gentlemen, she said curiously, 'Do you have aspirations as an artist, Lord Theo? I'm hardly an expert, but you, too, seem to have a true gift.'

'An amusement only. The debonair Lord Theo tarnish his image by doing something as plebeian as dabble in paints?' he retorted, mock-horror in his tone. 'I should think not!'

Though his sardonic tone was light enough, to her ear, an odd edge in his voice made the comment not quite ring true. She glanced over, but he had his attention firmly focused on the horses, his face unreadable.

Whatever she thought she'd heard, he obviously wasn't prepared to discuss it. Did Lord Theo have a secret desire to be a serious artist?

It was a tantalising thought, if improbable. Gentlemen were even less encouraged to paint or sketch than ladies, painting being an occupation reserved for the lower orders. Nothing would seem more out of character for an elegant, fashionable, much-admired society gentleman like Lord Theo.

Tucking away that riddle for another day and resolved, at least on this occasion, to give him all his due, she continued, 'Let me thank you again for treating the girls with such kindness and respect.'

'Ah, yes. Given your poor opinion of my character, I suppose you thought I would try to dazzle them with my magnificence. Perhaps, if I deigned to speak at all, I should look down on them through my quizzing glass.'

'The quizzing glass you don't carry?' She chuckled. 'Although you did dazzle. Isolated as girls like that have been from male magnificence such as yours, how could you not incite awe and admiration?'

He shrugged modestly. 'One does one's possible, though I suppose some of the credit should go to my tailor and valet.' The amused expression on his face fading, he added in a sober tone, 'It still seems sad to me to let a talent like Arabella's be buried under a regimen of cooking, cleaning and housework.'

'Few in our world have the means to do whatever they please. Especially females. For most, marriage is their only guarantee of obtaining financial security. A frail enough guarantee, tied as it is to the productivity and character of the husband. At least Arabella will have the chance to secure a future based on her own abilities. Though it is sad to think of her letting her artistic talent go undeveloped. Unless…'

A spurt of excitement energised her as a novel thought occurred. 'Would it be possible for a female with sufficient training to obtain work as an engraver, a colourist of fashion prints or an illustrator for one of the London magazines?'

'I have no idea. I suspect that a female could only obtain such positions if her father owned the business and brought her up in it, giving her the training and opportunity.' Lord Theo spared a moment from guiding his horses to give her a quick glance and sighed. 'From the hopeful expression on your face, I suspect you're going to task me with investigating the matter.'

'Do you think Arabella has the talent to be successful, if she were to have the opportunity?'

'I don't know that it's possible to determine that at this point. She would almost certainly need some instruction before one could judge how skilful she might become.'

'The Royal Academy has a school of art, does it not?'

'It does, but I have no idea if it would admit a female. I suspect not.'

'It has admitted female members. Angelica Kauffman and Mary Moser were among its founding members.'

'True. But they were already accomplished artists. For the most part, taught by and encouraged in the craft by their fathers.'

'So Arabella would need to find a tutor and then a sponsor to support her work,' Emma summarised thoughtfully.

She'd told Ellie Lattimar she would look for positions for the girls. Might she turn up among her society connections someone who had contacts in the artistic community, who might be able to find Arabella a teacher or a patron?

'I can almost hear the wheels turning in that busy little brain,' Lord Theo said after she'd sat for a few moments in silence. 'Planning to scour the halls of Somerset House hunting for a suitable mentor?'

'I might be. Just think how wonderful it would be, if Arabella were to become another Madame Vigée Le Brun!'

Lord Theo chuckled. 'Much as I admire your enthusiasm, that is getting a bit ahead of yourself. Miss Arabella might turn out to be a merely competent draughtsman, nothing more.'

'But shouldn't she be given a chance to see if she *can* be more? Even making a living as a competent draughtsman, if that skill gave her pleasure, might be preferable to a life in service. Not that it wouldn't be quite an achievement for a girl who began as an orphan on the streets to rise to the status of a housekeeper—if that is truly the height of her ambition. But when I think of how much I enjoy looking at the Gainsborough portrait of my grandfather, or how Havell's *Landscape in the Lake District* lifts my spirits every time I gaze at it… Imagine, having the talent to capture such beauty on canvas, to be preserved and admired, an inspiration to others! Imagine what a tragedy it would be never to do so because one never had the opportunity. How much beauty would be lost to the world!'

'How much indeed,' he murmured. 'Very well, I'll see what I can find out. But I don't promise miracles.'

'I don't expect them. Only reliable information. Since, as a gentleman, you can visit establishments and obtain honest opinions that I, as a lady, could never access. Though I shall be looking for such opportunities as I can discover.'

He chuckled. 'You may soon find opportunities—and me—in some surprising places.'

Before she could ask him to explain that cryptic comment, they reached a busier stretch of road, requiring Lord Theo to devote all his attention to his horses.

They lapsed into a companionable silence—though neither silence nor the unusually serious direction of their conversation were able to distract her from his sheer masculine presence, seated so close beside her in the phaeton.

Truly, Emma thought with a sigh, Lord Theo the society wastrel was already too appealing. Lord Theo the concerned gentleman, who'd undertake to help a girl of no birth or family, was even harder to resist.

The insidious desire to allow her body to brush against his when the curricle swung around a corner made her brace herself further away. As much as she suspected—hoped—the sensual attraction between them might be mutual, now was not the time to act on it.

There might never be a time. But she wouldn't worry about that now. Suddenly the Season had new purpose—to find positions for Ellie Lattimar's girls. And to see if Lord Theo followed through on his pledge.

The notion that they shared some common purpose created an even more insidious bond. She needed to remember that, though he apparently would humour her on the matter of Arabella, he could withdraw his support—and his sympathy—at any time. Most likely, as he'd just broken with his mistress, he was only bored and out of sorts.

Whatever the reason for his surprising willingness to help, she meant to take advantage of it while the mood lasted.

A few minutes later, they reached the Henley town house. As the tiger trotted over to help her down, she said, 'Thank you so much for driving me to Mrs Lattimar's school. I can now accept Mama's bargain with a sense of excitement, knowing I may use my last months in society to accomplish some real good. And thank you even more for agreeing to help Arabella.'

'You're very welcome.' Occupied in holding his horses still while she prepared to dismount, he spared her only a quick, oddly assessing glance. 'You are a remarkable woman, Emma Henley,' he said and nodded to the tiger to hand her down.

Chapter Eight

The following night, Emma stood with her friends Olivia and Sara at the side of the Lady Petersham's ballroom, watching the dancers while Olivia's mother and Sara's aunt, Lady Patterson, chatted nearby. Once seeing her safely moored next to her friends' chaperons, Lady Henley had given Emma's hand a squeeze and let herself be carried off by a group of her current admirers.

'I'm glad no gentlemen invited us to dance this set, so I may tell you both what transpired when I spoke to Mama about refusing Nullford,' Emma murmured, her voice pitched so only her friends might hear her.

'I hadn't dared ask,' Olivia said, her voice dropping to a conspiratorial whisper as she drew both friends closer, 'Now, you must tell all!'

In a few short sentences, Emma related her mother's contrition—which drew shocked exclamations from both Olivia and Sara—and her offer to allow Emma to begin looking for a house, as long as she agreed to remain in society. 'So you see,' Emma concluded, 'perhaps as early as the end of the Season, I shall have all in motion for the two of you to join me as soon as you are able.'

'That would be wonderful!' Sara exclaimed.

'That *is* excellent news,' Olivia said, her voice mirroring Sara's excitement.

'When might you be able to begin looking for a suitable house?'

'Perhaps as early as tomorrow. We're not quite ready to implement our long-cherished dreams yet,' Emma cautioned. 'But at least it's a beginning! Speaking of beginning worthy projects, I paid a visit to Ellie Lattimar's school yesterday.'

'How so?' Olivia asked. 'Did you coax your mama into accompanying you?'

'Actually, no.' Emma looked away, suddenly needing to straighten the lace on her sleeve. 'I met Lord Theo when I was riding yesterday morning and teased him into driving me there.'

Her two friends fell silent before Olivia said, 'I'd…forgotten I'd seen him speaking with you at several social events this year. You became rather well acquainted last Season, didn't you, when he was dancing attendance on Temperance Lattimar, before she married the Earl of Fensworth? I didn't realise you'd continued the friendship.'

Emma smiled wryly. 'I'm his verbal equivalent

of a hair shirt, I believe. When he tires of listening to the universal acclaim with which he's usually greeted, he comes to talk with me, knowing I can always be counted upon to roundly abuse him.'

The relationship was much more complicated than that, Emma knew. But not even to these dear friends did she wish to confess how much she had come to enjoy those 'sharp exchanges'. Or how strong was the sensual attraction that drew her to him—nor how deeply conflicted the feelings that attraction churned up in her.

'Appreciates plain speaking, does he?' Olivia said, raising her eyebrows. 'I've always taken him for a lazy, expensive fribble of a younger son. But if he values you enough to continue the connection, I might have to reassess that opinion.'

'He's certainly handsome, charming and well born,' Sara said. Looking at Emma thoughtfully, she added, 'You're not…developing a *tendre* there, are you?'

'Heavens, no!' Emma declared, forcing what she hoped was a light-hearted laugh. 'The Homely Miss Henley and the Divine Lord Theo? I should hope I'm not that stupid!'

'Didn't we all vow long ago to be sensible enough not to fall in love with handsome, shallow men who would spend our dowries and neglect us?' Olivia said.

'Speaking of the devil, isn't that him over

there, charming the beauteous Miss Fothergill?'
Sara said.

Emma looked in the direction Sara indicated,
to find it was indeed Lord Theo, looking down at
the enchantingly beautiful blonde who had been
declared the current Season's reigning diamond.
Miss Fothergill, who was fortunate enough to
possess a dowry as handsome as her looks, had
been wondrously popular with the gentlemen,
having always about her a large coterie of the
rich and titled, as well as less-fortunate swains.

With an uncomfortable pang, Emma noted that
the Beauty had not only accorded Lord Theo a
prime place right beside her, she was laughing
up at him in appreciation of some sally, her hand
draped on his arm.

Evidently their conversation had gone on for
some time, for the other members of her court
were looking decidedly disgruntled.

Emma had observed the potent power beauty
had to ensnare men often enough that this tab-
leau shouldn't have come as a surprise. Nor was
it less than the height of folly to feel somehow…
betrayed that Lord Theo was paying marked attention to another woman. *Ridiculous* folly, for
she knew, once his break with Lady Belinda was
complete, he'd soon replace that paramour with
another, equally lovely one.

Even if Emma hadn't misinterpreted his heated

looks and his suggestive words, it would be a long time before she'd have any opportunity to test their mutual attraction. He would probably make love to and discard a dozen women before then.

In any event, it was highly unlikely he would pay serious court to a beauty like Miss Fothergill, whose charms would be priced at marriage.

That she felt anything but amusement at watching him work his wiles should be a strong warning that she had given her foolish feminine side entirely too much leeway. Time to rein it back in and return to the more appropriate, and much safer, role of hair shirt.

As she reached that resolve, Lord Theo bowed, slipped Miss Fothergill's hand off his sleeve and offered it to one of the gentlemen hovering beside her. Before Emma could jerk her gaze away, he turned to walk off—and caught her watching him.

A broad smile creasing his face, he gave her a little nod—and headed in her direction.

'I believe he's coming to speak with you,' Sara whispered.

'Going from the beauty to the beast,' Emma quipped, trying to squelch the surge of excitement the annoying foolish female within her seemed to feel whenever Lord Theo drew near.

'We'll excuse ourselves and leave you to abuse him,' Olivia said. 'Considering the effusions he must have received from Miss Fothergill and her set, he should be in dire need of a comedown.'

And then he stood beside them, bowing. Half-delighted, half-irritated by the anticipation that sped her pulse and set nervous eddies swirling in her belly, Emma dipped a curtsy.

'Miss Henley. And—Miss Overton and Miss Standish, is it not? A good evening to you. A fine gathering, do you not think?'

'Tolerable,' Olivia said, exchanging a quick, surprised look with Emma. 'Kind of you to remember us, sir. I had not expected you would.'

'We've not met often, but Miss Henley has spoken so highly of her friends, of course I would remember them. If she holds you in esteem, you must be clever and charming indeed.'

'Olivia, I believe Aunt Patterson just signalled to me,' Sara said. 'Delightful to see you again, Lord Theo.'

'Ladies,' he said, bowing again as they moved away. 'Since the orchestra is presently taking a break, would you walk with me, Miss Henley?'

After nodding, Emma raised her eyebrows at him. 'You have scored some points with my friends,' she said as they set off. 'As seldom as you attend gatherings of eligible maidens like this, I didn't think you would recall them.'

'Ah, but last Season I received a signal lesson in the importance of remembering all the young ladies to whom I'm introduced,' he replied. 'It impressed itself upon my psyche so deeply, I shall never forget it. And you *have* spoken highly of your friends. Those are the ladies with whom you intend to stake your independence, I presume?'

'Yes.' All too conscious of him beside her, of her hand resting on his arm—the same arm Miss Fothergill had so recently been clutching—Emma had to concentrate very hard to ignore his distracting nearness. 'And what are you about this evening, Lord Theo? You've attended Marriage Mart events before, but generally devoted yourself to the safely married matrons. Surely you don't intend to raise the hopes of all these fond mamas by entering the matrimonial ring at last?'

Before he could reply, the answer to the riddle came to her, and she laughed. 'Ah, you must have broken with the Beauteous Belinda! So you completed your "onerous" task. Did you in fact send her a chatelaine?'

He chuckled as well. 'A pair of sapphire earrings seemed a safer gift. None the less, as she makes the rounds of social engagements, she might well be ready to spit in my eye, if not strangle me outright, should we chance to meet.'

'A woman impolitic enough to flaunt her lover in front of her husband could be capable of anything,' Emma agreed. 'Although even the outrageous Lady Belinda is unlikely to accost you in full view of a crowded ballroom like this.'

'True. So with her threat to my dignity neutralised, I must entreat *you* to be on best behaviour and not embarrass me in front of any society diamonds, the way you did with Miss Lattimar last Season.'

'As I am not friends with any other society diamonds, you may consider yourself safe. You don't truly mean to frequent this segment of society, do you? Charming debutantes like Miss Fothergill?'

To her surprise, a look of irritation creased his brow. 'I hadn't initially planned on spending much time at such entertainments. But you're not the only one who was recently closeted for a serious discussion with a parent. It seems Lord Ballister called on my father.'

'Oh, dear!' Emma said, immediately realising the implications. 'That must not have been a… comfortable interview. But surely the Marquess realises that you didn't encourage Lady Belinda's unfortunate behaviour at the opera.'

'Though Papa admitted as much, he also said it was time I mend my rake's ways and begin looking to settle down. Settle down!' he spat out, the sharp undertone of anger behind those words surprising Emma with its intensity. 'For years, I've dutifully played the rake, a role he urged on me, the pride he expressed at my supposed "mastery of masculine accomplishments" the only praise I ever had from him. But apparently Lady Belinda was one scandal too many and now I must turn from social lion to lapdog.'

Emma tried to picture him with some sweet young wife hanging on his arm—and couldn't manage it. 'Do you truly mean to change?'

'I'm not sure I could if I wanted to,' he replied ruefully. 'I've made myself into the man I am and lived the part for so long, I'd have no idea how to begin. Nor do I have much interest in trying, frankly. You'll abuse me for sounding like a coxcomb, but I've never managed to remain interested in one woman for very long. If I were forced to marry, my wife would have to be a society lady who understands the game.'

'You mean, a lady content to enjoy being the wife of a well-born nobleman, who wouldn't demand love—or fidelity?' she asked, somehow compelled to have him confirm what she already suspected.

'Would I want a wife who required me to dance attendance on her constantly?' He shuddered. 'Certainly not! It would be stifling. But fortunately, I'm not forced to the decision point yet. Once the contretemps over Lady Belinda dies down, I'm reasonably certain Papa will forget about me again. Whereupon I can resume my usual frivolous, wastrel life.'

Troubled by the self-deprecating scorn of that final remark, Emma couldn't think of a response before Lord Theo's brow cleared and he laughed. 'Enough melodrama! If I should decide it's time to beguile some eligible maiden, do you think my sins would be sufficiently forgiven by *ton* matrons that I would be invited to their entertainments?'

'A handsome, charming, rich young gentleman of good family?' Emma laughed. 'Nothing more quickly redeems a rake's reputation than the hint that he might wish to marry! If the matchmaking mamas suspected you were considering wedlock, past sins would be instantly forgiven. Although do you really think you could enjoy gatherings like this, filled as they are, not by clever and knowing matrons, but by the innocent and eligible sort of female you normally avoid?'

'Ah, but you are here. Isn't that incentive enough for me to attend?'

Once again, the look in his eyes sent little shivers through her. But the idea that he might be courting *her* was so ridiculous, she immediately squelched it. 'You'll not cozen me into believing you would come to gatherings like this with the express purpose of encountering me.'

'Would I not? How else am I to keep what is, according to you, already a massive ego from growing ever larger from all the adulation I receive? Especially if there are a bevy of matchmaking mamas present. Surely I must be in frequent need of a scathing assessment of my faults and character.'

'You make me sound…brutal,' she protested.

'But you are, Miss Henley, always! I end each encounter with you so cut by the slings and arrows of my inadequacies I can hardly prevent myself from bleeding to death with remorse and shame.'

She was laughing out loud now. 'Goodness! Doing it much too strong, my lord! As I recall, I bid you goodbye two days ago after having paid you several quite sincere compliments.'

'Did you?' He shook his head. 'The experience was so singular, I must have concluded I only imagined it.'

'Well, if you want to *seem* to accede to your father's wishes, but harbour no serious matrimonial intentions, joining Miss Fothergill's admirers is a wise choice. Her beauty and immense dowry make her court a large one. Despite your admitted charm, you're unlikely to win her away from titled men of larger fortunes.'

He clapped a hand to his chest. 'You are finally admitting that I have charm?'

'You *are* a coxcomb!' she retorted, slapping his arm with her fan. 'The beauteous Miss Fothergill might enjoy taunting her courtiers and triumphing over her rivals by parading herself on the arm of a man who's never previously shown any interest in virtuous maidens. But in the end, she values herself higher than to bestow her hand on a untitled younger son.'

'Trying to save me from the heartbreak of pursuing her, only to be rejected?'

Emma barely kept herself from rolling her eyes. 'Perhaps—if I were convinced you in fact possess a heart that could be broken. But since you just admitted you only intend to linger among the innocents until your papa ceases to concern himself with your activities, by all means, hide among Miss Fothergill's courtiers.'

'Hide? Might I not just wish to linger nearby to bask in her beauty?'

Emma knew the remark was teasing. Still, it touched so closely on her deepest vulnerabilities that pain slashed across her chest, as sharp as it was foolish.

'Don't let me keep you, then. Go back and bask.'

Suddenly desperate to quit his presence, she dropped his arm and whirled around. Before she could flee, he caught her elbow and turned her back to face him.

'Do you truly think me so shallow that I care about that silly, feather-headed bauble?'

His fierce gaze paralysed her, seemed to penetrate down to her soul, to all her needy and vulnerable places. The intensity of it sent a sensual current of awareness all over her body, shocking every nerve and creating a spiral of melting sensation at her centre.

Then his eyes dropped, as they had before, to linger on her lips, the gaze so potent she could almost feel it as a kiss.

Out of the corner of her eye, she sensed Olivia and Sara approaching, halting by her elbow. While she stood immobilised, barely able to breathe, he looked away and nodded at them.

'I'll leave you to your friends. Miss Henley, Miss Overton, Miss Standish, a good evening to you.' With a bow to them all, he paced away across the floor.

Still bedazzled, Emma watched him retreat, unconsciously raising a gloved hand to lips that still tingled. Even the cynical voice in her head was silent before the power of the desire he'd aroused.

He'd seemed almost—angry—that she'd sent him away to enjoy Miss Fothergill's beauty. Yet how could he not wish to?

Torn between hope and denial, she shook her head. How ridiculous she was, imagining that there might ever be something between the 'Homely Miss Henley' and one of most attractive, virile members of *ton*. She need only glance at the golden Incomparable that was Miss Fothergill or picture the voluptuous, raven-haired, blue-eyed siren Lady Belinda.

No, not likely. No matter how much *he* aroused *her*.

Belatedly nodding to her friends, she said, 'Shall we go in for some supper? I'm suddenly famished.'

Though they both looked at her in concern, doubtless able to sense the current lingering in the air, like the aura after a lightning strike, fortunately neither asked her what had occurred.

She wasn't sure she could have told them.

Very well, Lord Theo made her body sing. However, she reminded herself as she followed her friends to the refreshment room, if she gathered together all the ladies in whom he produced that reaction, she would have a group large enough to perform a rousing rendition of Handel's 'Hallelujah Chorus'.

And he would hum along with each one.

Chapter Nine

❧❧❧❧

Striding away across the ballroom, Lord Theo struggled to control his agitation. Bad enough to have his father harassing him. He didn't need the normally calm and rational Miss Henley to suddenly turn on him.

He'd thought he was making a light-hearted remark, in keeping with the banter they'd been exchanging, when suddenly her eyes had widened and her expression turned as hurt as if he'd…he'd *struck* her.

What in blazes had come over the woman? After all the jibes they'd traded, he wouldn't have believed she could suddenly become so *sensitive*. Up until this moment, she'd hardly shown herself to be a fragile soul whom one must handle with verbal kid gloves.

And after all the frank conversations they'd had, he'd thought she was canny enough to see beyond his polished society veneer—even to prefer the real man who lurked beneath. He'd been incensed to think she would actually believe him shallow enough to have been swept away by a chit of a girl who could hardly contribute a single intelligent comment to a conversation. A supremely self-absorbed beauty who'd been so courted, flattered and pampered her whole life, she took every man's adulation as her due.

Even as he willed himself to calm, he realised *his* reaction to Miss Henley's reaction was equally excessive—and wasn't sure whether he was more angry at her, or with himself. Despite their often sharply worded remarks, he would never have wished to hurt her. Though he hadn't intended to, clearly he had wounded her.

Seeing in her curt dismissal how obviously she rated her own charms as inferior to those of the fêted Miss Fothergill had also angered him. The 'Homely Miss Henley' indeed. Suddenly, he'd hated the nasty sobriquet the *ton* had hung on her. The attraction he always had to work to restrain had boiled up so fiercely, he'd wanted to prove to her how wrong that assessment was by kissing her, right there in ballroom.

He'd only just refrained. After which, the only prudent thing was to take his leave as quickly as possible.

By the time he'd gathered his hat and cloak, the intensity of his irritation had diminished. Still, if the blasted woman was going to evoke so strong a reaction that he had come seriously close to kissing her in public, he probably ought to consider terminating their friendship right now.

Though the simple word 'friendship' didn't begin to fully describe the complex relationship that had grown between them over the last year.

True, friends might snipe at each other as they often did, the needle-sharp accuracy of her comments sometimes truly making him feel he might bleed. But there was never malice behind her remarks, only a shrewdness, unhindered by any need to dissemble, that sometimes revealed truths he might not have enjoyed hearing, but that had made him think more seriously about himself and what he wanted than he would otherwise have been moved to do.

He had many 'friends'. But most of them spoke to him only of the everyday trivialities of life, of bloods and bruisers, horses, hounds and hunting, gaming or drinking or the pursuit of women not known for their virtue. No one but Emma Henley talked to him about things of true importance. The need for change in the way their country was governed. Supporting a school for girls who might otherwise have no alternative but the streets or the brothels. Trying to find a better future for a young woman of true talent.

And how his inner being had thrilled when

Miss Henley talked about the uplifting power of art! When she marvelled at how unique and precious a gift was the talent of those who could create works that delighted and inspired.

Most members of his class saw artists as just another sort of tradesmen, producing items to decorate their homes, their products no more special or different than a vase or a sofa.

He'd had to clamp his lips tightly together to avoid confessing he'd once yearned to devote his full efforts to that sort of creation.

He sighed. Perhaps if he'd dare reveal that to her, she wouldn't have accused him of preferring the company of the brainless Miss Fothergill.

Then there was that bedevilling, ever-intensifying physical connection that, like tonight, kept pulling him insidiously closer to doing something rash.

She truly was unlike any other female he'd known. The more time he spent with her, the stronger grew the flame of her uniqueness, luring him ever nearer.

Which could be both dangerous and frustrating.

Dangerous, because as much as she amused him, spending time with her always carried with it the possibility that society—or her mother—might consider some mischance of an encounter compromising. Which would mean a forced marriage.

Frustrating, for even if she accomplished her oft-stated plan to leave society and became an independent woman living according to her *own* rules, rather than society's, he doubted she'd truly be adventurous enough to take him for a lover.

Why continue to plague himself with a desire that could never be consummated?

Maybe he ought to untangle himself from his increasingly complicated involvement with her.

But then he couldn't completely cut the connection yet. He had pledged to discover for her what opportunities might exist for Mrs Lattimar's talented student to receive training as an artist.

They could hardly be more different—Arabella, the penniless street orphan, and Lord Theo, the wealthy, indulged member of aristocracy whose every wish—or most all of them—had been granted. But when they talked about drawing, the desire to instil more realism in the design, to create from what was merely chalk on slate an image that lived, breathed and had personality, he had felt his long-suppressed creative self begin to stir. Just that brief taste of discussing and sharing the suppressed passion he had for his art had excited him and given him a sense of satisfaction he hadn't felt in a long time.

Even now, he felt the strong urge to pick up his brushes again.

But what would be the point? A gentleman did not work as an artist.

Maybe he could offer Arabella the chance he had been denied. Somehow, he knew Emma Henley, if not his father, would be proud of him for that.

And somehow, it had become important to him that Emma Henley, whose appeal bedevilled him and whom society disdained, think well of him.

Despite his ambivalence over whether or not to continue their association, Theo was anxious to apologise for the distress he'd caused Miss Henley. He expected he might meet her riding in the park, where most of their encounters this Season had taken place. But the next two mornings passed without him catching sight of her galloping by on her big black gelding.

On both the following evenings, he dropped by several of the *ton* entertainments he thought Lady Henley most likely to attend, also without encountering her.

He did follow her good advice at several of the events by joining the court of admirers surrounded Miss Fothergill. That protective colouration had been sufficient to prevent any of the other matchmaking mamas present from harbouring the pleasant but erroneous notion that he was developing aspirations towards one of their daughters.

Marking time at his third soirée of the evening, he'd once again claimed a place at Miss Fothergill's side. Having discovered by now that the beautiful heiress was even more feather-headed than he'd first suspected, conversing with her required only a portion of his attention, a gentle flow of empty but practised compliments being sufficient to keep her entertained. He was thus able to devote the majority of his intellect to pondering the problem of apologising to Miss Henley.

Gentlemen didn't generally write to unattached ladies, but having had such bad luck encountering her in person, should he take the risk of sending her a note? Or perhaps he should stop by Mrs Lattimar's school, bring Arabella the paper and charcoal he'd promised, in hopes of encountering her there.

For the first time in memory, he'd left a lady on bad terms. Normally, he was able to smoothly extricate himself from the presence even of persistent, presumptuous or unpleasant females with practised ease, leaving the lady in question still smiling. This time, he'd walked away with the lady so visibly upset and himself so angry, an uncomfortable feeling had sat like lead in his gut ever since.

He was most anxious to rid himself of it.

He was still mulling over alternatives for doing so when he noticed Lady Henley and some gentlemen returning from the card room. Trailing in their wake was her daughter.

Offering Miss Fothergill a glib pleasantry and a bow, he quit her side and quickly made his way across the crowded floor towards where the group had paused at the opposite edge of the ballroom. As Theo wove in and out among the couples, he was aware that, for the perhaps the first time in his long experience with women, he was unsure exactly what to say.

And for perhaps the first time in his long experience, it mattered a great deal that he say the right thing.

When Miss Henley realised he was approaching and curtsied, rather than cutting him, as he'd half-feared she might, he felt an almost dizzying sense of relief.

As he rose from his bow, she angled her eyes briefly in her mother's direction. Taking the hint that she didn't wish to exchange more than commonplace pleasantries within hearing of that lady and her escorts, he reined in his impatience and said only, 'A good evening to you, Lady Henley, Miss Henley, gentlemen. I hope Lady Luck was with you tonight.'

Lady Hanley laughed. 'I didn't lose too much,

so I am content to take my leave. I trust you are ready as well, my dear?'

'Yes, Mama,' Miss Henley replied.

'Surely you don't intend to depart this early, ma'am,' one of her gallants protested. 'Several sets remain and I have not yet had the pleasure of dancing with you!'

'Much as I regret disappointing you, I promised Emma we could return home as soon as I finished that last rubber,' Lady Henley replied. 'You wouldn't want me to break my word, would you?'

While the swains argued over who should have the honour of escorting the ladies to their carriage, Theo said softly, 'Will you ride tomorrow morning?'

She nodded. 'I hope to.'

'Then I shall look for you.'

'Please do.'

The smile she gave him as she turned to follow her mother from the room was brief, but cordial. With relief—and an impatience to speak with her again that, he realised with a twinge of unease, was greater than it should be—he watched her walk away.

Chapter Ten

Theo arrived at Hyde Park the next morning just as the sun was cresting the horizon, topping the sky with a rosy halo. Though it was earlier than he would normally expect to encounter Miss Henley, he was eager not to miss her.

He'd intended to spend the remainder of last evening at his club. But after playing several hands of cards, he'd found his fellow members' usual excesses of brandy and their predictable conversation on the same predictable topics so irritating, he'd curtailed the night's revelry much earlier than usual.

There'd been a chorus of surprise and protest when he announced his intention to leave, his current partner pointing out that as it was barely midnight, the evening was far too young for him to be departing. But finding the mantle of debonair society wastrel wearing increasingly thin, he knew he needed to leave before he shocked his fellows by losing his control and snapping at someone.

He'd thrown in his cards and risen to depart, walking out to a chorus of boos and jeers, punctuated by several indecent suggestions.

Arriving back at his lodgings, he'd pulled his box of paints out of the back of his wardrobe and plucked paper, pencils and charcoal out of the drawer to which he'd consigned them months ago. After lighting more candles, he devoted several hours to doing a *nature morte* drawing of some apples, cheese and wine he assembled on his desk.

He'd awakened this morning, more eager and energised than he'd felt in months, ready to resume sketching—and purchase new oils.

Was it Miss Henley's influence, her sharp comments about him needing to find something more important to do with his life, that had deepened his dissatisfaction with the idle pastimes to which he'd devoted himself for years?

Though the encounter with Arabella had definitely sparked the long-dormant urge to create, the lady he waited to meet had certainly fanned the flame.

His musings interrupted by the tattoo of hoofbeats, he looked up—and, with a swell of anticipation, recognised Miss Henley on her black. Kicking his mount, he rode over to meet her.

Mindful of her attendant groom, they exchanged only conventional greetings until the servant dropped back a respectful distance. After directing his mount to walk beside hers, he began, 'Let me apologise—' at the same moment she said, 'I'm so sorry that—'

Both of them breaking off, Theo gestured to Miss Henley. 'Ladies first,' he said, the warm glow of her presence finally beginning to displace the cold lump that had lodged in his belly. Miss Henley had come as she'd promised—and appeared as anxious as he was to end the discord between them.

'I'm sorry to have been so—so missish at Lady Petersham's ball,' she said. 'It was silly of me to overreact in that way. I do realise you are too clever to be dazzled by beauty alone. If Miss Fothergill attracts you, it would be for her wit as much as her appearance.'

'Sadly, she doesn't possess both. But you must allow me to apologise, too. Though I meant my words only to be teasing, somehow they wounded you. I hope you realise that was never my intention.'

Even before he'd finished speaking, she held up a hand, shaking her head. 'No, no, you've no need to apologise. It was all my fault, being foolishly oversensitive.'

She sighed, remaining silent for a moment before continuing, 'You are a handsome man, Lord

Theo, a fact confirmed every time you glimpse your face in a mirror. I am…not a pretty female, a fact of which the glass would constantly remind me, if those around me hadn't been drumming that truth into me for years. And as a handsome man, you probably cannot understand what it is like for a plain girl living in a society where a female's worth is determined almost solely by her looks. It has made me…wary, I suppose. And so, in that instant when it appeared that even you, a man I'd come to know as more discerning than the idle society gentleman he appeared, would be swept away by looks alone, that touched at…a deep sensitivity in me. That sensitivity is my failing and you incur no fault for having inadvertently stumbled upon it.'

He'd intended to reply with a sally about being struck that she considered him 'discerning'—but so frank and personal an avowal deserved better than a flippant reply. 'You are right, I cannot imagine your position,' he said quietly. 'It did make me angry that you seemed to discount your own appeal, when you possess so many admirable traits—a piercing intellect, the ability to see beneath the surface, rather than just taking things to be what they appear, and the courage to speak out about what you believe important.'

'Those might be thought virtues by some—though I fear you have too often been at the sharp end of the speaking out! But you must admit, society seldom values a woman for her intellect, and most members of both sexes prefer not to look beneath the surface. They especially do not want to see the ugliness and want that exists outside the comfortable cocoon of our own prosperity—or even within it, our privileged life made possible by the service of others. Whereas beauty is easy to look upon, never taxing to the mind. I don't mean to sound dismissive! I appreciate the bright hues of a flower, a lovely piece of music—or the appeal of a handsome man—as much as anyone. But it is…dispiriting when what is on the surface alone is lauded, even when unaccompanied by any other virtues.'

He nodded. 'As it so often is. Did your own family not value you? Your mother seems to care for you'.

'Apparently, she does love me, although for most of my life that affection was expressed in laments about my lack of looks and worries about the difficulties that would create in getting me respectably settled. Which is why she has urged upon me men even she concedes would have been a poor match, in fear that I am not pretty enough to attract a better suitor.'

'Good heavens!' he exclaimed, appalled. 'She actually told you that?' When she nodded, with a disbelieving shake of the head, he said flatly, 'You were right. I cannot imagine that.'

She sighed. 'Some of my most vivid early memories are of my father, on the few occasions that he did not go out to his club, sitting in the drawing room as my sister and I were brought down by our governess. He would nod approval at a drawing I'd done or a paper I'd written, but it was my sister he called his "pretty little princess" and pulled on to his lap. Or the times we sneaked out of the nursery to peer down the stairs at Mama's elegant gentlemen callers, it was always my sister they would beckon to sneak down, call pet names or offer hair ribbons and sweetmeats—never me. My sister's whispering, while our governess praised some accomplishment of mine, that my being clever didn't matter, because I wasn't pretty and would never marry as well as she would, didn't help, either.'

He tried to think of something soothing, but the pain she'd expressed—that he felt for her, hearing about those experiences—was too profound and genuine to be assuaged by a quick quip or a facile remark.

As he remained silent, she said wryly, 'Don't worry, I've finished now with my far-too-detailed explanation on the subject of beauty. Though no explanation excuses my poor manners. Apology accepted?'

He nodded. 'Apology accepted—as long as you will accept mine for *my* poor manners, stalking off and leaving you alone on the middle of the ballroom.'

'To be fair, you left me with friends. Let us just say that we both behaved badly, are sorry for it and are ready to move on. So—friendship restored?'

'Friendship restored! It is regrettable, the damage mothers, fathers or siblings can do to an impressionable child,' he said with feeling.

'Surely you weren't abused by yours!' She cocked her head at him. 'Or, as the younger son, were you sometimes ignored in favour of the heir?'

'Always,' he confirmed. 'Although generally I considered it a blessing not to attract my father's attention.' His smile faded as he remembered. 'His scrutiny was all too often a painful experience.'

'Why so? You might not have been the heir, but you are intelligent, clever and handsome. What more could a father want of a younger son?'

He hesitated, but after her naked honesty in revealing her past, it seemed cowardly not to reply in kind. Besides, he found he *wanted* to reveal more of himself to the one person of his acquaintance who seemed to actually appreciate candour.

'You…asked me before if I'd had aspirations to be an artist. Once upon a time, I did.'

Sighing, he faced the memories he normally suppressed. 'We were at Wynchgrove Hall for the hunting season, the autumn I turned thirteen. Even at that age, I knew painting wasn't an activity my father would approve of, so I'd mostly dabbled surreptitiously, away from the family. But this one morning—ah, the light was so perfect! I got so caught up in working on a landscape that I lost all track of time and missed riding out with Papa. When he returned and discovered what I'd been doing, he gave me a thundering scold. After ordering that I give up this "disgraceful, womanish pastime", he tossed canvas, paints and all into the fire.'

'I'm so sorry,' she said softly.

Something painful shifted in his chest at her sympathy. Turning away from her too-perceptive gaze, he continued, 'I suppose every son craves his father's approval. Hurt as I was by his scorn, I resolved to devote myself to mastering the "manly" pursuits he admired—gaming and riding and charming women of questionable virtue.'

'You succeeded admirably,' she said drily.

'I suppose. Until the episode with Lady Belinda, my father seemed satisfied with my conduct. Certainly the lesson he'd taught was reinforced by my time at university and then in

London.' He shook his head. 'Let a gentleman drink all night, lose a fortune at cards, carouse with his fellows, fail to pay his tailor, and make a fool of himself chasing strumpets and society will smile upon him. But let him engage in a profession other than the law or the church and the *ton*, like my father, would believe he had betrayed his breeding and embarrassed his family.'

'Despite all that, you've never lost your desire to paint.'

'No. In fact, the session with Arabella has rather…revived it, stronger than ever.'

Miss Henley looked up at him, her expression earnest. 'Then you must decide what is more important to you. To be accepted, admired and lauded as an idle young man of fashion, going about the repetitive, mindless rituals of society? Or to discover whether or not you truly possess the gift to create work that can inform and inspire the world.'

While he fumbled for an answer to the question he'd deliberately shied away from asking himself for years, she continued, her eyes lighting with enthusiasm, 'Actually, as you *do* live on your own, out of your family's view, you could very well discover the answer without having to risk your father's or society's disapproval. Take instruction quietly, without letting anyone know. You could gain a true measure of how much talent you possess and *then* decide whether pursuing it is worth the cost to your reputation, position and standing with your family. Although, even if you should take up painting as a full-time vocation, since your wealth allows you to avoid becoming a tradesman by *selling* your works, you might not suffer as much socially as you fear. Society would think you odd, of course, and you would likely lose those friends who only wished to carouse, but I doubt you would be ostracised.'

He had occasionally considered the idea of finding a tutor—and shied away from making a decision about it as he'd avoiding thinking seriously about changing the course of his future. 'That I, with all the resources at my command, have not yet done so must make me look quite the coward to a lady like you, who is prepared to throw away the approval of society to do what you feel important, as soon as you can get your hands on the means to do so.'

She shook her head. 'It's not for me to judge someone else's choices. We must all find our own path.'

He felt humbled by the graciousness of that reply. Then, an instant later, he realised it also offered him a chance to redirect the conversation away from painful revelations towards a topic that was both more comfortable and one for which he had a burning question in need of an answer.

Trying to keep his tone casual, he said, 'You don't believe your path will include marriage?'

'I'm not *fundamentally* opposed to wedlock,' she replied. 'But I've seldom witnessed a union I would like to replicate. Since I have the financial freedom to live on my own, I see no need for a marriage like my parents', distant and polite, in which each spouse goes his or her own way. Nor am I prepared to indulge in—or tolerate in my partner—the casual infidelity so commonplace in our society. If I were to marry, I would give my whole heart, not just my person and my dowry. And since whatever wealth I possess would become legally my husband's, I would only risk marriage to a man who truly loved me, who believed in the causes I believe in and would allow me to support them. Whether it be funding schools like Mrs Lattimar's, lessons for a girl like Arabella or franking letters about pending legislation.

'However,' she concluded with a smile, 'having been in society for five Seasons without encountering any such gentleman, I might as well be fundamentally opposed to wedlock.'

He wasn't surprised to learn that a lady as idealistic as Emma required fidelity—and an all-consuming passion. In that case, she *was* wise to avoid marriage. He could count on one hand the unions he knew in which that wedding vow was honoured—or in which the partners were completely devoted to one another.

Having spent his adulthood in relationships that were decidedly more carnal than idealistic, he didn't think he was capable of either fidelity or devotion.

But that didn't answer his other pressing question.

'You said once you'd never belong to any man. I now understand your views on marriage. But… what of passion?'

There, he'd dared ask her. He held his breath, knowing if she chose to answer, she would give him the absolute truth.

She hesitated so long, he was convinced she meant to ignore his inappropriate enquiry. But then, keeping her face averted, she said softly, 'Passion…is another matter. Though experiencing it would be a tremendous risk for a female who did not wish to marry, I cannot say that I would never be tempted to do so, however unwise.'

So his instincts had been correct—there *was* a passionate nature concealed beneath her proper exterior—one she wasn't sure she was willing to live a lifetime suppressing. Delight soared within him at the possibilities the future might offer a discreet, careful, caring gentleman…when Emma was safely established in her own home, away from the penetrating glare of society, accountable to no one for her actions but herself.

'Well, enough serious discussion for so early in morning!' she said, pulling him from that provocative vision. 'I have a quite different and much more mundane topic for you, if you'll allow me to ask about it.'

Instantly curious, he waved a hand. 'Certainly. Enquire away.'

'You may remember that my mother gave me permission to begin looking for a suitable house to rent. I was so thrilled to begin! But it hasn't been nearly as easy as I anticipated.'

'Why so?'

'We always stay in Henley House when we're in London, so Mama had no suggestion about where or how I might find a property. I asked Haines, our butler, but though he could recommend registries where I might hire staff, he has no more knowledge than Mama about listing agencies that handle real estate.' Aggravation colouring her tone, she continued, 'Then I consulted Mr Mansfield, our solicitor—who did everything he could to try to dissuade me from using any of my funds to hire a house. If I had announced I planned to sing at the opera or perform upon the stage, he could hardly have been more disapproving.'

'You haven't a desire to tread the boards, have you?'

She chuckled, her irritation disappearing. 'No, even I am not that unconventional. But then I thought—you secured your own lodgings, did you not? Could you recommend a leasing agency that might handle suitable property? My experience of the city is so limited, you see. I am familiar with Mayfair, but really nowhere else. I wouldn't wish to live in one of the fashionable areas—even if I were prepared to stand the rent, which I imagine is the highest in London. But if I intend to pursue the life I want without causing undue distress to my family, I can't reside in an area full of aristocratic neighbours, who could watch my comings and goings and gossip about how I've disgraced my upbringing. Do you know the city well enough to recommend an area that would be respectable, but not so fashionable that I would be constantly encountering society *beldames* eager to harass my mama about her scandalous daughter?'

Grinning, he looked over at her. 'Are you going to be scandalous?'

Heat flared in her eyes at the innuendo in his voice. 'I might be.'

His own pulse kicked up a notch at that response, swelling his hopes for their eventual liaison. 'Then you must let me advise you. I could also give you a brief primer on the legalities of leases and rental agreements, what to look for, what clauses to avoid.'

She gave him a smile of such blinding delight, had they not been on horseback, he almost believed she would have kissed him. What a shame they were not walking alone down some secluded path!

'That would be wonderful! Mr Mansfield has been entirely unhelpful on that topic as well. It is really most annoying!'

'By offering to help, you shouldn't think I have designs on your virtue—yet. Bring along your maid, the butler, the solicitor, even your mama if you like.'

Her eyes widened. 'You're prepared, not to just recommend, but to actually accompany me?'

'It would be the act of a friend to make sure that you find a house in a respectable area at a fair price. I'm afraid there are far too many who would be prepared to take advantage of someone inexperienced in real estate dealings.'

'I'm sure you are right. I doubt that Haines and Mr Mansfield would be the only ones to disapprove of a single female seeking to rent a property. I imagine many men would think that a woman who steps out of her proper place gets what she deserves. So—you truly would help me?'

'You must have been ill, for I think your hearing has been affected. I just offered to, did I not?'

After rolling her eyes at him, she said, 'Very well, I accept your very kind offer. You will investigate, then, and send word to me?'

'I shall contact the leasing agent I used to obtain my current lodgings, who provided me very good service. Once he locates some suitable properties, I'll let you know.'

'Thank you!' she cried. 'That relieves me of a great worry! In fact, I am so humbly grateful, I shall henceforth endeavour to make only complimentary remarks about you.'

'Miss Henley, humble and complimentary? Oh, please, do not be! It would startle me so much, I might lose my concentration and fall right out of the saddle.'

Her eyes dancing with suppressed laughter, she drew a line over her lips with one finger before saying, 'You see, I am not even responding to that provocation! Now, before we head back, shall we have a good gallop?'

'I doubt My Lady Steeplechaser could bear leaving the park without one.'

'Excellent! As long as you don't sulk if I beat you.'

'You'd have to beat me first,' he replied, relieved to have their conversation return to teasing normality. 'To the end of Rotten Row and back?'

She nodded and turned to inform the trailing groom of their intentions before looking back to Theo, her eyes sparkling at the challenge. 'Ready? Go!'

At that signal, they both put spurs to their mounts.

As he flattened himself against his horse's neck, urging the gelding to more speed, Theo thought the meeting could not have gone more perfectly. He'd smoothed over the ragged edges of their friendship, ended the talk by indulging in one of his favourite pastimes and received oblique but tantalising encouragement that he might, at some later date, be able to indulge in another favourite pastime—with her.

He'd even be able to help her choose a suitable house—in a place where their discreet future rendezvous might take place without any danger of some *ton* neighbour discovering them.

Chapter Eleven

The next afternoon, Theo pulled up his carriage in front of Henley House. After instructing his tiger to walk the horses twice around the square, he trotted up the steps and rang the bell.

'Is Miss Henley at home?' he asked the butler who opened the door.

'Yes, but I don't believe she is receiving,' the man replied.

'I won't take much of her time. Haines, isn't it?' As the man nodded, Theo slipped a coin into his hand. 'Could you tell her I have some news for her and ask if she could join me in the parlour for a few minutes?'

'Very good, my lord. If you'll wait in here.'

After conducting Theo to the parlour, the butler disappeared. As he suspected, only a few minutes later, he heard a light footfall approaching.

Not for Miss Henley, he thought, smiling, to spend half an hour at her toilette, fussing with gowns and coiffeurs upon hearing that a gentle-man had called on her.

'Good afternoon, Lord Theo,' she said as she walked in, the butler at her heels. 'How kind of you to call.'

Only the presence of a hovering servant could have induced her to make such an innocuous re-mark, Theo thought. 'No need to send for your mother or ring for tea, for I can only stay a mo-ment,' he said, bowing in response to her curtsy. 'Will stationing Haines outside the open door pre-serve the proprieties?'

'I'm sure they will. Haines, if you would re-main in the hallway for a moment? Lord Theo will be leaving directly.'

The coin had done its work, for the man re-plied, 'Of course, Miss Henley. I'll also send John up for your maid, as Lady Henley would want me to, in case the gentleman decides to stay a bit longer.'

Apparently a single coin only went so far. For-tunately, his errand wouldn't take long.

'If you must,' Emma was saying as she ges-tured Lord Theo to a chair. 'Chaperons and maids!' she continued in a disgruntled tone after the butler had bowed himself out. 'I am *so* glad I shall soon be done with such ridiculousness. So, what is this mysterious news?'

'I could have conveyed this information when

we met at the Hollands' ball tonight, but as you said your mama wished that your desire to hire a house be pursued discreetly, decided it would be better to discuss the matter here. I sent a note to my leasing agent yesterday and received a reply this morning, with a list of properties in areas that are well away from the fashionable neighbourhoods, but safe enough for a single female to establish her own household. If you will be free tomorrow afternoon, he can obtain the keys and escort us to inspect them. Along with your maid, your butler and your mama, if you prefer.'

Emma laughed. 'I think the maid alone will do, although I will see if Haines is free. His expertise about what a property should include below stairs is much greater than mine. But—tomorrow! I didn't expect you would have results so soon!'

'Would you rather wait? Because I can—'

'Oh, no, I wish to proceed immediately.' A wondering smile slowly crept across her face. 'I'd begun to believe having a place of my own was only a schoolgirl's dream, never to be realised. I can hardly credit that in a single day's time, I might be close to making it come true.'

The faraway look leaving her eyes, she turned to focus on him. 'Thanks to you, Lord Theo. I'm so very grateful, I hardly know what to say.'

When she looked up at him like that, her hazel eyes aglow, enthusiasm and eagerness imbuing her body with a passion and energy that was almost palpable, it was all he could do to resist pulling her into his arms and kissing the full lips that had been taunting him for what now seemed like for ever.

Forcing himself to refrain, he said, 'You can do what you advised me. Choose what makes you happy and live that life to the fullest. So—you will be free to inspect houses tomorrow afternoon?'

'I will! Shall we say at two o'clock?'

Theo nodded. 'So I will see you at the Hollands' ball tonight?'

'Yes.' With a mischievous smile, she added, 'Shall I see *you* among Miss Fothergill's court?'

He laughed. 'Probably. Until I annoy her by coming to talk to you.'

'Ah, be careful! She may banish you yet for your impudence.'

Theo shook his head. 'My only regret at being banished would be losing my best camouflage for being able to talk to you.'

'Well, with luck, the subterfuge won't be necessary much longer. I'll see you tonight, then?'

When he nodded, impulsively she seized his hand. 'Thank you, Lord Theo. For helping me move closer to the dream of being more than another useless society matron.'

Her press of her small hand seemed to burn

through his gloves. Loath to let it go, he caught her fingers and kissed them. 'It is my privilege, Miss Henley.'

She walked him back into the hall just as her maid was hurrying down the stairs. 'As you see, it wasn't necessary to send for Marie,' she told Haines as they halted beside the open door. 'Until tonight then, Lord Theo.'

'Miss Henley.' With a quick bow, he walked out.

Once on the street, he soon caught up with his tiger and hopped back up into the vehicle. As he drove back towards his lodgings, desires, doubts and speculations kept circling through his head.

The idea of Miss Henley moving into her own house set off a maelstrom of enthusiasm and eagerness within his body, too, sparking an arousal he had a hard time controlling.

Taking a deep breath, he tried to halt his rampaging desire. Just because he knew the lady was attracted to him didn't mean that he was close to realising *his* fondest erotic dreams. Even after Emma moved into a house of her own.

She might be unconventional enough to live outside the constraints of society, but for an unmarried lady to take a lover went several leaps beyond 'unconventional'. True, there were radical women who advocated free love and the spurning of wedlock with all the legal restrictions it imposed upon women, but he didn't think Emma was one of them.

Despite the passion between them, he wasn't sure, after she considered the matter carefully, that she would choose to act upon their attraction. As certain as he was that he could bring her bliss, treat her with the affection and tenderness she deserved and take the precautions necessary to protect her, he didn't intend to urge their relationship beyond friendship unless and until he was convinced that she wanted to become his lover as much as he wanted to make her his. He respected her too much to try to beguile her into doing something she would later regret.

But if, after careful consideration, the lady wanted to proceed... Ah, he was prepared to put aside all his doubts and make that happen.

Midway though the Hollands' ball that night, blowing out a breath of relief, Theo sidled away from the group around Miss Fothergill and headed towards Emma Henley. While idling at the edge of the courtiers earlier, he'd spied her walking in with her mama, she joining her friends Miss Overton and Miss Standish, Lady Henley heading to the card room with the gallants who walked up to fetch her.

After the dangerous balancing act of the last

half hour, he was more eager than ever to reach her side. An odd little…twinge tightened in his chest when she looked up to see him approach—and smiled.

Instinctively he smiled back. What a relief to know, with appearances preserved, he could now look forward to some intelligent conversation!

'Ladies, good evening,' he said, bowing as he reached Emma and her friends.

'Good evening to you, Lord Theo,' Miss Overton said. 'We must thank you for Miss Henley's exciting news.'

'I just confided to them that you will very kindly be assisting me—along with my maid and the butler—to inspect houses tomorrow,' Emma said. 'Although I suppose we shouldn't discuss the matter in more than a whisper, lest someone overhear.'

'Goodness, yes!' Miss Overton said. 'You promised your mama you'd look for lodgings *discreetly*. The news that Lord Theo was escorting Miss Henley to look for a house would raise so many eyebrows the gossip would fly through the *ton* faster than the winner down the course on Derby day!'

'And since it would be hard for us to contain our excitement about the prospect of Emma finding us a home at last, we had better leave you two to discuss the details alone—or with as much privacy as a ballroom affords,' Miss Standish said.

'Your friends sound eager to make a start,' Theo said, watching them walk away.

'Yes,' Miss Henley said, her eyes aglow as she looked up at him. 'Leaving society, living on our own, doing something important…it's the goal we've longed for since we were at school together.'

'Three unrelated ladies living together? Do you think you will get along?'

Emma laughed. 'If we could survive the rancour and lack of privacy at Mrs Axminster's Academy for Young Ladies, I'm sure living on our own, each of us with a bedchamber to retreat to if need be, we will get along famously. Though I do expect I will have some time alone before they join me at the house.'

Suddenly Theo realised what she was implying. Though her friends were obviously as unconventional as she was, it would be much easier to allow herself the risk of taking a lover if that choice were known only by the two of them.

And if she expected her friends to join her, it also meant that she didn't expect the liaison to be permanent. Over the short-term, he had no doubts he'd be enthralled by her alone.

'How much time do you think you might have…alone?'

'I don't know. I only hope it will be…enough.'

His pulse leapt and arousal stirred again at her response, the clearest encouragement he'd yet received that she really did intend to embark upon the affair he craved so fiercely. 'I hope so, too,' he murmured.

For a long moment, he met her gaze, the desire he saw in her eyes further firing his need. Ah, how he burned to taste those wicked lips, run his hands along her lithe body and feel her tremble in response to his touch!

In truth, the only real question might be whether her friends dallied long enough that they were both ready to end the liaison. For as deep as his desire ran and as fascinating as he found the lady, he could already predict that he'd prefer the affair to be lengthy.

'But, premature to discuss that,' she said, looking away, her cheeks delightfully flushed. 'You must tell me about your progress with Miss Fothergill.'

He laughed ruefully. 'Ah, Miss Fothergill.'

'Who happens, at this moment, to be glowering at me in a most unfriendly fashion.'

'I may have to alter my strategy,' he said. 'This turning of my attention to a lady who, doubtless in her opinion, is a lesser female, has worked to pique her interest all too well. Tonight, she allowed that she might permit me more than one dance. And said that if I asked nicely enough, she might accord me the privilege of taking her in to supper.'

Miss Henley chuckled. 'That is favour indeed! Are you going to follow through on her invitations?'

'Good heavens, no!' he said with feeling, prompting her to laugh outright. 'Bad enough that the comment alone was enough to have several of her most diligent courtiers give me looks that promised pistols at dawn if I dared accept what she offered. But showing me such decided favour might make the old *beldames* who rule society start believing I have serious intentions towards the chit. I may have to make a strategic withdrawal and investigate joining the court of some other much-admired maiden.'

'Or you could simply abandon the Marriage Mart innocents and start paying attention to the dashing matrons you usually favour.'

'That would be just as dangerous,' he retorted. 'Pay attention to one of them and I may be offered an invitation that would be difficult to refuse without giving offence.'

'Ah, the lingering effects of Lady Belinda. Still not recovered enough to move on?'

He hesitated, not sure whether it was wise to make such a confession. But somehow he couldn't bring himself to make light of so deep a conviction. One that seemed to be gaining strength by the day.

'I…am no longer sure I want to move in that direction,' he admitted at last.

Obviously startled, all teasing fled, she angled her head at him. 'Not…in the direction of naughty matrons?'

'No. I'm very much afraid I'm inclined to go in a different direction altogether.'

For a moment she studied his face. He had no idea what she could read there—his desire, his fascination, his conflicted feelings about acting on it? But he couldn't make himself look away.

Finally, she nodded. 'I see. When one feels compelled to turn in a different direction, I expect the only thing to do is to follow where the path leads. Regardless of the risk,' she added in a whisper so soft, he thought perhaps she meant the words for herself alone.

'So tomorrow, take the first step?'

She nodded. 'Tomorrow, take the first step.'

The next afternoon, as the party was too large for his phaeton, Theo engaged a carriage to convey himself and Miss Henley, her maid, Haines—their butler—and the leasing agent to view the different properties.

By the time they'd inspected and dismissed the first and set out for the second, Theo was heartily

wishing he had never proposed the expedition—
or had dispatched the leasing agent to accompany
the group and stayed at home.

Though Haines remained scrupulously respectful, his frigid expression when he looked at Theo
clearly conveyed his opinion that, in encouraging
his mistress in the madness of leasing her own
house, the gentleman was leading her into ruin
as surely as if he planned to sneak up to her bedchamber and ravish her.

The fact that he did, at some later date, hope
to enter her bedchamber—by invitation, not by
sneaking up the back stairs—made the man's hos-
tility even more uncomfortable.

Then there was her maid, who began with
obvious admiration for Theo's handsome form,
progressed to delight that this elegant gentleman
was courting her lady and ended in tearful disappointment when, after studying Haines's frozen expression, she evidently realised Theo was,
in fact, merely assisting her mistress to look at
property and the tour was not the harbinger of an
imminent marriage.

Even the listing agent, at first babbling cheerfully about the attributes of the various properties, eventually noted the tension among the little
party trapped in the carriage and ceased his chatter. Theo caught him darting uneasy glances between Miss Henley, the maid and the butler.

Emma herself, of course, remained perfectly calm and seemingly oblivious, either looking out the window with interest as they passed through various neighbourhoods, or plying the agent with pertinent questions.

After the second property was dismissed, Theo was counting the minutes until the expedition ended as he handed Miss Henley out at the final destination. To his disgruntlement, after a glance at his expression, the wretched woman choked down a laugh.

Haines didn't need to worry about him ravishing her, he thought as the party trooped up the stairs. He was going to strangle her instead.

'This is a rather new part of town, isn't it, Mr Townsend?' she asked the agent. 'Bloomsbury, I believe it's called? The houses all look very recently built.'

'Yes, ma'am,' the agent replied. 'It's prime real estate, close to everything, but not so close that you will be tripping over persons…you might rather not see.'

'I've been informed that Bloomsbury is the abode of…tradesmen and shopkeepers,' Haines said, heavy disapproval in his tone. 'Not an area suitable for Persons of Quality.'

'I don't believe any of the Quality own property here,' the agent admitted. 'But the area is quite safe and perfectly respectable. A number of solicitors and business owners have purchased houses here. A piano tuner has taken the shop just opposite. And there are advantages to having a newly built house. The kitchen and work areas below stairs contain all the latest devices and the hearths will burn coal as well as wood.'

'I like the area,' Emma said, looking up and down the street with approval. 'Shall we go inside?'

To Theo's relief, this house was the most attractive they'd seen. The entry hallway was wide and welcoming, the front parlour spacious and boasted a finely carved marble mantel. A dining room and sitting room overlooking a small back garden made up the rest of the ground floor, with several well-appointed bedchambers and a private reception area on the first floor.

'This would do very nicely for a library,' Emma noted as they walked into the light, airy room just off the first-floor landing. 'I like the house very much! Though I note it doesn't contain much in the way of furnishings, beyond the sofa in the front parlour and beds and wardrobes in the bedchambers.'

'Those are only furnishings that convey with the property,' Mr Townsend said. 'However, the rent is lower than it would be if the house came with every room fitted out. It also allows you to choose the rest of the furnishings to suit your own taste. I can recommend several dealers where you could rent or purchase whatever else you require. Now, would you like to inspect below stairs, ma'am? Although I must caution you—the steps down are narrow and steep.'

'Haines, would you accompany Mr Townsend? I'd rather remain here, envisaging where I will install my bookcases. In any event, you have a great deal more knowledge about whether or not the facilities would be adequate than I do.'

'As you wish, Miss Henley,' Haines said, bowing. Sliding Theo another suspicious glance, he followed the leasing agent from the room.

Emma looked over at her maid, who was clasping her arms tightly under her cloak and stomping her feet, her cheeks marked by the tears she'd been silently shedding. 'Are you cold, Marie?'

''Tis no matter, mistress,' the girl said, pulling her hands out to wipe at her face.

'Goodness, you are frozen, poor creature!' Emma exclaimed, going over to chafe the girl's hands. 'Go down at once to the front parlour and stand by the window, in the sun. It was quite pleasant there.'

When the girl looked over at Theo dubiously, Emma laughed. 'Go on, now! Lord Theo and I shall join you in a minute. Don't worry, he has no intention of ravishing me on the bare floor of this chilly room!'

For a moment, she hesitated. 'Yes, ma'am,' the girl said at last, the lure of sunlight to warm her chilled fingers obviously outweighing the imperative of her duty to protect her mistress's virtue.

Or she might have concluded, Theo thought, watching the girl hurry down the stairs, that protecting her mistress's virtue was a lost cause. Should Miss Henley actually lease this house and commit the unforgivable solecism of leaving her family home, her virtue or lack of it would no longer be of any consequence. Unmarried, unchaperoned and living on her own, she would have permanently removed herself from the possibility of becoming a gentleman's wife.

As soon as the girl's descending footfalls faded, Emma clapped a hand over her mouth to muffle her peal of laughter. 'Lord Theo, I'm so sorry!' she gasped when she stopped to take a breath. 'Of all the ill-suited and uncomfortable group of people! I should have sent you home after the first house.'

Now that the ordeal was nearly over, Theo was somewhat better able to appreciate her levity. Managing a smile, he said, 'I'm not sure which more offensive: Haines's looks that accused me of being a vile seducer, or Marie's teary-eyed conclusion that I was responsible for encouraging you to do this, thereby rendering you ineligible and destroying her hopes of you marrying a gentleman.'

'Were I a playwright, this expedition would have made splendid fodder for a farce! But though I regret dragging you along, that is all I regret. Otherwise, I couldn't be more thrilled. This house will do splendidly! Spacious bedchambers, a front parlour large enough to allow the Ladies' Committee to meet here as well as at Lady Lyndlington's, even room for a library. My own house—with my own library!'

Laughing, she grabbed his hands and twirled him in a circle with her, until he had to laugh, too.

'Ridiculous female,' he said when at last she stopped, both of them flush-faced and a little dizzy. But looking at the sheer joy on her face, he couldn't remain annoyed.

'How pretty you are when you smile like that,' he murmured.

At once, she dropped his hands and turned away. 'Please, Lord Theo. I know you don't mean to mock. But I thought we were good enough friends for you not to offer me idle flattery.'

Exasperated, he caught her chin and turned her face back to him. 'I'm not offering you idle flattery! With your face rosy with happiness and your eyes glowing with enthusiasm, I *do* think you are pretty.'

'Don't be absurd!' she spat back furiously. 'You

couldn't. You will cease paying me ridiculous compliments before you make me any angrier.'

'And now you are going to make *me* angry,' he retorted. 'What gives you the right to decide what or whom I find attractive? I thought we were good enough friends for *you* not to assume I blindly accept the standards set by society. That you thought me intelligent enough to make my own assessments.'

He'd dented her assurance, for now she looked troubled. 'How…how *could* you find me pretty?'

'All right, I grant you that by conventional standards, your nose is too long, your chin too prominent and your cheekbones not high enough to be thought beautiful. When, ah, when some topic or cause arouses you! Those pale cheeks flush, your whole face glows, and your eyes! Large hazel orbs with glowing golden centres that announce this is a woman of courage and purpose, who neither tolerates fools nor allows society's artificial constraints to prevent her from doing the work in which she believes. You radiate a passion that is irresistible! Especially your mouth. I have a very hard time resisting those wicked lips.'

And then—he couldn't any more. Despite the ticking clock in his head warning that they might at any moment be interrupted, he had to taste them.

Bending quickly, his hands on her shoulders to

steady her, he brought his mouth down on hers. After a moment of shocked surprise, with a little murmur, she leaned up into his kiss.

Slow, slow, slow, he warned his ravaging senses. Most likely, she'd never been kissed before and he didn't want to frighten her. No, he wanted to lead her softly into the delight of passion, leave her tempted and wanting and eager for more.

So, after soft nuzzling kisses and one brief lingering touch of her lips with his tongue, he set her back on her feet.

Her wide eyes fixed on him, her breathing unsteady, she brought a trembling hand up to her mouth.

'See how dangerous it is to disagree with my judgement?'

And then he heard a tromping on the stairs that signalled the imminent return of the leasing agent and the butler. Stepping away to give her—and himself—time to regain some composure, he said, 'To be fair, at the next suitable opportunity, I give you leave to slap me.'

She chuckled unsteadily. 'And what if I'd rather have permission to kiss you again?'

He knew he was smiling broadly as a wave of sheer masculine satisfaction filled him. Well pleased with himself despite the unslaked passion

she'd aroused, he said, 'That could be arranged
as well. Soon, I hope.'

The wicked look in her eyes was both promise and challenge.

He was chuckling at her impudence when she
looked away to greet the servants. 'So, Haines,
did you find everything below stairs acceptable?'

Looking as if the words were forced from his
lips against his will, the butler said, 'I have to
admit, the entire downstairs is set up with great
efficiency. I think any staff you employ would
find the arrangements quite satisfactory.'

'Excellent. Mr Townsend, I am very pleased
with this property and would like to lease it.
Would you send all the particulars to my family's solicitor? Mr Mansfield, on Holborn Road.'

'Of course, Miss Henley. I'm so pleased to
have been of service.'

'I'm delighted with your service as well,'
Emma said. 'Lord Theo's high praise of your
work was well justified. How soon will the house
be available?'

'I should think you could take possession as
soon as the papers are signed.'

Miss Henley nodded. 'I shall probably not
move in for several months, but I would like to
obtain the key as soon as possible, so I may begin
furnishing the place and adding custom features,

like bookcases for the upstairs room that shall become my library.'

'I'm sure that will be entirely possible.'

'Thank you again, Mr Townsend, and you, too, Lord Theo, for arranging this tour. Shall we make our way outside?'

Allowing the lady to precede him, Theo followed her down, his senses still humming. Only a little longer—and with luck, he might make Emma his—in this very house.

Once they collected the maid and exited the building, Emma turned to him. 'Ungracious as it is of me to ask it of you, Lord Theo, might we take the liberty of absconding with your carriage, while you and Mr Townsend find a hackney? Haines has been absent from his post for quite a while and I know he is anxious to get back.'

She meant to save him suffering the butler's silent disapproval and the maid's despondency during the transit back, Theo thought with an inward smile. And phrased it to sound as though *he* was the one doing the favour.

'Of course, Miss Henley. I expect I shall see you again soon enough, perhaps at the Marshalls' musicale this evening. Mr Townsend, shall we set off?'

'Thank you again, Lord Theo,' Emma said as he handed her into the carriage, giving his hand a surreptitious squeeze before releasing it.

He closed the carriage door behind her, a dizzy sense of elation filled him, producing a euphoria that swept away all his remaining doubts. He couldn't remember ever being this excited about the beginning of an affair. Especially when he had no assurance yet there would actually be an affair.

Even if Emma chose to have him, it would be a month or more before their liaison could begin. Despite that, he felt as eager and excited as if the first tryst were to be this evening.

Selfish as it was, he was even gladder now she hadn't gratified her mother by marrying a man she could never love, though that choice might well have prompted her to commence a discreet affair immediately.

For one, he didn't like the idea of her wasting a particle of her passion and intelligence on a husband who could never appreciate them. Recalling the deprecating comments made about her looks and desirability by everyone from the *ton* to members of her own family, he felt another wave of sympathy and anger.

The marvel that was Emma Henley deserved a man who would appreciate all of her—the passion, the fire, the wit and the total devotion to the causes she found important.

He need only hold himself under control and

wait a while longer for the chance of winning the most magnificent of prizes—Emma's gift of herself.

Chapter Twelve

In the afternoon two days later, Emma readied herself to visit Ellie Lattimar's school for a session of reading to the girls. Sitting at her dressing table, looking in the mirror as Marie inserted the last pin into her braided coiffeur, she couldn't help but study her reflection.

Lord Theo thought her…pretty? She'd reviewed their conversation many times and she still couldn't fathom it.

After tilting her head at several angles and considering the results, Emma gave up with a sigh. She had to believe *he* believed it—his tone and the fire in his eyes had been too eloquent of honesty to doubt him. But it was quite impossible! She'd just have to consider that opinion the single flaw in his otherwise formidable powers of observation.

'Is there a hairpin sticking you, miss?' Marie

asked, obviously puzzled by Emma's gyrations in front of the mirror.

'No, no, all is fine,' she replied. Though maybe she ought to stick a pin in her head, if the pain would distract her from her absorption with Lord Theo. She'd become as bad as the brainless beauties at Mrs Axminster's, who thought of nothing but their come-outs and the handsome suitors who would court them.

But how could she put him out of mind, when each time she closed her eyes, all she could think of was that kiss?

Gentle, tender, sensual, the touch of his mouth had set off little lightning bolts of sensation that had shot to every corner of her. Just as she seemed to learn his rhythm and pressed upwards to kiss him back, he'd withdrawn. Leaving her bereft and trembling.

The danger in disagreeing with his judgement indeed! As she'd frankly admitted to him, all that simple kiss had done was make her want *more*— and tie her mind up in knots, wondering how and whether she should get it.

Instead, as the Season drew closer to its end, she ought to relegate that beguiling image to the back of her mind and focus on the more immediate imperative of finding more employment opportunities for Ellie's girls, while she still moved among the social class that would hire them. The debate over whether or not she would actually have the nerve to invite Lord Theo to become her lover could wait until later, once she was safely on her own.

She would certainly have the opportunity, if she could summon the audacity. This very afternoon, on her way to Ellie's school, she was to stop by Mr Mansfield's office to pick up the key to the house on Judd Street. Once the Season ended, she would be truly on her own—accountable for her behaviour to no one but herself.

As Marie helped her into her pelisse and set the bonnet on her braids, Emma suppressed a sigh. She wasn't sure which would be greater: her embarrassment and chagrin if she were to proposition Lord Theo and he refused, or her terror if he accepted.

After informing the driver of their destination and letting the footman hand her into the carriage, she settled into a seat by the window. With a sigh, she admitted what she didn't really want to acknowledge—the unfortunate fact that she'd grown far too attached to seeing Lord Theo. That his wit and the energising thrill of being near him heightened her appreciation and her enjoyment of whatever event they were attending. Even riding in the park, one of her chief joys, was raised to a new level of delight when she could share it with him, trading quips and information.

A dangerous fascination, whether or not she ever took the plunge into making him her lover. For if past behaviour were a reliable guide, his attention would focus on her only for a short time. She faced a bitter future if she committed the folly of basing her enjoyment of life on the necessity of experiencing it with him.

After a short drive, they reached Mr Mansfield's office. The solicitor had received the papers from the listing agent, reviewed them and informed her that he found the terms and conditions fair.

Though he—like Haines, who shook his head every time she passed him in the hallway—still obviously disapproved of her plans, she was his client and, in the end, he was obligated to do her bidding. His face solemn, as she signed the papers, he murmured, 'I hope you won't come to regret this, Miss Henley.'

Knowing the long-time retainer truly did have only her best interests at heart, she patted his hand. 'I thank you for your concern, Mr Mansfield, but I shall be quite fine.'

Looking as though he'd like to comment, but refraining, the solicitor simply nodded and handed her the key. 'The lease runs for a year. I've made arrangements with the bank for the funds to be transferred to the owner's account each month on the date the rent is due, so you need not concern yourself with the finances. There are also sufficient funds remaining in your account for you to purchase whatever you desire in the way of furnishings, along with the necessities of daily living.'

'Thank you for handling everything so smoothly,' she told the solicitor as she walked out, after consigning the precious key to her reticule.

An hour later, to the regretful sighs of the students, Emma read aloud the final sentence of the current chapter of *One Thousand and One Nights*, the book Ellie Lattimar had been reading to the girls. 'That will have to be all for now, ladies,' she said, smiling as she closed the book. 'Miss Wendell is signalling that it's time for your next lesson.'

'But you read almost as beautiful as Miss Ellie,' one of the girls said.

'Will you read to us again?' another asked.

'I would be delighted to! Now, off with you while I consult with Miss Ellie.'

As she approached the office door, a soft murmur of voices told her Ellie was not alone. Supposing she must be conferring with another member of the staff, Ellie had opened her lips to call out a greeting when she realised the other person in the office wasn't a resident of Dean Street, but Christopher Lattimar, Ellie's husband, a rising Member of Parliament whom Emma had met several times at Lady Lyndlington's home during meetings of her Ladies' Committee.

He must have slipped in through the back door—in order that a handsome man's arrival didn't distract the students, Emma surmised, smiling. She was about to revise her greeting when Christopher pulled his wife into his arms.

Not wishing to betray her presence during such a private moment, Emma froze.

A truly polite and well-brought-up maiden would have averted her eyes—but Emma couldn't. Warmth spiralling within her, she watched as Christopher cupped his wife's face, traced her lips with his tongue and then parted them to delve within. Moaning softly, Ellie opened her mouth to his kiss and pressed herself against her husband's body.

The passion and tenderness of their embrace held Emma spellbound. Immobilised and scarcely breathing, she couldn't look away, a single thought frozen in her dazzled mind.

I want that.

A few moments later, when Emma's brain began functioning again, she tiptoed backwards away from the doorway, not wishing the couple to look up after their kiss and catch her inadvertently spying on them.

Besides, she needed a moment to compose herself before she would be able to speak with anything resembling her usual calm. And though she succeeded in mastering her breathing and steadying her pulse, she couldn't push from her mind either her first, visceral response—*I want that*—or the one that now followed.

I'm prepared to do what I must to have it.

That need and that imperative were so strong, their voices completely drowned out the warning the wiser part of the brain was trying to whisper. *Acting upon that desire could be more dangerous than you can imagine.*

Finally shaking herself free of the sensual spell, she told herself sternly that for the present, she needed to focus her attention on furnishing her house and finding as many positions for Ellie's girls as possible before her time in society ended.

Walking with a heavier tread than normal, Emma retraced her steps to the doorway—relieved to note that, by the time she rapped on the door frame, Christopher Lattimar and his wife had moved apart. Hoping the expression she'd assumed was serene enough that neither would suspect she noticed their unsteady breathing and flushed faces, Emma entered.

'Excuse me, Ellie, I didn't realise your husband was here. And how nice to see you again, Mr Lattimar! Please, don't let me interrupt. Ellie, I just wanted to let you know that I've finished reading and the girls have gone on to their lessons.'

'Good to see you, too, Miss Henley, and you're not interrupting,' Christopher said. 'I'm due back at Parliament now, but having been given an hour's break, I decided to pay a visit to my favourite schoolteacher.'

He leaned down to place a quick kiss on Ellie's forehead. 'Before I go, let me once again express my thanks for the good work you are doing with Lady Maggie and her Ladies' Committee, Miss Henley. As we try to move this country ever forward, we depend upon efforts like yours.'

'If you could move it forward enough to allow women to vote, we could assist you in Parliament, too,' Ellie observed.

Mr Lattimar laughed. 'Now you sound like Lady Maggie! Let us secure the vote for every able-bodied *man* first, my darling. Then we'll work on extending the franchise to the ladies.'

'If you and your friends could get further provisions added to the Children in Factories Act to ensure all those potential voters receive the schooling that will enable them to vote intelligently, that would further the cause as well,' Emma said.

'We are working on it,' Christopher assured, giving Emma a bow before he walked out. 'I shall see you later at home, dear one,' he said as he paused on the threshold. 'It might be late evening, though.'

Ellie sent her husband a smile whose sensual promise Emma had no trouble interpreting. 'Don't worry, I shall be waiting, my love.'

What would it be like, Emma thought, to lie abed, awaiting the return of a handsome, virile lover? *I want that* echoed again in her head.

While she struggled to refocus on the immediate, Ellie said, 'Why don't you have a seat? I've just finished settling in a new student and would love some tea, if you have the time to join me.'

'That would be lovely. After the ball last night, I have a few more names to offer as potential employers.'

'Excellent! Excuse me just for a moment. I'll find Mrs Sanders and order tea.'

A short time later, they sat together, tea poured, as Emma had passed along the names of the matrons who had household positions to fill. Once the school's director had written those down, always curious about Ellie's rescue efforts, Emma said, 'You said you'd just settled in a new girl. Where did you find her?'

Pausing a moment, Ellie said, 'I don't mean

to embarrass you, but… I brought her from a brothel. Her mother is one of the girls there and neither of them want Alice to follow in her footsteps.'

'Heavens, I'm not missish!' Emma exclaimed. 'I think it's admirable that her mother wants a better life for her daughter.'

'Alice *is* a good prospect. She can already read and write a little, which is more than most of the girls when they first come to us. She's intelligent and quite eager to learn a respectable occupation.'

'How encouraging! Given the duties of the occupation, I wouldn't be surprised if you told me most of your students were the children of women who didn't wish their daughters to follow them into the trade.'

'Actually, not many are. The brothel girls produce fewer offspring than you might think,' Ellie said. 'Neither the girls nor the madams want them increasing, as it renders the girl unable to work during the final part of her confinement and for some time after the child is born. All the good houses encourage the girls and their clients to use various means to prevent conception.'

Emma raised her eyebrows. 'I didn't realise there were methods to prevent conception!'

Ellie laughed. 'It's not a topic generally discussed by genteel ladies. After all, most wives want children and husbands generally want as many sons as they can get. There are also still many who consider any attempt to prevent conception a sin.'

From the back of her mind rose the spectre of that sultry kiss. A guilty sense of excitement built as Emma realised the implications of possessing such knowledge.

Trying to keep her voice casual, she said, 'Just what sort of methods are there, then?'

Ellie tilted her head in surprise. 'You truly wish to know?'

'As you may have heard, by the Season's end, I'm going to be a lady living on my own. All sorts of knowledge could be useful.'

Ellie studied her for a moment, Emma hoping her cheeks weren't flaming red. At length, she nodded. 'Regardless of whether or not a female ever uses the knowledge, I think all have the right to know it. Has your mother talked to you about…any of the activities that take place in the marital bed?'

Emma tried to imagine her mother discussing such an intimate topic, and laughed. 'No. That's a conversation I'm sure she was reserving until the eve of my wedding.'

'A shame, for fewer girls would come to grief if they had a better idea of what to expect,' Ellie said with some feeling.

'I do spend half the year in the country, so I've

observed the mating of other species. I don't suppose the form practised by the human animal is much different.'

Ellie smiled. 'It's in many ways similar. Then you know, at the climax of the union, the male releases seed, which, if it finds a resting place in the female's body, develops into offspring. So the traditional method of averting conception was for the male to withdraw from the embrace before the seed was released.'

'Is that effective?'

'It can be—unless, in the ardour of the moment, the man neglects to withdraw. Some brothels prefer a surer method. It's a sort of sleeve called a French letter, made of fine gut, that is tied around the male member before insertion into the female's body. At climax the seed is spilled inside it and after the embrace is complete the member is withdrawn along with the sleeve containing the seed. Of course sometimes, in the grip of passion, the partners forget to use one. But in the main, if used correctly, it provides superior protection against conception.'

'You are certain?'

Ellie smiled faintly. 'I always found it so. Fortunately, my...protector had grown sons and no wish to antagonise them by siring other children. He instructed me in the use of the French letter and employed it whenever...necessary. So I escaped the shame of bearing him a child, for which I am very grateful.' Her smile broadening, she added confidentially, 'I had wondered if perhaps I were simply not capable, which would have saddened me very much after marrying my darling Christopher. But I've lately discovered that is not the case.'

It took Emma a moment to put it all together. 'You are increasing?' she cried.

When Ellie nodded assent, she jumped up to give her a hug. 'That's wonderful news! I'm so happy for you! But should you continue running the school? Shouldn't you retire and rest, let Miss Wendell—?'

Laughing, Ellie waved her to silence. 'You sound just like Christopher! Other than being rather tired, I feel fine. There's no reason for me to refrain from working here, not until very close to my confinement.'

'My congratulations to you both!'

Joy transparent on her face, Ellie nodded. 'When I think of the dark days when I saw no way out but death… Even once I was free, I expected the greatest happiness I could hope to attain was to establish this school and give other innocent girls the chance for a better life. Loving Christopher, bearing his child—it seems almost too great a blessing.'

'After all you endured, you are more than worthy of it,' Emma said with feeling. 'Now—just one more question. Where does one obtain French letters?'

Ellie studied her. 'Are you going to do something foolish?' she asked quietly.

Emma sighed. 'I am very much afraid I might.'

'I would advise against it, my dear. Intimacy involves more than the physical union. It can create a very powerful emotional bond. One hard to endure, if it is not reciprocal. Hard to break, if it cannot be permanent. However,' she continued briskly, 'if you are going to be foolish, at least be protected. But think very carefully. If you commit yourself to this, there is no going back.'

'I know,' Emma acknowledged. 'It just seems so unfair that passion is something a man can explore with neither risk nor regret, whereas a woman normally has to accept the restrictions of marriage to experience it.' Thinking of Mr Null, she added acidly, 'And some take on the restrictions of marriage and still don't experience it.'

'True enough. Very well, French letters are sold at apothecary shops. Generally, they are purchased by gentlemen, although I know the madams procure them, too. Now, I don't suppose I need to assure you that I won't mention our… interesting discussion to anyone?'

'I would appreciate it.'

As they rose to leave the office, Ellie came

over and gave Emma a quick embrace. 'Be careful,' she whispered.

'I will try to be,' Emma promised.

As she walked to the hackney her footman had summoned, Emma recalled the moment she'd come to Ellie's office and found her husband embracing her...and all she could think of was being in Theo's arms. Warmth and an aching need vibrated within her, along with the echo of her thought that day... *I want that.*

She'd felt the same imperative when Theo kissed her. Now, knowing there was a means to counter the greatest risk intimacy posed for a female, she wasn't sure she could resist the temptation to seize it.

If, of course, the gentleman was agreeable.

During the journey home in the hackney, Emma sat with her reticule in her lap, feeling the key within it like a burning coal. Memories of Ellie and Christopher's embrace alternated with the remembered feel of Theo's mouth on hers, Ellie's matter-of-fact description of French letters running as a soft-voiced commentary beneath it all.

She remembered the regret her mother had expressed that by turning away from marriage, Emma would never experience passion—or the joy of children. Might she be able to experience one without the other?

If the gentleman she chose for passion was Lord Theo, it would have to be. She recalled with painful clarity his absolute silence when she'd described what it would take for her to risk marriage—a man who loved her and would pledge his complete fidelity.

No, she was under no illusions that charming lady's man Lord Theo would ever pledge that to any lady. A man who attracted woman as he did—who enjoyed women as he did—would never want to restrict himself to just one. Even if he made a good faith attempt, there would be always ladies trying to seduce him out of that resolve.

And though she might actually consider a partnership with an artist who supported her reform work, nothing about his desire to paint would change his predilection for the ladies. So marriage and children with Lord Theo was out of the question.

However, that didn't mean that passion alone was without its risks. She would have to be very careful indeed, for, despite his aversion to matrimony, if she were to conceive a child Theo would almost certainly insist on marrying her.

The only thing worse than bearing a child she never meant to have would be the misery of marrying a man who would never be faithful. Wasn't that the prime reason she and her friends had decided long ago to forgo marriage?

Still, if she were going to taste passion with anyone, she wanted it to be with him.

Taking him as a lover might have more benefits than the physical, she reasoned. Maybe, once she'd satisfied her curiosity about lovemaking and slaked her desire, she would be able once again to consider him no more than a casual friend. Cheerfully go on with her life, as he seemed able to do after parting from his paramours. If she could have sensual satisfaction *and* end up free of the spell he seemed to cast over her, that would be the best outcome possible.

A giddy excitement fizzing within her, she nodded. Very well, she would do it. At the end of the Season, after she moved into her house and before her friends joined her, she would proposition Lord Theo.

Relieved at having finally made a decision and bubbling with excitement over what the future might hold—just a few weeks or a month hence—Emma tripped up the stairs to her bedchamber where, on her dressing table, she found a note from Olivia.

Humming to herself, she broke the seal and scanned it.

At first, she smiled in delight at the news that her dear friend had finally steeled herself to tell her mother that, at Season's end, she intended to leave home and set up a household with Emma and Sara. But as Emma realised the implications of her friend's victory over her recalcitrant mother, that smile faded.

Unless she were to put off her friends—and she didn't see how she could do that, when they'd dreamed and planned of this for so long—Olivia and Sara would move into the house as soon as she did.

There would be no interval alone in which to secretly entertain Lord Theo.

Well, that was a better outcome. A safer outcome. Olivia's triumph would protect Emma from herself.

So why did she have such a strong urge to scream and tear the letter into bits?

She supposed she could still invite Theo to become her lover, even if Olivia and Sara were in residence. They each had their own bedchambers. But their inevitable meetings—passing on the stairs, a chance encounter in the breakfast room—were bound to be awkward. She was pretty sure neither of her friends would truly approve of her trysting with Lord Theo. And as the house would be theirs, too, it wouldn't be fair for them to feel uncomfortable in their own home.

Then there was the matter of servants. It would be hard enough to limit the gossip with just her own maid, who had extensive contacts with the maids of other members of the *ton*, residing in the house during the affair. The chance of gossip getting back to the *ton* with two more lady's maids, plus the extra footmen and housemaids required for three occupants, would rise exponentially. And while Emma didn't exactly intend to sneak about during the liaison, neither had she planned to trumpet it abroad. She wouldn't appreciate lurid gossip getting back to embarrass the mother who'd been generous enough to let her go her own way.

With 'be discreet' her only request.

Apparently, she'd just have to give up the idea.

For another half hour, Emma sat at her dressing table, staring sightlessly at the note before her, her emotions churning chaotically.

It was wise to give up so risky a plan.

But if she let go the opportunity to taste passion with Lord Theo, she might never get the chance again. Might never meet another man for whom she would be willing to risk so much.

Sighing, she opened the reticule, took out the key and set it on the dressing table. So much potential, never to be realised, she thought, sadness a tangible ache in her chest as she pictured Theo's handsome face, relived the thrill of his kiss.

Then another thought occurred, galvanising her so that she sat bolt upright and clutched the key.

Why did she need to wait until the end of the Season? She had the key in her hand. She'd already intended to visit the house frequently, to see to completing the furnishing.

There was no reason she couldn't have Lord Theo meet her there now—while there were neither friends to feel awkward nor servants to gossip.

Just silence, space and opportunity.

She clutched the key so tightly, its iron teeth bit into her palm. She'd never thought of herself as wild or reckless, but once the idea took hold of her, all she felt was a fiery eagerness to see it through. It might not be wise, Lord Theo might not agree and she hadn't the faintest idea yet how she would phrase such an invitation.

All she did know was that if she were ever going to take him for her lover, it would have to be now.

Chapter Thirteen

The next afternoon, with an odd mix of excitement and trepidation, Theo tooled his phaeton from Mayfair towards Judd Street. Tucked into his pocket was the note he'd received this morning from Miss Henley, asking if he would meet her at her new house, as she wished him to advise her on the matter of its furnishings.

He'd been more than half-tempted to send back a refusal. For one, he had no wish to suffer through another session under the glaring eye of her disapproving butler or the tearful ones of her disappointed maid. Two, having been more unsettled—and aroused—than he should have been by the simple kiss he'd stolen on their last visit, he wasn't sure he could resist the temptation to try to steal another. Especially since the lady had announced herself eager for more.

In all his previous experience, *more* kissing had led directly to intimacy of a more serious kind than he wished to initiate on the sly in a house where maids and butlers tromped around, potentially barging in at any moment. He'd have preferred not to return to Judd Street unless— or until—he could take their relationship to the level he wanted, without fear of impediment or interruption.

On the other hand, since Emma Henley never did things in the usual and accepted manner, he was too curious about what she might need his opinion on to stay away.

The quantity of bookcases in the room she'd designated for a library, certainly, but what else? A trestle table from a tavern for her front room, so she would be able to accommodate a whole bank of workers from the Ladies' Committee, all writing letters at once? An apothecary's cabinet full of pigeonholes in which to store, not jars of herbs and medicines, but pending bills in Parliament? A desk in some anteroom where she might set up a hiring service, with a clerk to pair the names of students at Miss Ellie's school with offers of employment?

Chuckling, he patted the note in his pocket again. He had no idea what awaited him at Judd Street, but given that it was Emma who had summoned him, he expected to be both surprised and entertained.

Pulling up before the house, he turned the team

over to his tiger with instructions that the lad should lead them to the nearby livery and wait there, as Theo wasn't sure how long he would be. Standing on the kerb before the handsome brick town house, he took a deep breath and walked up the entry stairs to rap at the front door.

Which, to his relief, was answered by Miss Henley herself instead of the disapproving butler.

Pinking, he hoped with pleasure, but also seeming surprisingly nervous, she dipped a curtsy to his bow. 'Thank you so much for agreeing to come on such short notice,' she said, waving him towards the front parlour. 'I brought some tea from a local shop. Would you like some?'

Looking at her flushed cheeks and glowing eyes and delightfully rounded figure, alone for the moment with no disapproving faces looking on, he had to fight down the desire to tell her what he would *really* like.

She must have taken the garbled reply he did produce as assent, for she led him into the front parlour, where an upended crate served as a makeshift table, on which sat a tray, teapot, containers of milk, spoons and cups.

'Won't you have a seat?'

Theo looked dubiously at the single couch— which was much smaller than he remembered it. Not really seating for three—more like seating for two.

Two people who liked each other. A great deal.

Seated there, he would barely need to turn his head to be able to lean down and kiss her. Those naughty lips. That long, lovely swan's neck or the perfect little shell-like ears peeping out from beneath her elaborate twist of braids.

Heat flooded him and sweat broke out on his brow.

Maybe he should have heeded his first reaction and turned down the invitation.

Concentrate on something else, he advised himself a bit desperately as he perched on the sofa as close to the arm—and as far away from Emma—as he could manage.

He advised her in the mundane matter of cream and sugar and tried to balance his cup without spilling it—no easy feat, the way his hands were shaking. But though he waited impatiently for her to divulge some unusual request, like finding her a builder to construct an aviary in her garden, she continued to look down at her cup, strangely reluctant to begin a conversation.

This was Emma Henley, who was never at a loss for something to say?

Unable to bear the silence any longer, he said, 'I was pleased to get your note.'

He waited, but as that invitation to divulge her reason for summoning him was not followed by any explanation, he continued, 'In any event, I'm glad to see you again. If only to make sure that you're not still annoyed that I beat you when we raced in the park a few days ago.'

'Not a fair match,' she protested. 'My horse stumbled at the start.'

He lifted a chiding finger. 'All's fair.'

Which might have been an amusing comment, except for remembering the 'love' part of the quote. Which also reminded him of just how close beside him she was.

A fact his senses were nagging him to do something about.

'Well, then,' he said, shifting awkwardly, his momentary ease now completely evaporated, 'what have you been up to the last few days? Finding more sponsors to employ Miss Ellie's students?'

'Yes, that.'

Once again, she'd gone uncharacteristically quiet. When she averted her eyes and said nothing further, he said a little desperately, 'And you haven't yet told me what you asked me here to consult about.'

'Ah, yes. Well, you see...'

Exasperated as well as uncomfortable now with her unusual reticence, Theo decided this time he'd not try to force the conversation, but wait for her get out whatever it was that was troubling her. Which must be momentous, because he'd never seen her so hesitant.

He'd just taken rather too large a gulp of hot tea when she looked up at him and said, 'Lord Theo, are you familiar with French letters?'

He choked and spat out half a mouthful. Thrusting his cup on to the crate, he put a hand to his chest, coughing to try to clear his airway. 'What?' he gasped when he could breathe again.

Her pale face colouring, she said, 'I asked if you were familiar with French letters. Their… design and use. For if we are going to embark… on the relationship which I believe you've hinted might be of interest to you, that will be a point of some importance.'

All he heard was 'embark on a relationship…' Eagerness, delight and excitement warred with disbelief…for when it came to the decision point, he hadn't really thought Emma would choose that unconventional a path.

'So this is a…relationship on which you'd like to embark, too?' he asked, wanting to be sure he hadn't misunderstood.

She nodded. 'To speak more plainly, I would like you to become my…lover, Lord Theo. If you are agreeable.'

Seizing her hands, he kissed them avidly. 'You know I am. My dear Emma! As you must have been able to tell, having us become intimate has lately become my most fervent desire.'

It seemed only fitting to seal such a declaration with a kiss. But as, exulting, he bent to do so, Theo suddenly remembered their surroundings.

Hastily releasing her hands, he sat back. 'I would embrace you, but it just occurred to me that we've already been alone for some time, which must mean your despondent maid and disapproving butler are due to reappear at any moment.'

'I didn't bring the despondent maid, the disapproving butler—or anyone else. Just me. No one to overhear or overlook. You see, I should like to begin our liaison…immediately.'

'Immediately?' he echoed, surprised. 'In our admittedly euphemistic exchanges, I thought we'd indicated we would wait until after the Season, when you left your father's house for good and installed yourself here. Where you would no longer be answerable for your behaviour to anyone but yourself.'

'Yes, that is what I'd initially intended. But recent events have required me to…alter those plans. You see, enthusiastic about beginning the life we've dreamed about for so long, both Miss Overton and Miss Standish have now arranged to join me here as soon as the Season ends. There will be no period of…single occupancy, with the privacy and discretion that affords.'

'That's…disappointing. Even for a gentleman with my finesse, the idea of exiting your bedchamber some morning to stumble over two maiden ladies is…disconcerting.'

'Precisely,' she said with a sigh. 'I tried to convince myself that it was just as well and I should give up the idea of…exploring passion with a man who, I am sure, could show me every thrilling way to delight. But I found… I *cannot* give it up. If I am ever to experience passion at all, it must be now. And if I am to experience it, I want it to be with you.'

With exultation and excitement pounding in his ears and blood rushing to sensitise every part of his body, Theo struggled to remember what a huge step this would be for Emma. How he must make very sure that she had thought over every detail carefully before committing herself to him.

'That would be my dearest wish as well, but, Emma—are you sure? Have you truly considered all the implications?'

'It's a risk, I know, but one I am prepared to take—for the incomparable reward I expect. Do you not believe it would be…incomparable?'

'I am certain of it.'

'Isn't passion a…a unique experience? Something men and women treasure? Something that delights the senses and touches the soul like no other form of connection? Something you would bitterly regret having missed, if you had never experienced it?'

'I certainly think so.'

'I don't wish to miss it either, Theo. And since the next few weeks represent the best opportunity I will ever have to taste that about which poets write and librettists sing, I want to seize the moment. With you.'

She gazed up at him, her expression both fierce and oddly tender. 'If you truly want me, this may be our only chance. I travel about with much more freedom than most unmarried maidens. Mama is already accustomed to having me go to Ellie's school, where my maid does not like to accompany me. All I need to do is have a footman attend me, send him off to the local public house to await my summons when I'm at the school's doorstep and slip away here after he leaves. I think there's an excellent chance of conducting an affair without anyone ever finding out, even if we begin it before the Season ends.'

He nodded agreement. 'The neighbourhood is perfect. It's highly unlikely the piano tuner across the street or the law clerk on the corner would encounter Lady Henley at some social gathering and mention they'd seen a gentleman call on you. We would still have to be extremely careful, of course. But I agree—the chances are excellent that our liaison would remain undetected. But… are you *sure*?'

'You…are having second thoughts about wanting me?'

'Not at all! But…this is new territory for me, too. My previous liaisons have always been with experienced ladies. If you do this…you will no longer be a maid. If you were later to decide to marry, that would likely create problems.'

She shook her head. 'You already know I'd rather devote my energies to political causes than be tied down managing a husband's household or caring for his children. And if I *were* ever tempted to marry, I would choose a man who was willing to accord a single lady the same right to sensual freedom as an unmarried man. I know society's rules dictate that a gentleman may form liaisons with married ladies or widows, but never with virgins. I'll even allow it's a rule made to protect innocent maidens. But since I intend to leave society and its rules and make my own choices, shouldn't this be one of them? My maiden state— or lack of it—should concern only me.'

'You truly believe that? I would hate to proceed and have you later regret it, or think I took advantage of you.'

She gave him a sultry smile. 'Should I worry

that you may have regrets, or think I took advantage of you?'

Ah, how much he wanted to kiss those naughty lips again! 'You are entirely welcome to take advantage of me.'

'Then...you are willing to proceed?'

Certainly it was what he wanted, what he'd dreamed about. Taking her by slow degrees from the beauty of a simple kiss through every escalating stage of possession, paying homage to her neck and shoulders, the heavy roundness of her breasts, the smoothness of her ankles, calves and thighs, the sweetness at her centre. His mouth dried and his body hardened as he imagined it.

The long-ingrained taboo on seducing an unmarried lady of quality still niggled at him, but Emma Henley wasn't a shy innocent. No, she was a highly intelligent lady who knew her own mind. She had even taken the trouble to find out about French letters!

Besides, he'd fondly dreamed of claiming her after she moved into her own home at the end of the Season—when she would still, technically, be an unmarried lady of quality. Even though she was no longer living in her father's house. Even though, by leaving her father's house, unmarried, to live on her own, in the eyes of society she would forfeit her status as a lady and her right to protection.

If he truly intended for them to become lovers, did it really make any difference if they began now?

Then a happier thought occurred. What if he agreed to her proposal, but took things very slowly, very slowly? As an innocent, she would expect him to direct the experience. What if he led her in tiny steps, making sure she was comfortable with each increase in intimacy, promising himself he would break off the liaison at any point if she changed her mind?

No matter how difficult that would be. Having tasted her, he knew every sense would rebel at stopping short of full possession.

But making that vow to himself would dispel the rest of his unease over violating the unwritten gentleman's code so deeply ingrained in him.

Tipping up her chin, he whispered, 'So, Emma Henley, will you give yourself to me, freely and willingly?'

Desire and delight sparked in those dazzling hazel eyes. 'Freely and willingly.'

Looking at her glowing face, he let go of doubt and apprehension, as she had. 'I will bring you joy, Emma.'

She nodded. 'I know you will. But when? I cannot wait to begin.'

Thinking rapidly, he said, 'We ought to establish some guidelines. And should probably not chance meeting more than once a week.'

'Once a week?' she said with a frown. 'But that would only give us—six meetings?'

'Six for sure.' He smiled. 'You'll be amazed at what I can accomplish in six meetings.'

Her cheeks pinking, she said, 'I can't wait to find out. Very well, once a week. Are there any other conditions?'

'You must take a hackney from somewhere near the school. I don't want you walking here, alone on the streets.' He hesitated. 'Would you consider confiding in Ellie? She might be able to lend you Jenson, so you had some protection.'

'I should be fine by myself and, no, I don't want to involve Ellie. If…we should be discovered, I don't want her caught in the crossfire.'

He shook his head. 'I don't like it that you will travel unescorted.'

'I will be fine in a hackney. It would probably also be safer if I didn't always come from the school. Mama already knows I'll be visiting Judd Street to decide on furnishings and will need to be here to accept deliveries. I can have a footman come with me here, then send him off to collect items previously ordered from various suppliers.'

She threw him a smile. 'Given that most of the suppliers are located a good distance away, that should give us adequate time to meet. In addition to the fact that there are many other rooms you could slip into, if he should return before you departed. He wouldn't come into a chamber with a closed door without knocking for permission to enter.'

He sighed. 'First it was dodging innocent maidens. Now it's hiding in wardrobes from inquisitive footmen. You'll have us acting out a farce even more ridiculous than the one we played visiting Judd Street that first day, with Haines and Marie.'

'But it will be worth the effort, won't it? I know it will be worth it for me.'

Looking at that naughty mouth, those laughing eyes, the tempting swell of bosom, Theo had no doubt. 'I'll make sure it's worth it.'

'Then let the seduction begin,' she murmured.

At that come-hither smile, sensual delight flooded his body. Hell, hadn't he done foolish things before? If he meant to do this, and apparently he did, it was time to dispense with reservations and fully embrace the challenge—and the delight.

'What day is your mother most likely to be busy and least likely to notice what you are doing?'

She considered the matter. 'Wednesday afternoons. She always pays calls then and she long ago stopped trying to persuade me to go with her. It's also Marie's half-day, so she will not be about to notice when I leave and return. So, shall we say Wednesdays at three?'

'Wednesdays at three,' he confirmed with a nod. Day after tomorrow—and they would begin. A heady excitement swept over him.

'I must return home soon…but shouldn't such a bargain be sealed by a kiss?'

Smiling, he tipped up her chin again. 'Freely and willingly.'

If he meant to take this seduction slowly, he would have to hold himself under rigid control—beginning right now. So despite the desire thrumming in his blood, urging him to taste her deeply, run his hands over the body he would soon undress and stroke and come to know intimately, he made himself hold his arms at his sides and touch her only with his lips.

He brushed his lips gently against hers, then slightly harder, deeper, just grazing her mouth with his tongue. With a little gasp, she reached up to clasp his neck and pull him closer.

How could he resist when she opened her lips to him?

Fisting his hands against the cushions to prevent himself from embracing her, he deepened the kiss, letting her feel the soft wetness of his mouth, barely tasting hers.

And as he forced his hands to remain still, he found it strangely erotic to focus all his pent-up passion on this single point of contact, lips to lips, just a bare beginning of the exploration of her mouth.

Even so, his heart was racing and his breathing erratic when, after a few moments of teasing delight, he made himself move back.

'You'll get your first real lesson on Wednesday,' he murmured as he pulled her arms from around his neck.

Her normally pale cheeks were rosy and her eyes glazed with desire as she looked up at him. 'You won't regret this, Theo. I promise!'

Determined as he was to move forward, he only hoped she could make good on that pledge.

Chapter Fourteen

In the afternoon two days later, Emma arrived at Judd Street, her hand trembling as she inserted the key in the lock. After gaining access, she waved the footman trotting up the stairs behind her towards the front parlour.

'Put the basket in there, please. You have the list of the shops you must visit and know which supplies you need to pick up at each one?' When he nodded, she said, 'I'll take the linens upstairs. You may start running your errands. I shall expect you back in, say, three hours' time?'

'Yes, miss.' Looking down at the list dubiously, he said, 'I'll try to get everything and be back in three hours.'

'Very good. The Henderson ball is tonight and I know Mama will not wish me to be late returning.'

He bowed himself out. As Emma stood by the window, watching him set off towards the nearest hackney stand, excitement, trepidation and something near panic flooded her, filling her stomach with nervous eddies and making her feel almost faint.

Too late to panic now, she told herself. Walking into the front parlour, where James had left the basket, she pulled the linens from the top and looked approvingly at the provisions underneath.

She had no idea what one normally brought to a tryst, but she'd imagined that a bit of sustenance wouldn't go amiss. Telling Cook that she was likely to be at Judd Street for a few hours, she'd requested her to make up a packet with some cakes, a small jug of wine and a plate and glass. Though Cook, like the other servants at Henley House who'd learned that the unmarried daughter of the house had leased a property and intended to live on her own, was no more approving than Haines, the woman had done what she asked without protest.

If she disapproved of the house, Emma thought with a rueful laugh, she would probably have apoplexy if she ever learned what the wine and cakes were actually meant for.

First she'd deceived Mama and Marie, now Cook—to say nothing of the hapless footman. She, who had always prided herself on her honesty, she thought with a sigh.

She was beginning to realise just to what extremes a person would go for the sake of passion—and felt a sympathy for Lady Belinda she would never have believed possible.

Upstairs, she quickly put sheets on the bed and towels on the dresser, the silence echoing in the otherwise empty house sending the eddies in her stomach swirling ever faster.

Maybe Lord Theo wouldn't come.

He'd always said she was 'unusual'. Experienced as he was, she doubted he'd ever been propositioned by an unmarried lady of quality. She knew, after her offer forced him to look at seduction as an actual possibility, rather than a flirtatious temptation, that he remained somewhat troubled over taking her when she was still a virgin.

Would an attack of conscience cause him to rethink his agreement?

There had only ever been one man she wanted and wanted enough to go to such outrageous lengths. If Theo did have second thoughts and chose not to appear, she would sadly, but resolutely, plan to end her days still a maid.

By now, it should be nearing three o'clock. In a very few moments, everything she'd ever desired might become hers.

He would touch her…kiss her…take her. Warmth filled her, the now-familiar rush of sensation tingling through her body and causing a needy ache at the core of her.

Yet, when she heard the gentle rapping at the front door, she froze.

What was she supposed to do first? she wondered in sudden panic. Her arousal dissipating under a new flood of nervousness, she walked down the stairs and opened the door.

He entered and quickly she closed it behind them. 'Shall we begin…in here?' she said, gesturing towards the front parlour.

He bowed and waved, indicating she should precede him. She walked in front of him, acutely conscious of his eyes on her, wishing desperately for the practised allure of a Lady Belinda.

'Would you like to sit? I didn't bring tea this time, but I do have wine and cakes.'

He sat down, and acutely uncomfortable, she perched beside him. When he touched her chin to lift her face up, she jumped.

'It's not too late to have second thoughts, you know,' he murmured, his gaze on her face amused, but gentle. 'We can share some wine and I can leave, if you prefer.'

'No!' she cried. 'I don't prefer…at least, not if you don't. I… I just wish I knew what to do.'

'Nothing, Emma. You don't have to do anything. Only tell me what you like and what you don't.'

'I would like you…to kiss me again,' she said in a small voice.

'And I would very much like to kiss you. But why don't we have some of that wine first? To… relax you.'

'I'm certainly not relaxed,' she muttered and, when he chuckled, said, 'It's all well for you to be amused! You've visited a lady's home—and bedchamber—countless times. This is…all new to me.'

'Which is what makes it so precious. You offer me a priceless gift, Emma. I mean to be worthy of it. Now sit back and try to relax.'

She subsided against the cushions. If the circumstances were going to make her feel so horribly awkward and uncertain, she could at least lean back and take advantage of the situation to openly inspect and admire Theo in a way she'd never dared before, when there were others around to notice her interest.

And my, how worthy of admiration he was! His broad shoulders displayed to perfection in his well-tailored coat, she could see the muscles flexing as he pulled the wine flask from the basket, pouring some into the single glass. Her gaze roved appreciatively from the throat above his snowy neckcloth up to his strong, tanned face with its square jaw, high cheekbones and noble brow. The dark eyes that displayed a piercing intellect. The lips that had brushed hers when last they were at this house, and soon would do so again.

A wavy lock of dark hair fell over his forehead as he worked—the lock she'd so often longed to brush away. Soon, she would have leave to run her fingers through it.

'By the way, how long do we have?' he asked as he handed her the glass.

'At least two hours. Maybe more. So we should probably…begin.'

'Sip your wine first.'

Now it was he watching her, his gaze roving over her face. Not sure she would be able to swallow through her constricted throat, she took a tiny sip before handing him back the glass.

He set it down and turned back to her, his dark eyes serious as he touched a fingertip to the wine wetness of her lips. 'Do you know how often I've wanted to kiss these? Dreamed of tracing them with my finger?'

He did just that, moving a fingertip with barely perceptible pressure around the outline of her mouth, setting every surface he touched tingling. She sucked in a breath, her chest growing tight, a scintillating warmth beginning to build at her centre.

She wanted to ask again that he kiss her, but she didn't want to open her lips and risk losing the mesmerising feel of his slowly tracing fingertip. Sighing, she closed her eyes, wanting to devote every ounce of her concentration to feeling the effects of his circling finger.

Then, while she sat motionless, scarcely breathing, he moved his hand, adding another fingertip, the two fingers moving together to trace her chin, along her jaw and under it to the sensitive point where head joined neck. Back and forth across her neck, with fingertips alternating with nails, he caressed her from her chin to the ruff at the collar of her gown.

She arched her neck, wishing she'd worn a gown with a lower décolletage, so his fingers might reach lower, below her collarbones to where the swell of her breasts seemed ever more sensitised. Instead, after drawing a single fingertip along the collarbone and back up the column of her throat, he used his whole hand to trace the outline of her face, fingertips on one side, thumb on the other, from the heights of her cheekbone under her ear until fingers and thumb met at the point of her chin.

He rested the fingers of both hands on her cheeks, then moved them slowly upwards, combing them through the little curls beside her ears and up to lift the hair off her forehead, gently rubbing the skin there while his thumbs traced her eyebrows. And then traced a finger of each hand down her nose to rest them back on her lips.

'May I kiss you, Emma?' he whispered, his voice husky.

'Yes,' she breathed. 'Oh, please, yes!'

Tilting her chin up with one hand, he brought his mouth down on hers, brushing his lips against hers gently, as he had the very first time.

Now, though, she felt the wetness of his tongue against the seam of her lips, as he kissed her, its shocking, delicate heat. She gasped and instantly he moved away.

'Do you want me to stop?'

'Stop now and I shall strangle you!' she gasped.

Laughing low in his throat, he kissed her again with a nuzzling of his lips, the quick, wet brush of his tongue.

And then slowly touched again with his lips every place he had caressed with his fingertips.

Feeling like she was melting from the inside out, Emma was grateful for the sofa that kept her upright, else she might have slid bonelessly on to the floor.

For thrilling, wonderful moments he kissed her chin, neck, collarbones, forehead, brows, the curve of her nose, his hands caressing her face and neck when his lips went elsewhere.

At last, he moved his mouth on hers again. His

breathing rapid, he pressed down harder, his body leaning into hers, pushing her into the cushions.

She could feel his heart hammering under the jacket, his pulse as rapid as her own. She lifted her hands to clasp the back of his neck and pull him closer still.

He licked at her lips, probing at the corners, touching and withdrawing his tongue. When, on a sigh, she opened her mouth as he seemed to want her to, he slid his tongue within and sealed his lips to hers.

The liquid heat and velvet pressure sent a maelstrom of sensation swirling in her belly and lower, sparking a tingling in her nipples. Opening her mouth wider, she gasped when he caressed her tongue with his own.

Panting, she couldn't seem to draw air into her straining lungs. She wanted him closer, harder, devouring her, pressing into her until she could not tell where her body ended and his began.

When he suddenly pulled away, she whimpered in protest, but hushing her with a murmur, he lifted her from the cushions and angled her sidewise, easing her down so she was almost lying prone across the sofa. And then, ah, at that angle, how much deliciously deeper his tongue penetrated as he caressed every surface of her mouth!

She was swimming in sensation, drowning in

it, too drugged with delight to protest when he pulled his mouth away.

But he left her for only a moment. In the next instant, she felt his hot breath and the warm wet caress of his tongue on her chin, her neck, tracing down to linger at the hollow of her throat before going lower still. She felt the nip of his teeth on her collarbone, the wetness of his tongue as he slid it under the neckline of her gown, laving the skin beneath as far as the garment would allow him to reach.

And then, reclining his hard length against her, he took her mouth again, plumbing it with deep, hard, penetrating kisses.

Lost in sensation, her hands fluttering uselessly to her sides, she had no idea how long he went on kissing her, only that she wanted it to last for ever.

When he finally pulled away and gently helped her up, and reclined her against the back of the sofa, she could manage only a feeble protest.

'I d-didn't want you to s-stop,' she said raggedly.

'Glutton,' he said, though she was happy to note his breathing seemed as unsteady as hers. Reaching over to the table, he poured more wine in the glass and downed it. She was also pleased to note his hands were trembling.

He poured in more and handed her the glass.

Reluctantly, she took it. 'I'd rather you kissed me again,' she said as she took a small, token sip.

'I could go on kissing you all day, strumpet, but if this house had a mirror to inspect yourself in, you'd realise why we must stop.' His gaze amused and tender, he ran a thumb along her mouth. 'Your lips are already red and swollen. You'll need a brisk walk in the cold air of the garden, and possibly some salve, lest you return home looking thoroughly kissed.'

Her eyes widened. 'Is it that noticeable?'

'Yes, my sweet. So it is good that you brought some refreshments—perhaps you can blame some of the ruby colour in those oh-so-tempting lips on the wine. Now, drink up and have a cake.'

'Is that…all, then?' she asked, perplexed and a little disappointed.

'That will be all for today.'

'But…isn't there more? More than kissing?'

He laughed. 'Oh, much more! But when a marvellous banquet is laid out before you, you don't run to the table and gobble from every dish. No, you sample each thing in turn, savouring, appreciating.'

'We only have five more meetings, you know. You are sure we will have time to savour… everything by then? I know, it's silly of me, with no experience, to question the master, but I just want to make sure we end our time with me having tasted…every dish.'

'I assure you, you will taste everything you desire.'

'Very well, then.' She accepted a cake from him with a sigh, despite the protest deep within her body of a building imperative that was going to be denied. 'Although I suppose you are right. If I hope to continue these meetings undiscovered, I cannot go home looking thoroughly kissed.'

'We wouldn't want to do anything to jeopardise them, would we?'

'No. And thank you for—*that*. It was…wonderful.'

Tipping up her chin, he placed a gentle kiss on the end of her nose. 'You were wonderful, too.'

A sudden thought struck her and she gave a little laugh. 'I don't know how I'm going to meet you at social gatherings and not blush.'

'Making ladies blush is my speciality. I wouldn't worry about that.'

'What a master of deception I shall have to become.' She sighed. 'I am honest to a fault—that is, I used to be. I've recently discovered that in the pursuit of passion, I can be as devious as a moneylender.'

Chuckling at that, he said, 'Probably a good thing—if we want to *keep* pursuing passion. Unless…you want to stop now?'

'Stop?' she cried. 'Absolutely not! I'm already regretting we only have five more meetings. I don't intend to give up an instant of our time together.'

'Five more meetings.' His expression sobered. 'It doesn't sound like very much, does it? So we *must* meet in society—so I may make you blush and flirt with you and we can squeeze as much joy as possible out of the limited time available to us. Will you be attending the Armistead soirée tomorrow?'

'Yes. You'll be there?'

He nodded. 'I'll make a point of it. Now, I should slip away, so you have time to take that walk in the garden before your footman returns. Until tomorrow night, then.'

He rose and, setting down her wine, Emma stood up, too, and followed him to the door. 'One more kiss, before you leave?'

Smiling, he bent down and pulled her against him. Though the kiss began soft and sweet, using her new knowledge, Emma soon pressed harder, slipping her tongue into his mouth, seeking his tongue, suckling and caressing.

She was light-headed and dizzy again when he finally let her go. 'Kiss me like that and I'll never want to leave,' he said on a groan.

'Would that I could arrange that.'

Chuckling, he tapped her nose, set his beaver

hat on his head and, after a brief inspection up and down the street, slipped out the door.

Emma watched him walk away, the glow within her so bright she could scarcely contain herself. When at last he disappeared around the corner, with a little laugh she hugged herself and danced around the room.

It had been marvellous, wonderful, even more wonderful than she'd dreamed. And she had five glorious sessions more to touch him, taste him and have him show her every path to bliss.

No matter what happened, it was going to be worth it.

Chapter Fifteen

∽∾∿

You've done this numerous times, Theo told himself as he entered the ballroom of Armistead House. Walked into a room, expecting to encounter a woman with whom he'd begun an affair.

Except in his previous liaisons, they would have already become lovers. The lady would have been as skilled in dalliance as he was, ready to offer a knowing smile, to allow him a lingering touch of her hand or arm as he escorted her to dance, and to murmur words full of innuendo, all designed to make him eager for the next tryst.

But this was Emma. Inexperienced in dalliance, not yet truly his lover—and he had no idea how she would react upon seeing him again after sharing intimacy. The pattern of dalliance that had, frankly, become a little stale, was suddenly unfamiliar, new, exciting, sparking an unusual sense of anticipation and tension in his gut. He couldn't wait to see what she would do, hear what she would say—and discover whether or not she would blush at the mere sight of him.

But first, before he could allow himself to seek her out, he would have to titillate the gossips—and placate his father, if the Marquess happened to be keeping watch over his son's activities—by paying court to Miss Fothergill or some other equally sought-after damsel.

As he made his way further into the room, he noted Miss Fothergill in the far corner, surrounded by her usual coterie—and Emma, standing with her friends Miss Overton and Miss Standish beside the chaperons. Then she looked over and saw him.

The serene expression on her face didn't change, nor did her pale cheeks flush. But something heated and intimate flashed between them, wordless but so intense he felt the strength of it penetrate deep into his chest. Feeling his lips curve into a smile, he made a minute inclination of his head towards the group around Miss Fothergill, to which she replied with a barely imperceptible lift of an eyebrow. Yet he felt sure the message had been sent and received: *I must pay obligatory court...but then I will seek you out.*

Never had he felt less like offering empty compliments to a Beauty. Fortunately, Miss Fothergill's swains were even more numerous than usual, so he was able to let himself be shunted aside by an insistent young baron after just a few minutes of idle chatter.

Never had he been happier to leave a beauty's side.

Besides, he had news for Emma that he thought would make her almost as pleased with him as she'd been by his kisses.

As he crossed the crowded floor towards her, his body tightening with expectation and arousal, he thought perhaps they might have to rethink his dictate that they only meet once at week at Judd Street.

Next Wednesday seemed much too far away.

'Ladies,' he said, bowing as he reached the group.

'Lord Theo,' they chimed together as they curtsied.

'Miss Henley, could I have the honour of the next dance?'

'With *me*? But it is to be a waltz, Lord Theo,' she protested. With a wicked little smile, she added, 'Ah, I see. You were not fortunate enough to secure the hand of Miss Fothergill.'

Wretch, he thought. 'But my father will hear that I was most diligent in my attempt,' he said. 'Will you dance, then?'

She lay her hand on his arm, setting little tingles dancing along his skin. 'I suppose it is my

Christian duty to do what I can to assuage your disappointment.'

Ah, how he savoured the feel of her fingers twined in his, her waist under his hand as he moved her into the rhythm. Perhaps their own slow dance of seduction was more than a noble restraint that would allow her to draw back if she wished, before they went too far.

He'd told her to savour each dish, rather then grab greedily for everything at once. The sensual tension between them over what they'd already shared, the eager anticipation at knowing all the delights he had still to reveal to her, heightened desire and added a zest of freshness to the experience that he'd not felt in a long time.

'If you are my consolation prize, I shall expect you to entertain me,' he said.

'So you are still basking in Miss Fothergill's presence? You should have a care, though, not to seek me out too often after you've left her. Like Queen Elizabeth I, the Incomparable does not like her courtiers to smile upon anyone else.'

He shook his head dismissively. 'Her court is so large and my status in it, as you kindly pointed out, lowly enough that I wouldn't think she has either the wit to notice or the interest to care if I "smile upon" someone else.'

'She might not be capable of solving advanced equations, but when it comes to calculating the size of her court, she's as precise as a mathematician,' Emma replied. 'The night of the Norfolk soirée, when you left her and came over to speak with me after Mama and I exited the card room? She most definitely noted you approaching me. The look I got!' Emma chuckled. 'As if some scruffy commoner had been caught poaching on royal ground. I'm not sure what was stronger— her indignation that you would leave her, or her incredulity that you would leave her to talk with *me*. Though I doubt she was seriously concerned about having your attention stray for long.'

Lord Theo laughed shortly. 'I'm sure she was not. The silly chit has been encouraged to believe herself so dazzling, she'd doubtless find it unthinkable that a man accorded the privilege of her company would abandon her.'

'Perhaps she feels her beauty is *so* dazzling, mere mortals might need to turn away and focus a while on something commonplace, just to rest their eyes.'

'I would hardly consider you "commonplace", Emma Henley.'

She pinked a little at his compliment. 'How very kind you are, sir.'

'Not flattery—merest truth. And I really don't want to capture more of Miss Fothergill's attention. Since she contributes little to an encounter beyond offering her beauty to gaze upon, conversation soon disintegrates into a rather boring monologue.'

'A man with your famous wit? I'm sure your monologues are never boring.'

He grinned. 'And now it's you being kind. Enough about Miss Tedious Incomparable! First I have a question for you, then some information I think you'll be excited to hear.'

She fit into his arms so well, he thought as he swung her through the spirals of the dance, her superior height meaning he needed glance down only slightly to talk with her over the music. Putting his face oh-so-temptingly close to those oh-so-kissable lips.

She was gazing at his mouth, too, he realised. Remembering the kisses they'd so recently shared? The idea sent a bolt of heat through him.

Finally, she shook her head, as if to free herself from the sensual haze that surrounded them like a fine mist. 'And the question, Lord Theo?'

'I understand you are in the process of furnishing the house you just leased. I hope the goods you ordered for it have been satisfactory?'

'Yes, I'm quite pleased. With all the goods recently delivered to the house.'

'And Lady Henley was not upset by the amount of time you spent there, supervising?'

'In truth, I don't believe she noticed I was gone.'

Though she probably wouldn't be here, dancing with him, had anything untoward occurred, none the less, he felt better for her oblique confirmation that their meeting had gone undiscovered—and that she'd been pleased by her first lesson. 'I am very glad to hear it.'

'And the news that shall make me happy?'

Aside from the fact that he wished they could slip away to Judd Street this very minute?

'I spent yesterday afternoon enquiring about finding a tutor for Ellie Lattimar's student, Arabella. First at Somerset House, but as I expected, the Royal Academy does not take female students.'

Emma let out a huff of frustration. 'That's so short-sighted of them! After all, they have accepted female members! And are there not, even now, practising female artists of some renown?'

'True, but as we discussed before, most female artists were taught by fathers, or by a drawing master with connections to the family. And to be fair, the Royal Academy bases its ban on female students on the curriculum's inclusion of life-drawing classes. I imagine the directors fear there might be enough public outcry to jeopardise the continued operation of the school, were they to allow females to attend drawing classes with nude male models.'

'Although naturally, *men* attending a class to

draw nude *females* is not a problem,' Emma replied drily.

'Naturally,' Theo confirmed.

'Are there other options for her to receive instruction?'

'The classic method of studying art has always been to copy the drawings and paintings of master artists. While the Royal Academy stages its annual exhibition for the purpose of showing promising *new* works for sale, the British institution's annual summer exhibition displays only Old Master works. After the members have a chance to view the pieces, they are left on display for the express purpose of allowing other artists to study and copy.'

'A female artist could study and copy them, too?' Ellie asked.

'Precisely. And though females may not be admitted to the Royal Academy's school, they are allowed to study and copy the works displayed at the Academy's own yearly exhibition, as well. These are current works by living artists, rather than Old Masters, but every piece is reviewed by a jury of Academy members before being accepted for the exhibition, which assures a high level of quality.'

'Copying paintings on her own would be free, I imagine,' Emma said. 'But even so, Arabella would need funds to live on—to rent a room in a boarding house, purchase art supplies, food and clothing.'

'True,' Theo said. 'There is one other way she might get instruction—probably a better route, for it would allow the extent of her talent to be evaluated without her having to give up her place at Mrs Lattimar's, unless or until it's determined that she has skill enough to pursue art as a career. One of the directors at Somerset House told me that several of the artists who teach at the Academy school give private instruction as well. He referred me to George Inverson.'

'George Inverson!' Emma echoed, her face lighting. 'The student of Turner, who paints those wonderful landscapes? Whose portrait of the Lord Mayor was displayed at the Royal Academy Exhibition last summer?'

'Yes, *that* Mr Inverson. It took some time to track him down—and a bit of persuasion—but he said he would be amenable to taking on a part-time student. If Mrs Lattimar and Arabella find the arrangement acceptable, she can visit his studio two mornings a week, for a period of ten weeks, after which he will give his expert assessment of her potential as an artist.'

'It's a wonderful solution! I'm sure he will charge a fee, but I will be happy to pay it. Arabella will be over the moon when she hears about it! And I could take her to the lessons, so the school wouldn't have to spare a staff member.'

'I don't think that would be wise,' Theo said. 'Inverson's studio is in the city, located in an area I'm sure Lady Henley would not approve of you visiting with only a young girl as your escort.'

'I could take a footman,' Emma countered.

'And what would your mama's society friends think when they discovered you were regularly visiting a dubious location near Ludgate with a footman and a street orphan in tow?' Lord Theo asked. 'Bringing a footman means gossip would run rampant through the servants' quarters, and sooner or later, *someone* in the *ton* would find out. That on dit would sizzle through London society faster than fire down a lit fuse.'

Emma would like to disagree, but honesty compelled her to keep silent. Her mother would have palpitations if society began gossiping about her daughter, a footman and a girl from the streets. The embarrassment might be enough for Lady Henley to force Emma to cancel the lease on the Judd Street house—or decide to keep a much closer eye on her daughter's comings and goings. She couldn't risk that.

With a sigh, she admitted, 'You are probably correct. At the moment, it wouldn't be wise for me to excite *anyone*'s interest in where I go and how much time I spend there.'

'I'm perfectly able to take her,' Lord Theo said. Trying not to let his hopes about how Emma might react to the news get too high, he added in a casual tone, 'Inverson's agreed to take me on as a student, too.'

'That's wonderful!' Emma cried, smiling with true delight.

Theo felt his chest expand with a warmth that, for once, had nothing to do with lust. 'You approve of the decision?'

'Of course! You're actually going to study!' She squeezed the hand guiding her though the steps. 'I'm so pleased and proud!'

'Are you? I would never have believed I could do anything that would make the exacting Miss Henley proud of me.'

'Of course I'm proud of you. It's far easier to remain in one's easy, comfortable, socially approved role than to risk stepping into the unknown.'

'You don't seem to find it difficult.'

'That's because all the rewards that mean anything to me can only be gained after I take that step.'

'Then we must make sure you get every reward you desire.'

As they spoke, her delight and pride in his decision was gradually overshadowed by the strong sensual connection he'd felt the moment he claimed her hand. Her gaze locked with his, its warmth on his face almost like a caress.

Ah, yes, he could hardly wait to offer her every reward she sought.

Knowing he must stop gazing at her with such intensity before someone took note of it, he forced himself to look away—and scanned the ballroom to see if anyone appeared to be watching them.

Thankfully, no one seemed to be paying them any attention. He blessed the happy chance of having decided last Season to seek Emma out at society entertainments. His attentions to her might have excited comment the first few times he singled her out, but by now were commonplace enough not to arouse any particular notice.

Recapturing his usual, teasing tone, he continued, 'You needn't be *too* proud of me, lest the exultation go to my head. I'll be able to have Mr Inverson assess the level of my own talent without anyone in society finding out I've strayed from the narrow path of acceptable activities for a gentleman. If someone should happen to observe me going to or from the lessons, I can always come up with some glib excuse to explain away my presence in the city.'

'With a young girl in tow? Might that not give rise to some…unpleasant speculation about you?'

'What, the fashionable Lord Theo and some

street urchin?' he said, infusing his tone with such a perfect blend of top-loftiness and offended incredulity that she laughed.

'I can just see you depressing the pretensions of anyone who dared suggest such a thing. But… what will you do, if Mr Inverson confirms that *you* possess a superior talent?'

'Let's not be hanging my work beside the Old Masters just yet.'

'Make light of it if you will! But it would be a tragedy to waste a true talent. If you do possess one, I hope you will give it free rein—whatever the consequences.'

He shook his head wryly. 'You make it seem impossible to turn away from a path I would never have considered travelling again had you not teased me on to it. I'm not sure whether to be grateful—or furious.'

'For encouraging you to abandon the "narrow path" for something more important and fulfilling?' She smiled. 'If the artistic yearning is deep and true enough, it would have won out in the end, even without me.'

'I'm not so sure.' He laughed shortly. 'Submerging it in excessive quantities of alcohol and idleness worked well enough up until now to suppress it.'

The music ended and, after the obligatory bow and curtsy between partners, Emma placed her hand on his arm for him to lead her back to her chaperon. Knowing he couldn't dance with her again or even talk with her much longer without arousing speculation, he'd made sure they ended the steps on the far side of the ballroom from her friends, so he might draw out the time together as long as possible.

'When will you tell Ellie Lattimar about Arabella's lessons?' Emma asked. 'Or would you like me to inform her?'

'I'll stop by the school in the next day or so. I promised to bring Arabella some paper and charcoal, you remember.'

She bit her lip and his mind went instantly to the taste of her he'd sampled, distracting him so much he barely took in her next words. 'Much as I'd like to accompany you, it probably isn't wise for us to go anywhere together publicly.'

Unfortunate, but true. 'Not if we wish to continue meeting…privately.'

She uttered a shuddering sigh. 'Oh, how I wish it! I never realised how many hours there are in seven days! Perhaps we could meet, riding in the park. We've done that often enough that it shouldn't excite comment.'

Delighted she was as impatient for their next rendezvous as he was, he murmured, 'We shall have to content ourselves with anticipation. And ah, how much I do anticipate!'

'Not nearly as much as I,' she murmured. 'So, no visit to the school. I shall very much miss watching Arabella's face when she learns the news, though.' Her eyes brightened. 'Why don't we ride in the park two days from now, after you've talked with Arabella and Ellie Lattimar? You can tell me all about her reaction.'

'An excellent idea,' he agreed immediately. It wouldn't be as good as meeting her alone at Judd Street, but at least they would be able to talk freely…and he could tease himself with visions of just what he meant to do with her and for her once they finally were alone again.

'Arabella is going to be so excited, her feet won't touch the ground for days! She already thought you handsome. She will now believe you a hero.'

He shook his head wryly. 'It's humbling to be thought a paragon.'

She gave him a saucy grin. 'You needn't worry. I'll make sure to depress *that* pretention.'

'Will you? Do I not remember you promising me a few days ago that you would henceforth only pay me compliments?'

Shaking her head, Emma said, 'I can't imagine what prompted me to make such a ridiculous promise. I don't know how I'll be able to honour it.'

Chucking, he said, 'I never expected you could.'

Just before they reached her waiting friends, when he would be forced to surrender her hand and her company, Emma halted. 'And to think,' she murmured, looking up at him searchingly, 'only a short time ago, I thought you little more than an idle, purposeless society gentleman. I would never have guessed you possess such talent hidden within that elegant frame, or more than a sharp wit and a gift for amusing banter in that intelligent brain.'

Armoured as he was against her barbed comments and frequent scorn, he was completely unprepared for such glowing compliments. Humbled, he could think of nothing to reply...even as a soaring brightness filled his heart to think that he'd earned that heartfelt accolade by daring to stray from his society gentleman role—perhaps beginning to find his way back to his true self.

A man of whom Emma Henley could be proud.

'I'm not sure I deserve such praise,' he said gruffly. 'I hope I won't disappoint you.'

Smiling, she let her gaze slowly scan his face and then linger on his lips. 'Oh, I don't think there's any chance of you disappointing me.'

Relieved to revert to his more comfortable role of the *ton*'s leading rake, he smiled back. 'In *that* enterprise, you can definitely count on me.'

And then she was gone, welcomed back into

the fold of her friends and chaperons. Already counting the days until he might see her again, he made himself bow and walk away.

Chapter Sixteen

Two mornings later, Emma turned her mount into the gates of Hyde Park, anticipation and expectation swirling in her belly. She'd kept herself busy, attending evening entertainments with Lady Henley, focused on finding society ladies who had vacancies in their staff, then calling on them the following afternoon. Several matrons, after listening to a presentation subtly reinforced with mention of prominent school supporters Lady Lyndlington, the Dowager Countess of Sayleford and the Marquess of Witlow, pledged to consider Ellie's students for the openings in their households.

Once she moved permanently to Judd Street, effectively forfeiting her position in society, she would no longer move in the social circles where she would be able to search out such employment opportunities. But important as the work was, she struggled to contain the impatience that dogged her every hour, despite her excitement and anticipation, as if all her life now were just marking time for the next rendezvous.

Already, it seemed ages since she'd danced with Theo at the Armistead soirée—and centuries since their interlude at Judd Street.

What would he teach her next?

Smiling, she let herself recall each sweet moment of their first meeting. She was still impatient to grab for every delight—especially the delight of touching and caressing him. For a lady who seldom let anyone else lead her, it was sweet torment to put herself completely in Theo's hands, experiencing passion at the rate and rhythm he dictated. How anxious she was to proceed to complete fulfilment!

Her ear catching the sound of approaching hoofbeats, Emma gazed ahead—intensely conscious of the little shocks that danced over her skin when she saw Lord Theo riding towards her.

Eddies of anticipation swirling in her belly, she signalled her mount to approach his.

Halting a pace away, they exchanged conventional greetings, ever conscious of the attending groom. But as soon as they turned their mounts to walk side by side, Emma turned to him. She might not be able to touch him, but she could at least indulge her craving to devour him with her eyes.

He seemed just as eager to gaze at her, the molten look in his dark brown eyes sending a little thrill through her.

'Two more days,' he murmured.

'I know. An eternity!' she said with a laugh, selfishly glad he seemed as impatient for their rendezvous as she was.

'Since I cannot follow my inclination and lead you behind a convenient tree for some thorough kissing, I suppose I shall have to content myself with recounting my visit to Mrs Lattimar's school.'

'Since I cannot follow my inclination and beg for that thorough kissing, I suppose I shall have to content myself with listening. Although I truly am interested in what happened. Did Ellie think the lesson schedule would be feasible?'

'Yes, she said it would pose no problem and thanked me several times for looking into the matter. There was some heated protest about your paying for Arabella's lessons and about the inconvenience to me of transporting the girl to Inverson's studio and back, but I made short work of both. After informing her that I would be going to the studio anyway, as I will be taking instruction myself, I assured her I was very interested to follow Arabella's progress. Inverson has many important contacts within the art world and working relationships with patrons. If he believes Arabella to have enough talent, he will recommend her for commissions. So in the end, Ellie agreed to the arrangement, with another expression of her fervent thanks.'

'I'm so glad! I can only imagine what Arabella had to say when Ellie told her.'

'She was as ecstatic as you predicted.' Theo chuckled. 'If Ellie had not taken her in hand, I suspect she would have fallen at my feet. In any event, after thanking us both three times and promising me she would do her best and make all of us proud of her, she bounded out of Ellie's office to wait at the study table for the lesson I promised her.'

'I wouldn't have been surprised if she were too excited to concentrate.'

'Not at all. The prospect of soon being able to work under a real artist had her giving the work her complete attention. I had her do some studies of basic shapes and shadowing and a little work on perspective. She couldn't have been more eager.'

'I'm sure she was very grateful you took the time and trouble,' Emma said, impressed again by his care and consideration for a girl socially so far beneath him. 'I imagine your elegant society friends would be astounded if they could see the frivolous Lord Theo sitting at a wooden school table, instructing a budding artist who hails from the stews of St Giles.'

'Society would be astounded to see the frivolous Lord Theo doing anything of significance,' he replied, his tone acerbic. 'Besides, it was a useful refresher for me as well—since I, too, will soon be taking instruction from a real artist.'

'Thank you again—for caring about Arabella.'

'Thank you—for showing me a way to escape that "narrow" gentleman's path.'

She sighed. 'I wish we could escape propriety's path right now! But since that wouldn't be prudent, we can do the next best thing. How about a gallop? And I warn you, this time my mount will *not* stumble at the start. I promise I will not gloat when I beat you.'

'Careful what you threaten—lest I feel compelled to devise some…intimate punishment for when we no longer need to worry about propriety.'

A ripple of heat coursed through her, just imagining what he might have in mind. 'No punishment could be worse than the interminable wait until our next meeting at Judd Street. Now, ready? Let's go!'

In the early afternoon the following Wednesday, Theo stood cleaning his brushes. A landscape was propped up on the table beside him, his latest copy of it on the easel in front of him. This second attempt was going much better, and Inverson's critique at his first lesson had helped tremendously in correcting the problem he'd been having with the perspective. The master had also suggested better ways of mixing his colours to get closer to the shade he envisaged in his head.

He'd made definite progress, although he probably would have made more, if he hadn't had so much difficulty concentrating. His thoughts kept returning again and again to Emma and the delight of their clandestine rendezvous.

Just thinking about her brought a smile to his lips. He'd never before made love to a complete innocent and appreciated the great honour Emma had bestowed on him by allowing him to be the first to touch her. Though he expected it would be delightful to awaken Emma's senses, once he'd promised himself that the love-play would not reach fulfilment immediately, but progress through long, slow stages, he'd anticipated that for him, their first meetings would be exercises in controlling frustration.

To his surprise, he'd found that touching her, arousing her with his mouth and fingers, had been incredibly erotic, despite having to rein in his own reactions. He loved the way she responded, her little sighs, how she arched her body into his caressing fingers. She was as eagerly and intuitively passionate as his instincts had whispered she would be. And a fast study—that kiss she'd given him to send him on the way had been as arousing as the caress of a practised courtesan.

Perhaps it was the added thrill of knowing it was *Emma*—intriguing, unique, unexpected Emma—kissing him, the contrast between her prim maidenly exterior and the unbridled passion beneath, that intensified that most basic caress to a level of pleasure he usually associated with a much more intimate lovemaking.

All he knew was he'd existed in a state of semi-arousal every since, a condition that had progressed to aching hardness over this morning, knowing he would see her again this afternoon.

A glance at the mantle clock confirming that it was time to leave sent his pulse rate soaring, while arousal surged in his blood. Already his head was filled with her violet scent, his mouth with the remembered taste of her lips.

He couldn't wait to begin again.

After having his valet kit him out in proper afternoon dress, Theo left his lodgings and walked down the street to engage a hackney. Another precaution—experienced at assignations, his tiger wasn't one to chatter about where his master went and whom he visited, but it wouldn't be wise to drive his distinctive phaeton to Judd Street too often, lest someone notice and remember it.

He had the hackney drop him off several streets away, his excitement and anticipation building the closer he got to her house. And then he was there, rapping on the door—which was opened by a glowing Emma.

He stepped in quickly and closed it behind him, an echoing glow swelling in his chest.

When she drew him close and lifted her face to him, he was more than happy to oblige. He bent to give her a kiss that started sweet and then turned passionate, as she opened her mouth to him and eagerly greeted his tongue. He pulled her closer, giving himself up to the pleasure of tongue dancing with tongue.

His heartbeat was thundering when he gently pushed her away. If she meant to start where they left off, he'd better find a way to delay.

'Did you bring sustenance this time?'

She made a little moue of displeasure. 'Must we have sustenance? I was hoping for more kissing.'

'In good time, wench,' he said, secretly delighted that she seemed so ravenous for his touch.

'Very well, I suppose I shall have to first be a good hostess. Shall we adjourn to the parlour, then?'

She led him to the front room, where the sun through the windows filled the space with soft golden light. 'You see,' she said, gesturing into the room, 'I have been busy. We now have a proper table, side chairs, even a rug. I discovered that coming here to work on the furnishings provides excellent camouflage. I've visited the house several times, so now when I tell Mama where I'm going, she makes no more comment than to remind me at what time I must be back to change for our evening engagements.'

'So the footman is out collecting items again?'

'Yes. Glassware, this time. Cook is still providing the basket of food, but after today, we'll have more than one glass. Wine?'

'Please.' While she set out the wine, glass and bread on the table, he took a seat beside her on the sofa.

She poured a glass, but instead of handing it to him, she dipped a fingertip in the liquid, painted it along his mouth and pulled his head down to lick the wine from his lips. 'Ah,' she murmured. 'Now that is how I should like to drink my wine. Or like this.'

She took a small sip, put her lips to his and coaxed his mouth open with her tongue. He felt the heat of her tongue gliding against his, the chill of the wine, the taste of her lips and the wine mingling as she sipped and suckled at his mouth.

They both swallowed and she broke the kiss. 'More wine, my lord?' she asked with a wicked little smile.

'Yes,' he breathed, this time ready when she took the tiny sip and shared it with him, wine and lips and tongues mingling. Snuggling against his side, she leaned her head back against his chest before taking another sip, letting him bend down to open her lips and partake of the wine nectar from her mouth.

They continued the game until they finished the glass, Theo delighted by her inventiveness. And he was the one who was supposed to be doing the tutoring!

'I have only to tell you what I like—is that right?'

Knowing that might soon land him in trouble, none the less he nodded. 'Tell me what you like, or don't like.'

'I would like you to touch me again, like you did last time. Only here—' she smoothed her hands from her neck over the swell of her breasts '—and here,' she murmured, rubbing them over the round of her belly.

Desire thick in his throat, he leaned her back against the cushions. Watching her watch him, he put his hands on her shoulders, rubbing and kneading them, then behind, to massage up the column of her neck. She opened her lips, probably to protest that he'd strayed from the area she indicated, but as he kneaded and soothed, whatever she'd meant to say exited her lips in a long sigh. Following the line of her shoulder to her collarbone, he massaged there, then slowly lower until his fingertips reached the top of the swell of her breasts.

She arched her back, lifting her breasts up to him, and finally he obliged, smoothing his hands over the tops and then cupping them while his thumbs sought the nipples hidden under bodice, stays and chemise. Despite the layers of clothing, he felt the nubs peak and intensified the pressure of his thumbs, drawing out a gasp.

'Kiss me now,' she urged.

'Very well, my lady.' He leaned down and took her mouth, gently at first, then with increasing pressure, his tongue seeking hers and laving it to the rhythm of his caressing fingers.

Her breathing accelerating, she took one of his hands and slid it from her breast down her belly, towards the junction of her thighs. 'Here,' she gasped. 'I ache here.'

He caressed her stomach, down to the top of her thighs, desperately trying to ignore the little voice that urged him to rub, not down over the unproductive arc of stomach trapped under thick gathers of skirt and petticoat, but upwards.

Finally, he could resist the siren call no longer. He reached down and tugged a handful of voluminous skirt up to bare her knee, quickly sliding his hand beneath.

This was delight, warm skin under only a thin layer of gartered stocking. He cupped her knee, traced the round of the upper calf, and then, unable to resist the temptation, moved his hand upwards to where the stocking gave way to warm, bare skin.

Ah, the heat and devilish temptation as his fingers caressed the velvet warmth of thigh! By a supreme effort of will, despite every sense shouting for him to slide his hand ever upwards until his fingers met the wetness of her centre, he forced his hand to remain where it was, playing just at the edge of stocking and garter.

Murmuring, urgent, she pushed her leg against his hand. He kissed her mouth, her chin, her neck as he caressed first one thigh, the other, not slowing his pace until they were both gasping. Ending the kisses at last, he pulled her to lie against him.

'I love it…when you touch…bare skin,' she said unevenly, her head against his chest. 'But… I would like to touch you, too.'

She reached towards him, but with danger warnings flashing through him, he caught her hand. 'That's for…another day,' he said, his voice as ragged as hers. 'Now it's time to straighten your clothing, have some more wine and that restorative walk in the garden, before your footman returns'

She sighed. 'If I must. But I'm getting rather

greedy to taste more of this banquet. We haven't much time left and I know there is so much more to experience.'

'Patience. Anticipation will make the pleasure even greater.'

To his relief, for he wasn't sure how much longer he would have been able to withstand temptation, she sat up straight and allowed him to act as her lady's maid, straightening her bodice, pulling the stockings straight and ordering her skirts.

Straightening a ruffle on her bodice, she said, 'There were too many garments today. Next time, I want to meet you in the bedchamber. Have you remove those annoying layers so I may feel your hands on my naked skin. Everywhere.'

He had to stifle a groan. He could picture it all too easily—and eagerly. But how could he unwrap the present that was Emma and avoid having her lure him into taking her completely? He wanted to draw out the process so that full intimacy didn't occur until their very last meeting, in the admittedly increasingly unlikely case that she suddenly decided she didn't want to limit her future marriage options by losing her maidenhood now. But previous experience hadn't given him any guidelines on how to conduct a limited lovemaking.

He had no idea how he would satisfy her request without losing either his control or his mind, but he'd have to figure it out. And he had only until next Wednesday to do it.

But ah, how she continued to surprise him! Despite being a maid, she not only met each increasing level of intimacy without shyness or embarrassment, she boldly told him what she wanted. Hearing the demands from her own lips made her requests doubly erotic.

Pulling his mind from thoughts that would be more likely to have him kissing her again than preparing to leave, he said, 'Pour me some wine, won't you? You're perhaps the only person in London who will truly understand the significance of this, so I wanted you to know. I took my first lesson with Mr Inverson yesterday.'

She set down the glass she'd just filled, her gaze lifting to his and her mouth widening in a smile. 'I'm so glad! Was it as fulfilling as you'd hoped?'

'Even more,' he said, delighted to expand on the only topic of conversation that might actually distract him from thoughts of kissing her. 'There was such a sense of…*freedom* in openly acknowledging my desire to paint! In being able to show my work to someone who understands the burning need to capture with my pen or brush the marvels before my eyes, and who is knowledgeable enough about the process and the techniques to really *see* it. See, evaluate and offer suggestions for improvements.'

Picking up the glass, he laughed, remembering the sheer thrill of it. 'I couldn't stop asking questions! At the end of the hour, I expect he was glad to send me along to the gallery to copy the works he'd hung there for his students to study. Frankly, I became so absorbed that I totally forgot the time. Not until the servants came in to light the lamps and told me the master had returned home for his supper, and I should do the same, did I put down my pencil.'

'That's wonderful!' she exclaimed, her excitement and approval buoying him further.

'After going home to change, I dined at my club, but having already offended several members by repeatedly refusing to join them for cards, I felt it prudent to leave. I had some vague intention of dropping by several entertainments…but then it struck me that the techniques Inverson had demonstrated—that I'd been practising by copying the works in his gallery—are masterfully on display in a landscape by John Sell Cotman that hangs in the back parlour at Father's house. I just knew it would be an excellent tool to study! However, having no wish to alert the Marquess—yet—to my revived interest in art, I knew if I wanted to borrow it, I ought to remove it while he and Mother were away for the evening.'

He grinned, recalling it. 'I felt almost like a housebreaker, slipping into the back parlour and standing on tiptoe to take it from the wall.'

Emma chuckled. 'Did you truly sneak the painting away like a thief?'

'Not exactly. I thought it best to tell Richards, the butler, that I wanted to borrow it for a while and have him get a picture from the storeroom to replace it.' With a touch of irritation at the indignity of it, he added, 'I knew as long as he chose something of similar size and colour to hang in its place, Father would never notice the difference.'

'And did you in fact go home and study it?'

'Yes. I spent the rest of the evening sketching, then, in daylight, when I could better evaluate the colours, I spent the early morning selecting oils. Of course, then I had to go back and try them out.'

'Are you happy with the work?'

'Not yet. There's something off with the perspective and I haven't got the colours quite right. I'm going to bring both Cotman's oil and my copy to Inverson to my next lesson, to get his advice.'

For a moment, her eyes roved his face, approval and fondness in her gaze.

'I believe you look happier and more excited than I've ever seen you.'

He nodded. 'I feel more alive than I have in years…as if, after merely sleepwalking through life, suddenly I've awakened, to find everything newer, fresher and more colourful. And, yes, I believe I am happier and more excited than I can remember.'

'You see, there can be advantages to wandering from the narrow path of the idle society gentleman.'

'Just as long as I don't forget how to be society's most skilful lover,' he murmured, waggling his eyebrows and giving her an exaggerated leer.

She laughed at that, as he hoped she would. Much as he loved the thrill of kissing her, touching her, he was glad they hadn't lost *this*—the witty repartee he shared with no one else.

'And now I most definitely need to take my leave, lest I encounter your footman on the doorstep.'

She sighed. 'I suppose you are right. But I hate that it always seems our time is so limited.'

'We must take what we have and be glad of it,' he replied. On the one hand, he would like hours…days to explore her body with his mouth and hands. On the other, he was very glad for the restrictions that buttressed his sorely tested control—else he would never be able to stretch out this seduction through four more sessions.

At least, he thought with deep satisfaction, she had given absolutely no sign that she was worried or regretful about the liaison upon which they'd embarked. No, she was patently eager for more.

After giving her another lingering kiss, he rose. Linking her arm in his, she walked him to the door.

'I shall be counting the hours until next Wednesday.'

'So will I,' he admitted before giving her a bow and walking quickly out—only to walk back inside even more quickly and shut the door behind him.

'Am I to hope you couldn't resist another kiss?' she asked, smiling—until she looked up at his face. 'What is it?' she demanded. 'What happened?'

'I shall have to linger a bit longer. I just saw my old school friend, Kensworth, walk into the shop of the piano tuner across the street.'

Chapter Seventeen

⁓⁓⁓

Emma's eyes widened as she realised the implications. 'Did he see you?'

'I don't think so. But his tiger is walking his vehicle outside the shop. I'd better wait here until he leaves before I try to make my way back. I wouldn't want to slip through the mews on to the main street and then have him pass me in his carriage while I walked to the hackney stand.' He gave her a strained smile. 'Hopefully he'll depart before your footman returns and I have to hide in the wardrobe.'

'Yes, I'd rather you avoid that indignity,' she said, trying to lighten his mood that had gone from sensual and joyous to withdrawn and guarded in the time it took him to walk out the door and back in. 'Besides, I don't think we need be too concerned. If he had seen you, surely he would have hailed you, or waved.'

'Let's hope so.'

'Fortunately, we haven't yet finished the wine and I believe there are a few of Cook's cakes left, too.'

She led him back into the parlour, but despite her plying him with wine and trying to tease him out of his worry, he remained distant and distracted.

Finally, exasperated by the failure of her attempts, she said, 'Very well, out with it! Spit out whatever dark thoughts are putting that thundercloud look on your face and that frown on your brow.'

'Sorry, Emma. I know I haven't been good company.' He smiled at her, but it didn't reach his eyes, which remained bleak.

The first icy little niggle of panic rippled through her. 'So…what *are* you thinking?'

'That we've been hopelessly naive. And that I've been both thoughtless and careless.' He shook his head. 'Trysting with a well-bred virgin in the city limits of London! What was I thinking?'

'That you were too polite to refuse a lady's proposition?' she said, terrified that she knew where this discussion was going and trying to head it off.

At least that drew a reluctant laugh from him. 'Politeness had nothing to do with it, as you very well know. It was fascination and a craving I could not master. I should have thought it through more carefully.'

'The way you are now?' she said. *He's going to end it*, she thought, pain already lancing through her.

'I'm sorry, Emma. But this whole idea was madness from the start, you know. When I consider what would have happened, had Kensworth seen me, hailed me? He would have demanded to know what I was doing here. Despite whatever glib excuse I devised, he would have noted the number of the house from which I exited. And when word reached him, as it eventually would, that Miss Henley had rented that property… He's not the sharpest quill in the drawer, but he'd have no trouble putting that together. And you know what that would mean.'

'Other than embarrassment for me and my family?'

'*Embarrassment?*' he echoed. Jumping up to pace the room, he turned back to say, 'A good deal more than that, you can be sure! Your father would demand that you marry me, with good cause. Isn't that what you've always wanted to avoid, a forced marriage?'

She shrugged. 'I would simply refuse.'

'It would not be that simple and you know it! The news would sweep through town like a hot wind in July! Causing intense distress and embarrassment to your family the longer it circulated without an engagement being announced. With the pressure on you to capitulate growing stronger every day.'

She shook her head. 'You don't know how resolute I can be. Papa would never beat me, I can be quite deaf through a harangue and there's nothing he could threaten me with that would make me change my mind. I already have this house and a competency to live on, which he cannot take away.'

'What of the work that means so much to you? Do you think you could persuade matrons to hire Ellie's students, or influence politicians, if you were living in disgrace?'

She shrugged again. 'My ability to find places for the students will end soon anyway, at the end of the Season, when I disgrace myself by leaving society. As for my letter writing, those missives go out under the aegis of the committee, not in our individual names. And since the group already includes a former courtesan and is run by friends who, I trust, would never abandon me, regardless of how scandalous society might consider me, that wouldn't be a problem.'

'Very well, if you could withstand the scandal, what of me? I grant you, I've earned my reputation as a rake, but even the highest stickler in society knows that my *amours* have always been knowledgeable and willing matrons. I've never taken advantage of an innocent. Were it to be known that I'd debauched you and failed to marry you, it wouldn't be just your good name that suffered. I might be somewhat careless of my reputation, but I am a gentleman. I value my honour.'

'I'm sure you'd manage to live down any scandal. Rich, well-born gentlemen always do. It might even enhance your appeal to the naughty matrons.'

After falling silent for a moment, he said quietly, 'What if your father threatened to denounce me to the *ton*? Accuse me of seducing you and refusing to marry you? He knows my father—who, you may remember, is already unhappy with me. I can guarantee you, for turning my back on honour and besmirching the family name, the Marquess would cut me off completely. I wouldn't be indigent—I have funds of my own, as you do. But he'd see me blackballed from my clubs, ostracised by society and prevented from seeing my mother, brother and sisters. Would you stand by and let him do that?'

Her dear Theo humiliated and shunned over something she had driven him to? She couldn't!

But…to marry him if they were discovered? As much as she could not now imagine her life without him playing a role in it, she'd never envisaged that role to be 'husband'. Lover for a time, and maybe, once the flame of passion had gone out, a dear friend.

What crushed her heart was the idea of marrying him, having that flame die and having to look the other way when his passion ignited for another.

The very thought made her feel sick.

Surely there must be some other way—something other than marriage, or parting.

Ignoring his question, she said, 'So…you propose that we end our liaison.'

'You think I *want* to give it up?' He shook his head. 'But when you weigh the very real risks… Who knows when some other of our acquaintance will take it into their heads to get a piano tuned, or turn out to have a solicitor who resides in this neighbourhood? Whereas if, pray God, our meeting today goes unremarked, you will be safe. How can you ask me not to protect you from the one thing you've always said you dreaded—being forced to marry?'

She had no right to complain. She *had* persuaded him to violate one of the core tenants of the *ton* gentleman's dubious moral code. Nor could she argue with his assessment of the result, should they be discovered. But beyond logic, the fierce desire to fulfil the promise of passion he'd given her made her think furiously of some other way out other than capitulation—and the loss of all she'd treasured and anticipated.

He came to stand beside her and tipped up her chin. 'Say *something*.'

Despite the scare today, she still felt confident that, with a few further precautions, they could continue their liaison and avoid detection. After all, it was most unusual for a gentleman to visit a piano tuner, rather than summon the man to his home. And though she knew several physicians and solicitors resided on the street, they kept offices elsewhere. No member of the *ton* would normally make a social call on a tradesman.

Not that she expected it would do her any good to argue that case with him now, she thought, glancing at the implacable look on Theo's face.

Feeling like the bones inside her chest were crumbling, she looked away. Until another idea occurred. A daring idea, an outrageous idea, an idea that most likely would ultimately prove ineffective.

But with only a few weeks of freedom left before the Season was over and her friends joined her, ending for good any chance for further intimacies with Theo, she would try one last ploy, dubious as it was.

'So that's it, then?' she said flatly. 'It's all over between us?'

Clenching and unclenching his fist, he shook

his head. 'Believe me, I don't find that idea any more palatable than you do. Let me think about it for a while. Maybe there could be some other way for us to be together. Perhaps after you're living on your own.'

'What, you'd have me come to *your* rooms? How long do you think *those* visits would remain secret? And would your reputation be spared then? Gossip would say my parents forced me to leave society, abandoning me because you'd ruined me—so you could have me without having to marry me.'

Flummoxed, Theo blew out a breath and walked back to the hearth. He didn't even try to argue, for he knew only too well that was exactly what the gossips would think.

While he stood there, gazing sightlessly into the hearth, she laid her final card on the table.

'If you're not prepared to risk continuing our affair, then I suppose I shall just have to find someone else.'

Theo whipped around to face her. 'Find someone else? What do you mean?'

'Surely you see how unfair this is. You've led me into intimacy and I have loved every step of the way. But you promised me the full banquet and I don't intend to be denied it now. Of course, I'd prefer to share the ultimate act of possession with you. But I have only a few short weeks before the Season ends. If you will not permit that, I would rather find another who will initiate me than never experience passion at all.'

He stared at her, as if trying to gauge whether or not she was serious. She met his searching look with an implacable look of her own.

'Find another?' he said at last. 'Another, who?'

'There's Lord Chapuys,' she said, naming one of the most dissolute young men in London. 'He seems not to find me…totally unappealing, and goodness knows, he hasn't any scruples to overcome.'

'Exactly!' Theo said furiously. 'No scruples at all—either against trysting with you, or bragging of it all over town.'

'Well, Mr Charles Anderson, then. He's equally without scruples, but perhaps a tad more discreet.'

'Anderson! Chapuys! You've just named two of the most unprincipled rakes in the *ton*!'

'Which would make them the most likely men to oblige me with an affair, without suffering attacks of conscience over my unmarried state.'

'And equally unlikely to refrain from boasting of it, though I grant you Anderson is a bit less of a braggart.'

'Perhaps. Perhaps not. They, too, believe themselves gentlemen and might not want to incur a black mark on their reputations by spreading news about that sort of indiscretion. That "gentleman's code", you know.'

'You would really give yourself to man you couldn't respect or care about?'

Emma nailed him with a look. 'Men care about and respect every female with whom they tryst? Oh, yes, I know, it must be different with a female. Only *men* are allowed to experience passion freely, with no strings attached.'

His expression aghast, he kept staring at her. 'You're truly serious about this, aren't you?'

'I am seldom less than serious about something that affects my life and future so profoundly.'

Which set him off on another round of pacing the room. Finally he halted before her, anguish— and a trace of anger—on his face.

Would he fall for her bluff?

Another look at his expression told her he wouldn't—at least, not here and now. 'You're not going to agree, are you?'

'You know I want to. But, Emma—what you want could end up ruining your life. How could I live with myself if I did that to you?'

'Very well, finish your wine. I shall not tease you again.'

'Promise me you won't go forward with this with someone else.'

Giving him a look of sadness and longing, she declined to answer.

With a muttered oath, Theo stalked over, seized the wine glass and downed the contents in one swallow.

'What I ought to do is carry you up and lock you in one of the bedchambers until you put that nonsensical idea out of your head.'

She took the wine glass from his hand and set it back on the table. 'It appears that your friend's carriage has departed. It should be safe for you to leave now. Dear Theo,' she said softly, touching his hand. 'Thank you for what you've given me and good luck with your lessons.'

With that, she stood and walked him back to the door.

'Please, don't do this, Emma.'

She gave him a cryptic half-smile. 'Goodbye, Lord Theo.'

She walked away and mounted the stairs up to her library, leaving him in the hallway, staring after her.

By that evening, Theo's mind had been going round and round in such agitation for so many hours, he had a pounding headache. He'd intended to forgo society entertainments again and work on his painting, but he found himself continually distracted by thinking about what Emma Henley might be up to.

Surely she'd just mentioned Anderson and

Chapuys to try to persuade him to grant her what she wanted. Surely she wouldn't actually offer herself to men like that.

Though they both did have a reputation, among the scandalous matron set, of being excellent lovers.

Was that why she'd chosen them?

Surely she *hadn't* chosen them!

Theo jumped up and paced the room, his mind racing. On the one hand, the risk of discovery, brought home so vividly when he almost walked down her front steps straight into the carriage from which his friend had just exited, was real, despite the fact that Judd Street was in a middle-class neighbourhood where neither had expected to encounter any members of the *ton*. But if Kensworth had shown up there, someone else might as well.

If they were discovered the furore, the gossip, the outcry would be just as deafening as he'd warned her.

Everyone, from Emma's outraged parents to society matrons indignant that a gentleman had broken the sacred rule not to trifle with innocents, to his clubs where a level of honourable behaviour was expected from its members, would be clamouring for a wedding.

He'd endured his father's verbal abuse over Lady Belinda, but he didn't even want to imagine what the Marquess would say to him under those circumstances.

Sighing, he crossed back to the easel and picked his brush back up.

Granting her wish was impossible…and yet the idea of letting her go, never tasting her, never sweetly, gently initiating her into the rapture of that most intimate embrace, was like a sharp knife to the gut.

The idea of letting the smarmy Anderson or the oily Chapuys perform that act for her made him want to take that knife to their guts instead.

Theo had tried to lose himself in his work, but after putting far too many brushstrokes awry and having to redo them, he gave up in disgust. Grabbing the rag and linseed oil, he quickly cleaned his brushes, his hands, and had his valet bring him hot water and his evening gear.

He took a hackney to the first entertainment, tapping his hands on his thighs in impatience during the transit. Should he just give in and agree to her request?

Surely she didn't want to experience pleasure at the hands of a womaniser like Anderson or a casual fornicator like Chapuys.

Would she go that far, to gain the knowledge she craved?

Were she a normal female, he'd know without question that she wouldn't.

But this was Emma Henley and he truly wasn't sure to what lengths she was prepared to go to get what she desired.

I'd prefer to experience it with you.

He uttered a sigh that was more like a groan. If she couldn't be dissuaded, maybe it would be the act of a gentleman to accept her bargain and, by doing so, protect her from men like Anderson and Chapuys. They would neither appreciate the gift she gave nor be at all concerned about guarding her reputation.

If he did agree, that wouldn't eliminate the risk of her being compelled to marry him if they were discovered.

She might try to withstand the pressure Lord Henley would bring against her, claiming it was only her reputation destroyed. But the Baron would be sure to impress upon how her being ruined in such a manner would disgrace the entire family—to say nothing about what it would do to Theo's own reputation.

Given those harsh truths, she might well relent.

If forced to marry, he couldn't imagine anyone who would make a more interesting and entertaining—to say nothing of passionate—partner than Emma Henley. Though he would hate to marry her knowing she was unwilling. Knowing, in his heart, he couldn't give her what she'd told him she needed in exchange for giving her hand and giving up her freedom. *A man who truly loved her—and would not tolerate casual infidelity.*

He wasn't so sure he *couldn't* love her, given how much she already fascinated him. But when, in his entire life, had he ever remained faithful to any woman?

And if he pledged that to Emma and couldn't make good on that vow...

The risk of her affair being discovered was just as great if Anderson or Chapuys accepted her offer—probably greater. Could he really stand by and see her forced to marry one of them?

To keep her from the likes of Anderson and Chapuys and give her the experience of passion they both wanted, maybe he would *have* to accept her request.

Because if Emma Henley were forced to marry anyone, it had better be him.

That solution didn't completely soothe the acidic mix of anxiety, anger and frustrated passion churning in his stomach. But his intention to go forward settled in with such finality, he knew it was the only answer he could live with.

Now that he had come to the decision, Theo burned with impatience to find Emma and set up a meeting—safely riding in the park—to discuss it. Immediately, before she had a chance to talk with Anderson or Chapuys. But, to his annoyance, she was not present at the Wendover ball.

Curse the alarming events of this afternoon! After that shock of their near-discovery, enquiring about such mundane matters as which *ton* entertainment Lady Henley planned to attend this evening had gone right out of his head.

His irritation and anger building, he was forced to drop by two more parties before he finally ran her to ground at the Throckmortons' *soirée dansante*.

Where, to his utter fury, he discovered her waltzing—with Lord Chapuys.

The Earl's son held her far too close, looking down at her with a leering expression that immediately made Theo want to punch it off his face.

Wending his way across the dance floor, narrowly avoiding collision with several dancers, Theo reached Chapuys and grabbed his elbow, arresting the couple's motion in mid-turn. 'I'm sorry, the lady promised this dance to me.'

Pushing the man back, he seized Emma's arm. Practically dragging her three steps away, he placed her hand on his shoulder, put his arm at her waist and swung her back into the rhythm of the dance, leaving Chapuys staring after them in disbelief.

'Good Heavens, Lord Theo, you could have just asked!' she protested, her tone half-annoyed, half-amused. 'There was no need to sweep me away like a post rider intent on delivering an urgent message.'

'You are the most aggravating, unreasonable, impossible woman in the universe!'

'Now, now. If you don't want me yourself, it's not fair to scare other contenders away.'

'Have you asked him yet?'

Her face colouring, she said nothing for a moment. Just as he was about to demand an answer, she said, 'No. Although I don't see why it is any business of yours. You had your opportunity and you refused.'

'What if I've...reconsidered?'

She raised startled eyes to his face. 'You mean—you will agree?'

'I mean I would like to...reopen the discussion. But not here, in a crowded ballroom, where anyone might overhear. Will you ride in the park tomorrow morning?'

'I could.'

'Good. I'll see you early. And bring your deafest groom.'

Restless, impatient and too distracted to work on anything, Theo rode into Hyde Park early the next morning through the usual swirling mist. His agitation wasn't calmed by the fact that he'd barely been able to sleep, or by the headache induced by the quantity of brandy he'd imbibed trying to capture that elusive state.

On the one hand, his randy body was in alt, making it hard for him to stop thinking of anything but the many delightful ways he would pleasure Emma, from more kissing and touching all the way up to ultimate possession.

On the other hand, his brain kept warning him in no uncertain terms that giving in to her—and his own, he admitted—desires should be grounds for getting him clapped up in Bedlam with the other lunatics.

His only reply to that withering truth was, better Bedlam than letting an innocent like Emma proceed into dangers she couldn't possibly image with the likes of Anderson or Chapuys.

Enough agonising, he told himself, clenching his jaw against the pounding in his head. He'd decided to do this and he would. He'd take as many precautions as he could to avoid disaster, which was all he could do.

As long as he could keep Emma safe with her reputation reasonably intact, the risks would be worth it.

A few minutes later, he heard the sound of a rider approaching out of the mist. When the form revealed itself to be Emma Henley, Theo spurred his mount forward to meet her.

'Lord Theo,' she said coolly, nodding as if

this were just an ordinary encounter in the Park. 'Good morning to you.'

'And to you, Miss Henley. Ride with me, won't you?'

Having identified the rider addressing his lady as the gentleman she'd frequently met at the park, the groom dropped back to let them proceed side by side, ahead of him.

If only he knew the dangerous nature of the plans about to be made, he'd grab his mistress's reins and lead her back home, Theo thought.

'So, you've reconsidered, as you told me last night?' Emma asked as soon as they'd drawn far enough ahead to be out of earshot.

'I still think it's madness. Are you sure you can't be dissuaded?'

She frowned. 'If all you meant by asking me to meet you was to try one last time to talk me out of this, there's no point in conversing. Good day, Lord Theo.'

'Wait, Emma,' he called with an urgent undertone. 'If you insist on going forward then, yes, I've reconsidered.'

Her face brightened. 'You will truly do this?'

'I suppose it's safer than risking a charge of murder. If you were to promise yourself to either Anderson or Chapuys, their dead bodies would later be found floating in the Serpentine. I'm not completely sure, but I think I'd be less likely to hang if I were only accused of being a vile seducer.'

'You mean it, then?'

'I mean it.'

'Quite honestly, I didn't really believe you would agree.' Her face transformed by a joyous smile, she said, 'Thank you, Theo!'

When she looked at him like that, as though he'd just granted the dearest desire of her heart, something warm and aching squeezed in his chest. How he wanted to give her everything she desired! He couldn't help feeling as humbled as he was eager.

'I just don't want to do anything that would bring you harm.'

'You won't! Moving forward, we'll be even more cautious. Perhaps have you arrive and depart via the mews, after a careful scrutiny of both the alley and the street outside. After all, I may be careless about my own reputation, but I'm no more anxious than you to create a scandal that would see us both excoriated in the full glare of society, to the humiliation of my family and the destruction of *your* reputation. But instead of focusing on the risks, won't you think about the delights that still await us?'

'I might still be able to come up with a way to meet later, when you're on your own. Not at my rooms, of course, and not anywhere your friends would discover us.'

If, by the end of the Season, she still wanted him to continue tutoring her. Quickly, he shook out of his head the unpalatable idea that by then she'd be ready to dismiss him. He knew instinctively it would take far longer than a few halcyon weeks for him to tire of her.

'And where might that be?' she said sceptically. 'No, all I can be assured of is that we will have Judd Street to ourselves for four more meetings. If you could figure out some way for us to continue our liaison later, that would be wonderful. But I don't intend to give up this time...and risk never experiencing it at all.'

'Very well. I shall see you at Judd Street next Wednesday?'

That glorious smile lit her face again. 'I shall count the days. Won't I see you somewhere in the interim?'

'I didn't know whether you'd noticed my absence from social events at the end of last week.'

'I did.'

'It wasn't from a desire to avoid pleasant company.'

'You were not off...pursuing naughty matrons?' she asked, not meeting his eye.

'No!' he exclaimed, surprised she would ask, after he'd already confessed that activity had lost its appeal. 'I do *hope* to attend a few this week—unless I'm forced to flee to the Continent.'

'Flee? What do you mean?'

'Late last week, my aunt, Lady Howard, gave her annual ball. Though I've been spending most of the last several evenings painting, I knew she'd be offended if I failed to drop by. A large number of the *ton* were present, including Miss Fothergill.'

'Did she scold you for neglecting her?'

He laughed. 'Oh, the self-centred arrogance of a beauty! No, she didn't scold. In fact, she accorded me the first waltz. I could almost feel a blade pressing against the back of my neck when I turned away from her entourage to lead her on to the floor! While dancing, she *encouraged* me, telling I must not give up just because I didn't possess a title or as much wealth as her other suitors. She told me that despite my lack of attributes, she found me "very handsome and charming"—so much so, that she might be prepared to overlook the fact that I could never make her a titled lady.'

'Good heavens!' Emma exclaimed. 'Was she making a declaration to *you*?'

'Not quite! She begged me to call on her—I presume so I could go down on bended knee in a setting more fitting than my aunt's ballroom.'

Looking as entertained as he'd hoped, she said, 'And what did you reply?'

'I told her that I was unworthy of such an honour. That being the pinnacle of grace and beauty that she was, the universe itself would cry out unless she bestowed her hand on a man of the greatest wealth and highest degree, just as her mama had always told her she must and as all society expected. That she couldn't allow a *tendre* for an unworthy supplicant to keep her from her destiny. Then, after getting her to agree that one must make sacrifices to fulfil one's destiny, I handed her off to a duke's son and exited the ballroom with all speed!'

She laughed and he revelled once again in the banter they shared. 'So, I may not see you at social events?'

He grinned at her. 'Possibly not, until I hear the announcement of Miss Fothergill's engagement to some other unlucky fellow.'

'It would probably be safer to concentrate on your painting.'

'I think so. And I'll give you a full report on what Mr Inverson has to say about it—and about Arabella's work.'

'I shall be waiting anxiously to hear about both.'

'Until Wednesday, then?'

'Until Wednesday,' she confirmed. 'That is, after we've had our customary gallop.'

'You think to beat me twice in a row?' he scoffed, delighted to have not just their camaraderie restored, but also the promise of making love to her. Damn the risks! He would squeeze every drop of joy from every moment—for them both. 'You may dream of it.'

Chuckling, she put spurs to her gelding, calling out, 'I'd rather just let you eat my dust.'

And she was off, Theo spurring his own mount in pursuit.

Chapter Eighteen

The next Wednesday afternoon, Emma unlocked the door at Judd Street in a fever of anticipation. Closing it behind her, she walked over to run her fingers over the balustrade of the stairs leading to the first floor and inspected with approval the hall table and carpet she'd had delivered the day before.

Ah, how she loved this house, this place that was hers alone, where the only rules and expectations were those she set herself!

A self that was showing itself to be wilder and more uncontrolled than she'd ever suspected. Even now, she sometimes had trouble believing that she, plain Miss Emma Henley, had mustered the audacity to proposition Lord Theo, one of the handsomest, most sought-after gentlemen of the *ton*. She had gathered the courage to actually go through with fulfilling the outrageous desire to experience passion outside of wedlock, a freedom normally exercised only by men.

Then, when he'd been assailed by quite reasonable doubts, she'd virtually blackmailed him into continuing their arrangement, obviously against his better judgement. She could still hardly believe that her gamble had worked, that the possibility of her turning to men he couldn't help but disdain had forced him into reconsidering.

Not that she would ever admit it to him, but though she'd been prepared to flirt outrageously with Anderson and Chapuys, she would never have given herself to either of them. She found it both thrilling and endearing that Theo had been so uncertain whether or not she would act on her threat that he'd felt compelled to protect her.

Nor would she ever have predicted, propelled by the urgency of desire, how bold she could be in asking for what she wanted.

Today would be even better, she thought, a thrill running through her to tingle in that hot, needy place deep within her. That place where pressure seemed to build and build when he touched and kissed her, until she felt she was trembling on the verge of some dramatic culmination.

Maybe it would happen today, when he'd agreed to satisfy her desire for him to touch her bare skin—everywhere. Though he'd not yet given his consent, today she intended to strip him of his garments as well, so she might caress and explore his body as thoroughly as he had caressed hers.

Would that touching be followed, finally, by the full possession she yearned for? How ravenous she was to consume that final, most delicious dish on the table of delights!

She took the basket of provisions up to the bedchamber, checked linens and pillows, the bowl of water on the washstand, to make sure all was in readiness—including inspecting the supply of French letters that she'd had Theo procure for them and secreted in the drawer of the bedside table.

The eddies of desire intensified as she took one from the drawer, smoothed her fingers down the thin sheath. Perhaps today, he would show her how to use one. How to mould it around his rigid member, before lying down to receive him...

The sound of a light rapping on the side entry door made her pulse leap.

Soon...she might have all she desired.

Knowing it wasn't wise to have him lingering on the doorstep, even in the relatively deserted mews, Emma ran quickly down the stairs and opened the door to admit him. Once it safely closed behind him, she threw herself into his arms and raised her head for his kiss. Which was long, deep and passionate.

'Ah, I've missed you!' he exclaimed. 'I'm also thirsty. Shall we have some wine? I'm very fond of the way you prefer to drink it.'

'Of course. Follow me.'

As she headed towards the stairs, he hesitated. Looking back over her shoulder, she said, 'I've put our provisions upstairs this week.'

'In the bedchamber?'

'Yes. Isn't that the best place to disrobe? It might not be prudent in the still curtainless front parlour.'

Still he paused, looking so uncertain Emma had the sudden fear that he was going to refuse. Had he tired of her already?

Despite the dismay that thought produced, she made herself say calmly, 'If you've come only to tell me you've changed your mind and wish to discontinue meeting me after all, please do so quickly.'

'Discontinue meeting you?' His eyes widened in a surprise that looked genuine. 'Whatever made you think that?'

'You seem…reluctant to proceed. I thought perhaps your concern about all you risk coming here outweighed your desire after all. Or perhaps… I've been too bold in my requests.'

'I've hardly had time to grow tired of you and

I love your boldness! I just don't want to…take advantage of you by going too fast.'

Giddy with relief, she retorted, 'You cannot go too fast for me. If that is all that troubles you, let's go have some wine.'

He followed her up the stairs and into the bedchamber she'd chosen as hers. 'Charming,' he pronounced, his gaze moving from the small table and grouping of chairs near the hearth where she'd set out bread, cheese and wine, to the wide windows admitting a warm glow of afternoon sunshine, to the tall bed with its crisp linen coverings. 'Perhaps you'd better also show me the wardrobe I'll hide in if the footman returns early.'

'No footman today. This time I had him escort me to Ellie's school, where I dismissed him, telling him Ellie would have Jenson take me back when I was ready. So there will be no time limit, no one coming to interrupt. For once, we can have all the time we wish.'

His eyes darkening as the implications sank in, he said, 'That will be…wonderful. But how will you get home? I don't want you walking alone.'

'As you know, there's a hackney stand not far away. I'll let you leave first, then follow you. Even if we linger as long as we like, I expect it will still be daylight when I depart. As you remember, we chose this neighbourhood because it is safe. I can walk a few streets down to the hackney stand without coming to any harm.'

He grimaced. 'I don't like it, but I suppose a hackney will serve.'

'I shall be fine. And now, my lord, can I pour you some wine?'

'Only if you will share it with me.'

'As my lord commands.'

Luxuriating in having all the time she wanted, Emma was content to linger over the wine kisses, to delight in feeding Theo, who drew her fingers into his mouth and sucked all the bits of bread and cheese from them. When at length the food had been consumed, she came and stood before him. 'Now, I may ask for what I want?'

The smouldering heat in his dark eyes said he knew exactly what was to come. 'You may ask.'

'Then, my lady's maid, please remove my bodice.'

She turned to give him access to the laces at the back of the garment. Nuzzling her neck, he slowly loosened them, until he could pull them free.

'Now the skirt,' she instructed.

He skimmed his hands down her stays to her waist, rubbing and caressing as he went. Unhooking that garment, he held her shoulder to steady her as she stepped out of it.

And so she proceeded, having him remove

each layer in turn. She'd thought he might start kissing her as flesh was revealed—her wrists, her elbows—but he did not, only watching her until she stood before him clad only in her chemise and stockings. His breathing a little uneven, he helped her to pull the chemise over her head and peel down the stockings so she was fully displayed to him, the afternoon sun through the bedchamber window playing over her naked skin.

Slowly, he inspected her from toes to hairline, his gaze coming back to rest on her breasts. She felt her nipples pucker.

'How beautiful and fearless you are,' he murmured. 'On to the bed with you.'

He helped her up, guided her so she was lying propped up by the pillows and sat beside her. Only then did he lean over and kiss her.

As he took her mouth gently, only gradually increasing the pressure, his fingers explored her body—the neck and shoulders he had caressed before, then the curve of her belly before he moved back up to touch her tight, sensitised nipples. As she gasped into his kiss, he grasped them between thumb and finger, gently pulling and squeezing.

The sensations he aroused seemed connected directly to the aching place between her thighs, for something seemed to spark within her each time he rubbed his thumb across the top of her nipple. That curious, spiralling pressure began to build, winding her breathing tighter and tighter, making her feel once more like she was approaching a precipice.

Then he moved one hand down to let his fingers play at the top of her calves, rubbing above and under her leg, as he had before. This time, though, as one hand caressed her nipple, he moved the other to the silky inside of her thigh and slowly up. Urging her legs apart to expose the aching centre, he touched her there, right at the apex of her desires.

That small, acutely sensitive ridge of flesh was already moist with her need for him. Murmuring approval, he rubbed his thumb over it as he inserted a finger into her passage—that needy place where, later, she wanted that filled sheath to go.

As his fingers stroked in and out, he broke the kiss and brought his lips to her breast. 'I just have to taste you,' he murmured and took the nipple in his mouth.

If the sensations created by his thumb had been exquisite, the hot, wet suckling of his mouth was almost unbearably intense, coiling the tension within her so tightly she could barely breathe. And then, as his mouth suckled and his fingers stroked, that tension released in a shocking pulse of erotic energy that vibrated to every corner of her body.

For long, exquisite minutes, waves of pleasure washed over her, before at last dissipating.

She wasn't sure how long she lay there, limp and boneless. When at last her jaw worked well enough to produce speech, she murmured, 'That was wonderful. Almost as wonderful as I'd dreamed it would be.'

'Almost?' he repeated with a frown.

'But there is more, isn't there? And, yes, I know, that must be saved for another day. But I'm feeling very selfish, that after giving me such pleasure, you are still…unsatisfied.'

'Giving you pleasure is satisfaction enough.'

'Could I not touch and kiss you to the same level of pleasure? Or do you require—another day's lesson—to reach your peak?'

'Are you not satisfied enough with today's lesson?' he asked, an odd note of desperation in his voice.

Why should she be, when he was obviously still in need, but with infinite patience and tenderness had denied himself to give everything to her? Such unselfishness shouldn't go unrewarded—even if she had to trick him a little to give him the prize.

'You said I can ask for what I want, didn't you?'

Looking both dazed and wary, he nodded.

'Then I want to look at and touch your unclothed body—just as you have looked at and touched mine.'

She thought for a moment he was going to re-fuse, but at length he said, 'Just look…and touch. Yes, I suppose you may do that.'

'Then stand before me, so I may play valet as you played lady's maid.'

As he had for her, she methodically removed each garment—although she did *not* refrain from sliding her hands over bare skin as it was re-vealed, his eyes riveted on her face as she did so.

When he stepped out of his breeches, reveal-ing the hard shaft of his erection, she sucked in a breath.

Mistaking that for alarm, he said hastily, 'Don't worry! I won't hurt you, I promise.'

She shook her head. 'I'm not afraid. Only thinking how beautiful and fearless you are. Now, you must get on to the bed. Just recline against the pillows and relax.'

His laugh sounded disjointed. 'Relax?'

'Well, the relaxation will come later,' she said with a chuckle. 'First, there will be pleasure.'

Shaking his head, muttering something about Bedlam, he subsided against the pillows.

A rush of excitement filling her, she began at his forehead. With a sigh of delight, she ran her fingers through the lock of hair that always tumbled down there. 'If you only knew how long I've dreamed of doing that.'

'Combing my hair?'

'Yes. Just like this. It's wonderfully soft and sensuous, just as I thought. Like braided silk.'

'Silk,' he echoed, his eyes falling shut as she combed her fingers through the hair on his forehead and brow. Then used both hands to run her fingertips over his face, as he had done to her. Licked her fingertip and traced it across his lips, then inserted in his mouth, where, groaning, he suckled it, spiking a jolt of sensation in that place between her thighs that had so recently quivered with pleasure.

Perched on the edge of the bed, she bent over and kissed him, moving lips and tongue slowly, leisurely over his, outside and within, nibbling and suckling while she smoothed her hands over his shoulders, arms, wrists, fingers, the hard plane of his abdomen, the furred surface of his chest. He groaned again when her fingers played with the flat, hard disks of his nipples.

And then she abandoned his mouth and slid to the foot of the bed. Stroking first his toes, his ankles, the upward arch of calf and round of knee, she followed with her lips the explorations of her fingers.

She tasted salt now on his slick, heated skin as she moved upwards, her hands finding the sharp angle of hipbone while her tongue traced the top of his thigh. He was murmuring now, his hands clutched on the bedclothes, his neck arched, his shoulders moving restlessly against the pillow.

And then…the ultimate goal. His whole body jerked when her fingers clasped the shaft of his erection. Satin over iron, she marvelled, devoured with impatience to know the feel of it within her. But first, she would taste—

Before she could, with a garbled sound, Theo elbowed himself off the pillows, seized her and laid her down on the bed under him. Crouching over her, he kissed her with feverish urgency, as if he could not get enough of her mouth and tongue.

That imperative was building within her again and now she knew its ultimate, glorious destination. Sliding her feet on either side of Theo's, she wrapped her legs around his, trying to pull him ever closer—and felt his erection prodding at her belly.

She needed only to shift upwards a fraction to direct his shaft lower, into the wet cleft where she most wanted him. Driven by an urgency that drowned out every other thought, she thrust her hips upwards and felt the stretch and smooth glide of him as his member penetrated her.

He felt it, too, and broke off the kiss. As he lifted his torso on his arms, obviously intending to pull away, she wrapped her arms around his shoulders, desperate to hold him close.

'No, Theo, don't stop. Please, please don't stop now,' she cried, underlining her plea by arching her hips upwards again, taking him deeper.

For a moment, he hovered over her, the locked arms supporting his torso vibrating with tension. Then, with an anguished cry, he pressed his chest against hers and slid his shaft deeper.

As if that motion had freed him of all restraint, he kissed her with unbridled passion as he moved his member in a steady rhythm in and out, gradually delving still deeper. She gasped at a momentary pain, but wrapped her legs to keep him from withdrawing, wild to keep him moving within her.

For a few moments he stilled, his kisses gentling. Teasing and nibbling at her mouth, he waited until her body relaxed enough to permit him easy movement. He then resumed the rhythm of advance and withdrawal, each time penetrating a little deeper, until he'd sheathed himself completely.

By now she'd learned the rhythm and matched her hips to it as the indescribable bliss of heat and friction quickly rebuilt the pressure within her. Until, once again, she crested the precipice and the world came apart in starbursts of pleasure.

Vaguely she felt him tense, heard him cry out

and knew that he had found release as well. Replete with joy and rapture, she hugged him tighter.

She must have drifted to sleep, for her next sensation was the prickle of his stubbled jaw against the softness of her cheek. She opened her eyes to find herself cradled against his shoulder, his gaze watching her.

With a smile of utter contentment, she reached up to touch his lips. 'How can I ever thank you?'

Chapter Nineteen

He ought to thank *her*, Theo thought, kissing her fingertip. What a marvel she was indeed! Love-making always relaxed and satisfied, but never before had he experienced such an expansive feeling of well-being. Of *joy*.

Lying in his arms was not just a lovely woman or a skilful seductress. It was *Emma*—blunt and opinionated, passionate and generous, pushing him beyond the limits he'd imposed on their intimacy and carrying him to a level of bliss he'd never before experienced. Pushing him beyond the boundaries he'd long ago set for his life, too—and encouraging the man who'd begun to emerge.

The one woman he'd ever met that he might actually be able to love.

He was about to open his lips and tell her so

when the voice of caution suddenly emerged from his cloud of contentment.

Tell her he loved her? Whatever was he thinking?

He dared not confess what she'd made him feel. Even if, in fact, it was 'love', although how would he know, since he'd never come close to such an emotion before? True, the feeling was purer and more intense than anything he'd ever experienced.

But the thrill of *everything* he'd ever experienced had dimmed, sooner or later. Emma had made it very clear that she wanted love to be for ever. With his history, he was the last man in London who could promise that.

So, stuffing back inside the admission he'd been about to make, he said, 'I should beat you, though, wench. You skipped a few dishes and grabbed the most exotic with both hands.'

'I was a bit worried you would keep me nibbling hors d'oeuvres for ever.'

With a sigh, he replied, 'I should have kept you nibbling.'

The smile on her face faded. 'It wasn't…as good as you had hoped?' she asked in a small voice.

Emotion wanted to claw its way free and shout out how much he cared for her. With some difficulty, he reined it in, hugging her close instead.

'Never think that, Emma! You were marvellous! Everything I've dreamed of and more! So much more that I was unable to hang on to my resolve and, despite my intentions to initiate you gently, was as greedy as you in wanting to gobble that final dish.'

Another factor that had made their union so unique suddenly struck him—with a chill much colder than his confusion over his feelings for her. 'So much so, that, as neither of us noticed at the time, we neglected one important step.'

Her eyes widened. 'The French letters.'

'Sitting uselessly in the drawer,' he said drily. 'I'm so sorry. I can't imagine what came over me—well, you did, I suppose, wretch. I have never before neglected to take the proper precautions.'

'Oh, dear.' She frowned as the implications of that neglect registered. 'Well, too late to worry about that now. We'll take proper precautions in future. Conception can't happen *every* time, or every married female in England—and many of the unmarried ones—would be *enceinte* constantly. Besides, I refuse to let such a marvellous experience be tainted by worry or regret. You did…truly think it was marvellous?'

Though he was less successful than Emma in pushing aside his worries, he had no trouble avowing that. 'Wondrously marvellous. So wondrously marvellous that, were it not so late, my fondest wish would be to begin all over again.'

She glanced up at the mantel clock and sighed. 'I suppose you will have to leave. But perhaps my wanting to consume the whole banquet today was a good thing. For our last three meetings, there need be no restraint at all.'

He touched the tip of her nose tenderly. 'No restraint, but more precautions.'

'Definitely precautions. Besides, I've heard that having the lady fit her lover into a French letter can be made quite arousing. I shall have to consider all the possibilities.'

Feeling himself hardening at the very thought, he groaned. 'Don't you dare speak of it, or I shall not be able to leave until you give it a try. And Emma, bewitching Emma, you know I must leave. It's already late afternoon and I must take a very circuitous route to avoid any streets with shops some errant friend might turn up at.'

She gave a frustrated huff. 'I know, I know. I suppose we must tidy up and help each other dress. Though, fortunately, I am not accompanying Mama out tonight, I mustn't return so late that she—or Marie—questions me too closely.'

'One more thing. If, despite your optimistic assessment, there should be…consequences from our lack of caution, please say you'll consider marrying me. I'm not such a bad fellow after all, am I?'

For a moment, he saw in her eyes something that looked almost like...pain. Whatever the expression signified, it passed too quickly for him to positively identify it.

'Well, I suppose marrying you might be *somewhat* preferable to wedding Mr Null. None the less, I shall pray there are no such consequences.'

'Wretch!' he said drily. 'I'm ecstatic to know I still rank ahead of Mr Null. Now, milady, your maid is ready to serve you.'

Still unsettled by the unexpected strength of his emotions—and the need to contain them—Theo tried to laugh and smile while they helped each other wash and dress, Emma taking advantage of every opportunity to touch and caress him as she helped him back into his garments.

But with the ever-perceptive intuition she seemed to possess, once they were ready to head downstairs, she stopped him with a touch to his shoulder.

'Is something wrong?'

He hoped the dismay he felt that she'd somehow noticed the subtle change in him didn't show on his face. 'No, there's nothing wrong,' he replied, making himself smile at her. 'What makes you ask?'

'Just that you seem to have somehow...withdrawn, now that our time is almost over. Are you…regretting that I pushed you beyond the boundaries you'd set?'

It was a perfect opening to confess what was troubling him…but he knew his tangle of emotions, all the conflicting desires and vague intentions, were something he needed to get straight in his own mind before he could discuss them with her. 'How could I regret that, when you brought me such bliss?'

She smiled at that, though she didn't look completely reassured. Thankfully, she dropped the subject, asking instead if he wished to finish the wine before he left.

And then, far too soon, she was walking him down the stairs to the side door leading to the mews.

'Shall I see you any time before next week, or will you be occupied again with your painting?'

'That depends on whether or not Miss Fothergill's engagement is announced, I suppose,' he teased, delighted to bring another smile to her face, which was already looking as forlorn at the thought of their imminent parting as he felt. 'Will you be at the Longchamps' soirée on Friday, or the Everson ball Saturday?'

When she nodded, he said, 'I'll try to see you there. And perhaps I'll meet you out riding. But now…'

'Now you must go,' she agreed, nodding.

Before he could turn the latch, she pulled him back and gave him a deep, soul-touching, body-arousing kiss, so rich with the remembered feel of possession that he almost changed his mind about the need to leave.

She broke the kiss and gave him a little push. 'Goodbye, my marvellous Theo.'

'Keep yourself safe, my incomparable Emma. I'll be missing you.'

'And I, you,' she said.

Then he walked out the door and closed it behind him.

Too filled with the euphoria of their meeting to want to venture into society, where he would have to resume the role of slightly bored *ton* gentleman, Theo decided to remain at home that evening. Besides, since Emma had told him she wasn't going out, there wouldn't be a chance of encountering her and escaping the façade for a few minutes of delicious repartee.

He needed to watch himself even more carefully now when they did meet in public, he told himself as he set out his canvases, pulled out his brushes and arranged the array of candles that would allow him to continue working after the daylight faded. He remembered all too vividly how quickly gossip had developed about his previous *amours*. Not that he'd been particularly concerned, beyond displaying the expected level of discretion, whether or not those affairs became public knowledge. But once a man and a woman became lovers, the intimate rapport they felt for each other became increasingly difficult to conceal.

And despite her wry confession of how devious passion had made her, he didn't expect Emma, always honest Emma, would be particularly skilled at concealing it. Especially not since they'd become lovers in truth.

And what a wonderful lover she was! Everything he'd suspected, and more, he thought, awe, delight and an expansive sense of well-being warming him.

Perching in front of his easel, for a few moments he allowed himself to revel in memories of seduction and possession—though, he thought wryly, given how completely he'd lost his grip on control, at the end it had been more Emma seducing him than he leading the inexperienced lady.

However, he couldn't enjoy the sensual memories without also recalling the unprecedented upswelling of emotion, so unexpected and so unexpectedly intense, that had overcome him after their lovemaking.

A truth that had the smile fading to a frown.

He'd managed to keep from giving it voice this afternoon—but if it recurred? Grew stronger?

Perhaps that intensity was only the product of the bliss of first possession. But somehow, he suspected that he would be just as overwhelmed, sated and disarmed each time she pleasured him. Could he continue to hold his tongue and refrain from expressing feelings that might lead her to expect a devotion and constancy he was not at all sure he could offer her?

Much as he would like to push away those troubling thoughts and simply anticipate the pleasure to come at their next two meetings, the uneasy conviction began to settle over him that he was going to have to force himself to figure out what was happening, before he said or did something that would end up hurting Emma.

He might not understand what bewitchment had come over him, but he knew he would do almost anything to keep from wounding her.

He absolutely would not, at this point, consider the possibility that if their relationship grew ever more intense, the kindest thing to do might be to end it before she grew too enamoured of him. For she would want for ever and he wasn't sure he could give her that.

But he certainly could give her *right now*. Turning his mind from the painful prospect of their eventual parting, he refocused on the fact that they had only three more rendezvous at Judd Street.

He already knew that he would not be ready to end their affair *that* soon and was pretty sure she felt the same.

What were they to do, then, once the Season ended and her friends joined her?

Another burning question to which he must soon find an answer, he thought, still frowning as he began mixing paint on his palette.

As it turned out, Theo was not required to carefully watch his behaviour when he met Emma at the Longchamps' soirée on Friday. Thursday morning, he had received an invitation from the Marquess requesting his presence that night at dinner.

An invitation which was, of course, really a summons. As he only dined with his father occasionally, his first reaction was a deep dread that somehow the Marquess had discovered his liaison with Emma—though their new precautions included him taking such a circuitous route to and from Judd Street, he couldn't imagine how that could have happened.

He soothed himself with the thought that perhaps the Marquess had merely discovered he'd resumed his interest in art. Despite Theo's scepticism, maybe his father had actually noticed that he'd borrowed the Cotman landscape. If so, he might be in for a jobation, but since he had also acquiesced to his father's demand to attend *ton* events and pay court to a marriageable beauty, he didn't think his father should rake him over the coals for too long.

None the less, he dressed with particular care and presented himself at the family manse at precisely the hour his father stipulated. Somewhat to his surprise, the invitation appeared to be for a family dinner, for his mother and both his married sisters and their husbands were also in attendance.

He was able to relax and simply enjoy teasing the girls, hearing about the latest exploits of their children and listening to his brothers-in-law exchange news with the Marquess about the progress of spring planting at their various estates and the problems being experienced by their tenants.

Not until the ladies left them to their brandy and cigars did his father turn to Theo.

'I hear you've been courting the Fothergill chit. With her excellent dowry and good looks, a fine prospect, but not a trout you're likely to land, given that men of equal wealth and higher status are also casting for her. Still, I'm pleased that you took my advice to heart.'

'Given Theo's famous address, he may win out in the end anyway,' Compton, his elder sister's husband, said.

'Perhaps,' his father allowed. 'In any event, I don't expect the girl—or her family—will make a choice before the end of the Season. Why should she? Might as well enjoy her moment in the sun as the most sought-after unmarried female in London. Which means, my son,' his father said, turning to Theo, 'you'll have plenty of time to complete the little project I have for you and still get back to London to put in your bid with Miss Fothergill.'

'Project, Papa? What project?' Theo asked, biting his tongue on the immediate protest he wanted to utter. With the time he had left for meeting Emma so short, the last thing he wanted was to be sent out of town.

'I've been keeping tabs on the results of the spring meeting at Newmarket. There are several prime horses I'm quite interested in acquiring. Now that the meets are over for the year, they are being stabled and trained in the area. Only one of the three that interest me most will be brought to Tattersall's. The other two will not go on the market at all.'

The Marquess smiled. 'Not only do I trust your expertise when it comes to evaluating horseflesh, you are, as Compton just mentioned, possessed of a good deal of address. I want you to go to Newmarket tomorrow and look over my three top choices. If they are as fine as I've been led to believe, buy the one before it's brought to London, and persuade the owners of the other two to sell them to me.'

Damn and blast, Theo thought, having a hard time maintaining a pleasant expression. He had no excuse for turning down his father's request that he dared express—not that the imperious Marquess would accept a refusal, no matter how valid a protest he could muster.

All he could hope to do was race up to Newmarket, check out the horses, sweet-talk the owners and get back to London as quickly as he could. With any luck, within a week or ten days.

So, burying deep the smouldering but useless anger at having a precious week of his already limited time with Emma stolen from him, Theo nodded and replied, as expected, 'I'll leave first thing in the morning.'

He tried to ease his disgruntlement by observing that it might actually be a good thing to leave London for a time. Being away from Emma's distracting and beguiling presence—the anticipation that, on any particular day, he might encounter her riding in the park or at some evening entertainment—ought to allow him the distance and perspective to figure out exactly how he felt about her—and determine out what he envisaged for their future.

* * *

Not until he made his way back to his lodgings after the few hands of cards his father had proposed to the company after dinner did he realise that, not only must he leave London, he'd have to leave without seeing Emma again.

It was much too late to call at Henley House, and if he really wanted to get to Newmarket and back again as quickly as possible, he needed to leave London tomorrow at first light. Well before the earliest hour he could reasonably call on her.

He damped down another flash of useless irritation at his father.

Once back in his rooms, he penned her a quick note explaining his unexpected departure from town—and a euphemistically expressed hope that he would return in time to enjoy their next rendezvous at Judd Street.

Hopefully, by the time he did return, he would have worked out a perfect plan for their future.

Chapter Twenty

Emma drifted awake out of a soft cloud of dream where she lay entwined with Theo in her bedchamber at Judd Street. Aglow with the memories, she wrapped her arms around herself, wishing that she were back in that sunlit room, awakening in his arms after more wondrous lovemaking.

What was she to do with herself before she saw him again at the Everson ball tonight? She found it increasingly difficult to concentrate on formulating her list of potential employers to call on. And yesterday, during the letter-writing session for the Ladies' Committee, she'd twice drifted off, becoming so absorbed in her daydream that she'd made a blotch of ink on the paper and had to start over again.

She was becoming just as much a silly idiot as those marriage-obsessed girls back at Mrs Axminster's, she scolded herself with a smile. But perhaps she had some excuse, since the subject distracting her was not speculation about some potential future mate, but the irresistible allure of the incomparable Lord Theo.

She was enjoying her morning chocolate when Marie knocked and walked in. 'A note came for you, miss,' she said, offering the letter on a silver tray.

A note in a decidedly masculine scrawl. Hope and curiosity, mixed with a niggle of dread, went through Emma as she picked the missive off the tray. 'Thank you, Marie. I'll be ready for you to help me dress in half an hour.'

She waited until the curious maid had left the room before unsealing the note and quickly scanning it.

As she'd suspected, it was from Theo. And to her great disappointment, he informed her that his father was sending him out of London to discharge an errand he couldn't refuse to perform. He apologised for not informing her of this in person and expressed his regret for having to miss meeting her 'at the various upcoming social events to which we were both looking forward.'

Various upcoming social events to which they were looking forward, she thought, trying to accurately interpret the phrase he deliberately left innocuous enough not to raise eyebrows, no matter who might chance to read it.

Did he mean just the Everson ball? Or would he not return in time to meet her at Judd Street next Wednesday?

An automatic protest lanced through her. She was having a hard enough time waiting until tonight! How was she to be patient through what sounded like days and days? And she absolutely couldn't face the prospect of losing one of the few precious meetings they had left.

Take yourself in hand, Emma Henley, she scolded sternly. *You are more than a silly chit hopelessly beguiled by the most fascinating man in London. You have matrons to visit, friends to consult with and a school full of girls who would love to have you read to them.*

Yes, she'd stop by the school today. Perhaps Arabella would have some drawing to show to her. Visiting with the girl about her lessons would make her feel closer to Theo, who took her lessons at the same master's studio.

And what a poor honey she sounded, to be grasping at such flimsy straws to feel near to him!

Emma managed to keep herself reasonably busy for the first week of Theo's absence. But when one week stretched into two, the vague disquiet she'd felt upon noticing his change of demeanour during their last time together at Judd Street began to haunt her.

Despite his quick denial, something *had* changed in him after they'd become lovers. She'd felt as if he'd…withdrawn from her, once the euphoria of satisfaction faded.

Had he really left town at his father's behest, or had something happened to make him decide he didn't wish to see her any more?

Surely, if that were the case, he would have had the courtesy to tell her face-to-face, rather than dispatch an impersonal note. Surely they were better friends than for him to end their liaison in such a cold fashion.

But then, what did she know about ending a love affair?

Or the conduct of it, for that matter. He'd fully possessed her. Perhaps he didn't find the prospect of repeating that experience very exciting and was already keen to move on.

With a sinking feeling in the pit of her stomach, she remembered their banter over his decision to break with Lady Belinda. The baubles he'd bought, which he'd delivered—with a note.

Though she told herself she was foolishly overreacting, his absence and her worry over it brought her face-to-face with a dilemma she'd very carefully avoided thinking about.

What was she going to do when Theo *did* end their affair—whether he'd already done so, or would some time in the future?

He'd only ever promised they would be lovers…
for a time. And after that, if she were lucky, they
might remain good friends.

Would that be enough?

She was very much afraid it would not.

It was ridiculous to feel so desolated. As if her
whole life were crumbling around her and her last
chance of happiness had evaporated into the mist.

It was quite possible that whatever errand had
taken him out of town had lasted longer than expected. He'd taken a chance sending one note.
She understood that it wouldn't be prudent for
him to send another.

But even if he had no intention of breaking
with her—yet—eventually having him walk away
when the affair was finally over was going to
make her feel just as awful as she did right now.

What was wrong with her? She'd known from
the beginning the liaison would only be tempo-
rary. She had her work with the Ladies Committee, students at Ellie's school to mentor and the
task of completing the furnishing, then moving
into, her house on Judd Street to occupy her.

But somehow, reminding herself of the activities she'd expected to keep her happy and pro-
ductive all her days was unable to stave off a
bleakness that made her want to curl up in a little
ball on her bed and howl with anguish.

Because, she realised in a blinding flash, she

had been utterly stupid, even more stupid that those silly girls at Mrs Axminster's Academy. More reckless than a clinging Lady Belinda. She'd camouflaged her fascination with Theo under the guise of the desire of a modern woman to have the freedom to taste passion.

While, in fact, she'd been falling in love with Lord Theo Collington.

She'd hoped that having him make love to her might cure her of her fascination. That after her needs were slaked, she'd be able to dismiss him and move on, return to her plans and her causes with her usual quiet, practical self-sufficiency. But that taste of passion had only made her want more.

She saw now that the insidious, seductive voice of desire had drowned out the whispers of prudence and common sense, masking the dangerous truth of how much she'd come to depend on having Lord Theo in her life. Lord Theo, who didn't dismiss the causes that meant so much to her, but urged her to support them. Who admired her for refusing to conform to a standard of behaviour she disdained. With whom she had been able to truly be herself—and be valued for who she was.

He'd even, foolishly, thought she was pretty.

Oh, how deep down the rabbit hole she'd fallen! Thinking herself reasonable and detached, when all the while she'd been blind to every sign of her increasing preoccupation. Ignoring all the warnings of danger as foolishly as a maid who believes a rake's promise of marriage before he seduces and abandons her.

When she should have listened to Ellie, who had tried to caution her. *'Intimacy can create a powerful emotional bond. One hard to endure, if it is not reciprocal. Hard to break, if it cannot be permanent.'*

She knew Theo cared about her. She wouldn't have been able to blackmail him into continuing their liaison if he hadn't.

But caring for her, and *loving* her, were two very different things. Now that the shock of intimacy had pulled the veil from her eyes about the true nature of her own emotions, she knew how much more powerful her feelings were than a tepid 'liking'.

She couldn't take Theo as a lover again and then watch him walk away. Could she be around him now, as a friend?

Chatting with him during an occasional ride in the park. Seeing him in town, at the theatre or the opera, exchanging a few light words while his latest paramour hung on his arm, bored and impatient that he was taking time to speak with a dowdy spinster.

After possessing him, being possessed by him,

the idea of having him move on to love others jabbed at her gut with an intolerable pain.

She didn't think she could tolerate it. For if she'd recently discovered previously uncharted depths of passion and boldness, she also realised her emotions ran equally deep. She would have it all—passion, friendship, camaraderie, devotion—or nothing.

She simply couldn't be Lord Theo's casual friend.

What if he returned in a day or so, ready to resume their affair? Would she have the strength to refuse him?

An equally awful thought occurred. How was she to walk into the Judd Street house, the house she loved and had been so impatient to live in, when the very air would remind her of his presence? How could she sleep in that bedchamber, where the softness of the mattress pressing against her back, the faint lavender scent of the sheets, would recall his making love to her?

Jumping out of bed, she paced her chamber, her mind working furiously.

If she couldn't trust herself to avoid the temptation to renew an affair that would only mean heartache…if she couldn't bring herself to complete a task she'd bedevilled her mother for months to allow her to begin…if she couldn't be sure, once he broke with her, that she wouldn't trail after him with the humiliating tenacity of Lady Belinda accosting him at the opera…then the best thing was to be elsewhere.

She would leave London—and go to Aunt Emma in the Lake District.

Mama might object, but she'd tell her she needed to consult with her aunt over the monetary details of her gift so she could continue completing the furnishing and removal to her new house. Papa, if he noticed her absence at all, wouldn't care. To Olivia and Sara she would offer a version of the same story she told her mother. Anxious as they were to join her and claim their own independence at Season's end, they would speed her on her way.

No reason to mention to Mama that she had no idea when she would return. Being in London meant the near certainty of encountering Theo and, right now, she didn't know how she could bear it.

As for telling Theo… Better that the break, already so painful, be clean. To Theo, she would say nothing at all.

Besides, she thought, smiling wistfully, with her out of London, he'd soon forget all about her. And there'd soon be a new bevy of pretty ladies clustered around him, making sure he didn't remember.

* * *

Ten days later, exhausted and anxious to see Emma again, Theo rode back into London. After meeting with his father to report the ultimately successful completion of his task—trying not to clench his jaw in irritation at an errand that had run into delays at every turn—he pressed on to his rooms, intent on bathing, changing and going at once to visit her.

He'd initially welcomed some time apart in order to figure out exactly what he meant to do about their liaison. Ponder over whether the exceptionally deep feeling he'd developed for her was real and whether it was possible it might endure.

He'd quickly come to realise how much she had become interwoven into the fabric of his life, how much he enjoyed and looked forward to their almost daily interaction. In the three weeks they'd been apart, his life seemed…flatter, less satisfying, the only conversation available to him the usual trivialities uttered over dinner by the gentlemen he'd been charming into selling their horses to his father. He'd missed Emma's intelligent commentary, her tart observations about society's silly rules and foibles, the way her whole body became energised when she spoke about political reform or finding places for 'Ellie's girls'.

How he loved to watch her eyes widen and passion animate her face, transforming it from plain to compelling! It was like magic anew each time he saw it. And it gave him great satisfaction when some comment of his made the magic happen.

Although he hadn't troubled to bring paint and canvases with him, he had taken his charcoals and a new sketchbook—which was now almost full. Recalling the assemblage of drawings, he wondered what Emma's reaction to them might be—and had to smile. Whatever she thought, she would give him her honest opinion, no matter how much it might sting.

Soon, now, he would have to acquaint his father with the fact that he had begun lessons and intended to take up painting again.

The Marquess was certain to disapprove, perhaps harangue him as he had years ago, trying to shame him into once more giving up his 'unmanly pursuit'. However, he now found the prospect of his father's—or society's—disapproval no longer bothered him.

Emma approved and she was right. When one felt a calling, one needed to recognise it and treasure the gift—not hide from it in a haze of alcohol and frenetic, empty activity.

We must all find our own path.

He had her to thank for prompting him to rediscover his. For the joy with which he looked forward to exploring his talent and utilising it to the fullest.

How could he not love a woman who had led him back to finding his own soul?

An even more blinding realisation had followed hard on that fact. True, he had for so many years played the role of careless rogue that it had become second nature. The women with whom he had casual affairs had wanted only the handsome lover, the amusing companion, the wastrel who drifted along the frivolous current of *ton* life.

Why should he have felt any inclination to become attached to any of those women, who prized only the shallow façade? Who would have found his passion to paint as incomprehensible as his father did, who would have been as appalled as the Marquess at the idea of a gentleman pursuing a vulgar tradesman's calling?

Whereas Emma knew the whole man—both the amusing companion who enjoyed a battle of wits and the iconoclast artist whose soul burned to create. And she admired them both.

How could he not be faithful to a fascinating woman who valued him for who he truly was?

In fact, he'd decided that he wanted no more of secret trysting at Judd Street. He intended to court Emma with serious intent and, if he could, persuade her to marry him.

Arousal rippled through him at the very idea

of being able to make love to her openly, without subterfuge or caution. Their three, time-constricted sessions had been far too short to even begin to tap the enormous reserve of passion he felt for her.

What would it be like to awake with her beside him and make love to her as daybreak lightened the sky? Discuss art and politics over the breakfast table before she went off to her Ladies' Committee and he resumed his painting. Meet in the afternoon for tea and kisses, attend dinners with her political friends where matters of importance were discussed. Return to end the day as it began, with her in his arms.

How eager he was to see her! He wondered what progress she'd made in furnishing her house, how her campaign of finding positions for Ellie's girls was going, and which Parliamentary bill the Ladies' Committee was currently writing letters to promote.

After taking so much care with his appearance that his valet had the impertinence to observe he must be setting out to seduce some new lady, Theo tooled his phaeton to Henley House and bounded up the entry steps, filled with excitement at knowing that, in a very few minutes, he would finally see her again.

Unfortunately, the door was answered by

Haines, whose icy demeanour upon recognising him told him the butler had not forgiven him for encouraging his mistress to leave her family home for Judd Street. Rather than usher him inside, the butler stood blocking the doorway.

Theo gave the man his most charming smile, followed by asking whether Miss Henley was at home and accepting calls.

'No, my lord, she is not.'

'Is she not at home, or just not accepting callers?'

After a pause, Haines said, 'She is not at home, my lord.'

'Do you know when she will return?'

'I'm sorry, my lord, I am not a party to that information.'

Theo clenched his jaw, recognising now the price he was going to pay for having antagonised the butler. In full protective mode, Haines would probably make him drag out every last bit of information.

Unfortunately, his first reaction—putting his hands around the man's neck and trying to choke him—probably wouldn't make the butler any more forthcoming.

Unable to summon a smile quite as pleasant as the first, Theo persisted, 'Do you expect her back this afternoon?'

'I really couldn't say, my lord.'

'Tonight?'

'I don't think so.'

Maybe, in the course of furnishing the house, she'd decided to spend the night at Judd Street. Holding on to his patience with an effort, Theo said, 'Then when do you expect her? Tomorrow morning?'

'I really cannot say when Miss Henley will return to Charles Street.'

Frowning, Theo tried to make sense of that titbit. Piecing it all together and coming up with a rather unbelievable conclusion, he said, 'Has Miss Henley…left London?'

Again, that infinitesimal pause, after which Haines said, 'Miss Henley's friends and family are cognizant of her whereabouts.' Then, giving him the briefest of bows, the butler shut the door in his face.

Furious, Theo stalked back to his phaeton and flung himself up. Frustrated as he was, he'd eked out at least one pertinent bit of information. Though he could not imagine why, it appeared that Emma was not presently in London.

For a time, he drove around aimlessly, the irritation of coping with the heavy afternoon traffic preferable to proceeding to the park, now that it was the height of the promenade hour. He knew he would have no patience for answering the interested enquiries about where he'd been and what he'd been doing for the last three weeks.

Why had Emma left London? Even more important—why had she left without even sending him a note explaining the reason and giving him her whereabouts?

He thought he'd left her as eager to see him again as he was to see her. Had he misjudged her interest in their relationship that badly? And if not, what could he have possibly done to so offend her, that she'd left him without a word?

He could return to Henley House and try to pry some information out of Lady Henley—though given the butler's animosity, if there were any way for the man to prevent him from seeing Emma's mother, he would surely do so.

While he stood impatiently as the tiger stood at his team's head while the road was cleared of a collision between a heavily loaded brewery wagon and a farmer's cart, he suddenly thought of another avenue to explore.

He didn't think Emma would leave London without letting her two best friends know of her whereabouts. One in particular, the acerbic Miss Overton, had impressed him as being just as honest and plain-spoken as Emma.

Theo wasn't acquainted with the Overton family—but the porter at his club was a fount of information about every aristocratic member of the *ton.* As soon as the blockage cleared, he turned the phaeton around and headed for St James's Street.

After a short stop at the club, where the porter proved as helpful as he'd hoped, Theo returned once more to the phaeton and headed for Hanover Square.

Halting before the handsome brick town house, Theo handed his team over to the tiger, telling the lad he would take a hackney home, and trotted up the stairs. After the frustrations of the day, he sincerely hoped his luck would be in at last and Miss Overton would be home and willing to receive him.

He was conducted to a pleasant salon done up in gilt and cream. To his infinite relief, a short time later, Miss Overton entered the room, curtsying to his bow.

'Should you like some refreshment before I enquire to what I owe the honour of this visit?' Miss Overton said, an edge of irony in her tone.

'No need for refreshments. I merely wish to ascertain where Miss Henley has gone.'

Miss Overton stared at him for a long moment. 'She did not send you a note informing you.' A statement, not a question.

'Obviously not,' he replied, resisting the urge

to shake her, too. 'But I imagine she would not have left London without telling you.'

Miss Overton sighed. 'I don't wish to be unkind, Lord Theo, but I can't help thinking that if Emma wanted you to know where she is, she would have informed you herself.'

'That may be true, Miss Overton. Although I thought we had parted on good terms—indeed, as good friends—the fact that she did leave London without informing me forces me to believe that I must have in some way offended her. Which would never have been my intention. I value Em—Miss Henley's friendship greatly and am anxious to make amends for whatever wrong I have committed.'

Once again, Miss Overton studied him. Theo had the sense that he was being evaluated, her response to be based on the outcome of that assessment.

Finally, with a sigh, she said, 'Perhaps you'd better have a seat.'

After they'd both taken a chair, she continued, 'As I'm sure you are aware, I know Emma rather well. And knowing her well, I could not help but observe that her behaviour…altered when she was around you. Despite her protests to the contrary, I did not believe she was indifferent to you.'

'I believe she came to value me, as I came to value her,' he answered carefully.

'That may be so. But in the last month before she left London, I noticed a marked change in her. There was an…urgency I had never seen before. She also became somewhat…evasive about her movements. After initially being so enthusiastic about her house in Judd Street, she discouraged Sara and I from coming to visit, claiming she didn't wish to show it until she'd cleaned and furnished it. Was she…meeting you there?'

He hoped his surprise didn't show in his expression. But as he hesitated, unsure what to admit, Miss Overton said, 'Come now, Lord Theo! Emma is my dearest friend. I would never say or do anything that would cause her harm. Perhaps she was meeting you, perhaps not. But when I got her note, I suspected something about her leaving so suddenly involved her feelings for you. The fact that you've sought me out, concerned about that very thing, confirms that impression.'

'When did she leave?'

'Eight days ago.'

'And where has she gone?'

Miss Overton remained silent, as if gathering her words. 'Would you like my opinion, Lord Theo?'

'Give it if you must. But I'm more interested in learning Miss Henley's whereabouts.'

'I believe she left London because for her,

your *friendship* had become something else. Something that threatened her resolve to remain independent and never subject herself to the humiliation of becoming a neglected wife. Although, forgive me for being so blunt, I doubt there was ever any chance that you'd consider making her your wife. In that case, haven't you caused her enough distress? If you do consider yourself her *friend*, leave her alone.'

'Thank you for your opinion,' Theo said, not sure whether he was more alarmed by having the girl confirm his suspicion that Emma was upset or incensed by her obvious disdain.

The rewards of having created such a persuasive image being no more than a rakish society wastrel.

Rising, he said, 'You clearly don't consider me worthy to be a friend to Miss Henley. You may also choose not to reveal her location. But rest assured, one way or another, I intend to discover it and go to her.'

'You are that determined?'

'I am.'

With a sigh, she said, 'If you insist on intruding yourself upon Emma despite what I've said, I may as well give you her location. She's gone to visit her Aunt Emma—Lady Emma Baines-Thornton—at Thornton Place, a manor near Bowness-on-Windermere in the Lake District.'

'Thank you, Miss Overton. I shall trouble you no longer.'

'As long as you don't trouble *her*. I'm an excellent shot, you know.'

Despite his anxiety, that brought a glimmer of a smile. Miss Overton was a worthy friend to Emma. 'I'll keep that in mind. And earnestly hope you will have no need for that pistol.'

Chapter Twenty-One

In the morning eight days later, Emma set out from her aunt's rambling manor on her daily walk, climbing the path that led to the crest of the hillside overlooking the long stretch of water, sparkling in the distance. Early summer had arrived in full force to the Lake District, leaving the windswept hillside verdant with new grass and sprinkled with wild flowers.

Her nearly three weeks' absence from London had not diminished her longing for Theo, nor had she yet come to a decision about when to return and how she would deal with him when she did.

Though she'd lately begun to fear there would be a different and much more serious complication than mere heartache.

Her courses, normally clockwork-regular, should have begun two weeks after their intimate rendezvous at Judd Street. Now, almost five weeks later, she'd begun to feel a strange heaviness and sensitivity in her breasts. She'd awakened the last two mornings to become immediately sick and, even later in the day, certain smells, like fish or woodsmoke, could bring on a return of the nausea.

She remembered the summer she'd spent with her elder sister, when Cecilia had first suspected she was increasing. She'd complained of the same tenderness in her breasts and hadn't been able to make it to breakfast without first being ill.

She had only lain with Theo once—so single-mindedly intent on experiencing the full range of passion, she'd swept him beyond control—and both of them beyond thought of taking precautions. And now, she very much feared she was with child.

Stupid enough to have fallen in love with him—but now she might be compromising the future of an innocent babe. As furious with herself as she was heartbroken, she put her hands on the slight curve of her belly.

Was she sheltering new life there, a precious melding of herself and the man she loved?

Was there any way she could keep such a child?

How could she keep it and subject a child she loved to the disadvantages of being born a bastard? Though she didn't care if she were infamous, she had no right to consign an innocent babe to that fate.

Would having their child at her side, and having Theo for a time, be enough to make up for not having him for ever? Was it fair for her to decide such a life would be unendurable, when having the child born in the sanctity of marriage was so important to its future?

How long ago and far away it seemed that she'd thought herself an independent woman with the power to choose her own destiny. Facing the dilemma that had cursed womankind from time immemorial when passion was indulged outside wedlock, she no longer felt so powerful and her destiny might well soon be taken out of her hands.

Though when she'd broken down and confessed her fear to her aunt, that lady had suggested there might be another way to protect the child and avoid a marriage to man she loved who could never love or be faithful to her.

A marriage that would be a recipe for lifelong misery.

Despite the mildness of the breeze and the beauty of the landscape spread before her, Emma felt tears wetting her cheek. Just wonderful, she thought, swiping them away angrily. Not only was she stupid and reckless, now she was turning into a watering pot.

Normally she walked until she reached a rock near the crest, where she could sit and drink in the serene beauty of the landscape all around her.

Now, angry with herself and feeling a wave of weariness overtaking her, Emma turned around before reaching the crest and headed back to Thornton Place.

Tired and dispirited, Emma entered her aunt's house, intending to take the stairs to her chamber and rest as soon as she handed her pelisse and bonnet over to the elderly butler. To her surprise, though, as he accepted those garments, Lawson told her that her aunt had requested that Emma join her in the back parlour as soon as she returned.

It appeared her nap would have to wait. Wondering why her aunt would need her with such urgency, Emma walked down the hallway and entered the parlour. Where, as she stood on the threshold, the question she'd been about to ask withered on her lips.

Seated in the wing chair by the fire, sipping tea, was Lord Theo.

Her heart leapt and all she wanted was to run over and throw herself into his arms. Until she remembered the many good reasons why she didn't dare display her true feelings to him—or give him any hint of her true condition.

'Ah, here she is now,' Aunt Emma was saying. 'I've just been getting acquainted with your London friend, Emma.'

Surely Aunt Emma hadn't told him anything! To the panicked look she fixed on her, that lady returned a tiny, negative shake of her head.

Reassured, Emma told herself to stop acting like a ninny and recapture her normal calm, composed demeanour—no matter how agitated her nerves or how much her stomach roiled, threatening to embarrass her by having her cast up her accounts in front of him.

Taking a slow, deep breath to calm the queasiness, she said, 'Lord Theo, what a surprise to see you here.'

'I found I had unfinished business in the area.'

'He told me he intended to do some shooting,' Aunt Emma said drily. 'Though I do hope you'll take care, Lord Theo—since to my knowledge, the season here is not yet open for game. And you'll stay for dinner, of course. My cook puts together a much finer roast than you could hope for down at the Shepherd's Crook.'

'I'd be delighted.'

'Emma, I know you've just returned from a walk, but why don't you show Lord Theo the view from Thornton's Crest? Unless you are too weary?'

Torn between wanting to spend time with him and needing to end the interview as quickly as possible, before he suspected anything, Emma felt the distractions afforded by the landscape and the view were worth the fatigue of the climb.

Anything was better than being closeted in this small room with him. 'No, I am fine. And the vista is magnificent, Lord Theo.'

'Excellent! I'll expect you back in, say, half an hour, Lord Theo?'

'Of course, ma'am,' Theo said. 'And thank you again for your hospitality.'

As they headed up the trail, determined to keep the conversation light and prevent it from veering into anything personal, Emma said, 'I trust that the errand which took you from London prospered?'

He laughed shortly. 'Lay that unexpected absence at the door of my "manly achievements". One of the few things about me that my father values is my knowledge of horseflesh. He took it into his head to buy some racehorses that had done well at the spring Newmarket races. So of course, I must be dispatched at once to evaluate them and negotiate their sale. And, yes, after having to run halfway around England to track down one of the owners, I was finally able to secure all the horses my father desired. But why—?'

'Were you able to do any painting while you were away?'

'No, but I did take along a sketchbook. I did a

number of charcoal sketches of landscapes and some portraits of the working people I observed on the journey. I'm eager for you to see them, but first, I must ask why—'

'I'm sure the sketches are admirable. Do you intend to turn them into oils?'

Before he could respond, they reached a turning in the pathway, from which one could see the summit. Pointing up to a large, flat outcropping of stone, she said, 'That's the Crest. The stone makes a fine seat and the view is incomparable.'

The slope was steeper now and, continuing to walk as she gestured, her uphill foot landed on a loose collection of pebbles just as she transferred all her weight to it. The foot slid and she lost her balance, falling heavily, her side striking a rock that protruded on to the trail.

Theo scrambled up to kneel beside her and offer a hand. 'Are you all right?' he cried anxiously. 'You haven't injured yourself, have you?'

'No, I'm fine,' she assured him. But she couldn't help grimacing as he assisted her to her feet—and putting a hand to her belly, not realising what she'd done until she saw his eyes follow her actions.

Tightening his grip on her arm when she would have pulled away, he said, 'Emma, are you carrying my child?'

Her obvious surprise and the soft gasp that

escaped before she could stop it most certainly confirmed his suspicion, so there was probably no point trying to deny it. But not ready to confess it outright, she said instead, 'Is that why you wanted to see me? And how did you find me? I can't believe Haines would have given you any information.'

'No, he still hasn't forgiven me for Judd Street. I convinced Miss Overton to tell me where you'd gone.'

Conversation halted for a moment as they both watched their footing on the last steep bit of the trail approaching the Crest. Once he'd helped her take a seat on the rock, she said, 'What difference does it make if I am? You don't wish to marry and neither do I.'

'You're wrong. I do want to marry you, Emma. Very much.'

Of course he did. Hadn't he already made her a qualified proposal, that wonderful, infamous day she'd given him her maidenhead, pledging to marry her if there were 'consequences'?

'There really is no need.'

'But there is! Not just because of the child. But because I've come to realise that I love you—truly, deeply. I've missed you so much, these five weeks we've been apart. Missed asking your opinions and receiving your insights. Missed hearing about your work with the Ladies' Committee and at the school. Missed laughing together and riding together. I even missed you abusing me. And especially, I missed this.'

Leaning over her, he cupped her face in his hands and kissed her. At first she drew back, but, unable to help responding to his magical, beloved touch—especially when this might be the very last time she ever experienced it—she gave in to irresistible desire.

They were both trembling when he finally broke the kiss. 'Ah, how I have missed that!'

Just because he still desired her now didn't mean the eventual death of his passion would be any less agonising. Better, as she'd told herself before leaving London, to suffer the agony immediately and try to move on, rather than live with the inevitability of heartache hanging over her head.

So she replied, as coolly as she was able, 'Indeed. Once initiated into passion, it is very hard to give up.'

'It's my passion for *you*, Emma, that I find hard to live without.'

She gave him an expression of polite disbelief. 'There's no need to make me pretty speeches, Lord Theo. If you are concerned about the future of…of the child, you needn't be. My aunt is acquainted with a squire in a neighbouring county. He and his wife have lost two babies and she cannot have another. Although Aunt Emma hasn't yet spoken to them, she believes that they would be thrilled to adopt the child and bring him up as their own. The squire owns a fine property that brings in a handsome income, so the child will lack for nothing. Given the circumstances, I think that would be the best solution for all concerned.'

'Best for all concerned?' he echoed. 'How can you say that? How can you cavalierly talk of giving away our child? Emma, I know you've always been leery of marriage. You want a life of freedom and purpose, but you must know by now that I would support you in that aim. I'll make sure that having a household and a baby doesn't prevent you from participating in the political work you love. And despite your brave talk of a woman's right to experience passion, I don't think you could have loved me so sweetly if you didn't truly care for me, at least a little. Won't you let us build on that?'

Lovely, beautiful lies, all designed to break her resistance—so he could 'do the right thing' and safeguard his gentleman's honour. She wasn't sure she could stand hearing many more of them without running down the hill, screaming.

Knowing she needed to end this before the tears welled up, she said, 'Please, Theo, I think you've said enough. Said what you needed to say, so you may leave, knowing you have fulfilled your duty.'

'I didn't come here to fulfil a duty,' he retorted, his tone exasperated. 'I came because I love you and I want you to be my wife!'

'Well, we don't always get what we want, do we?' she snapped, swiping the tears off her cheeks.

He stared at her for a moment. 'You don't believe me, do you?'

'Oh, stop, Theo! You know what *I* want in a marriage. Do you think I've forgotten what you told me—with passionate conviction hardly more than a few months ago—about *your* view of wedlock? That if you were ever forced to marry, you would be stifled by a woman who wished you to dance attendance on her? That you couldn't imagine being faithful to any woman?'

He exhaled a frustrated breath. 'Very well, so I told you that. But that was…before. Before we'd spent so much time together.'

'Before we'd conceived a child together.'

'That, too, but mostly because I love you. Don't you believe people can change and grow? Change their minds, find deeper truths?'

'It's possible. I just don't think it's likely in this instance.'

'So you'll refuse me without even giving me a chance to convince you? Condemn our child to being born a bastard because you doubt me?'

'He would be adopted into a good family. And

have the most important thing a child needs—two parents who love each other.'

'Adopted or not, he would still be born a bastard.' The exasperation in his tone turning to anger, he cried, 'Emma, you know I could never permit that to happen to a child of mine! I can't believe you would permit it for a child of yours. Dam—dash it, you must marry me!'

'And now you're turning dictatorial as well as insincere! I think you'd better leave before… before either of us gets any angrier and says something we might regret.'

Blowing out a frustrated breath, he fell silent. Looking away from him, out over the valley, she wasn't sure what hurt more—the idea of him leaving, or the sweet pain of having him woo her with sentiments she didn't dare believe.

'So there's nothing I can say to convince you my feelings are sincere?' he said at last, his voice calm and quiet once more.

'No.'

'Just one more thing. Do *you* love *me*? Tell me you don't care about me and I'll go, let you do what you think best for the child and not bother you again. Can you tell me that?'

She took a struggling breath and looked him in the eyes. 'I don't…' Her words trailed off and tears filled her eyes. Even to end this, she couldn't make herself utter such a lie. 'Please, Theo, don't make this any harder. Just go.'

Ever perceptive, he picked up immediately on her hesitation. 'So if you do feel something—'

'No, Theo, enough!' she interrupted. 'I can't bear any more.' Pointing down the pathway, she repeated, 'Go. Just go!'

She turned away again, willing him to leave… and in a small, aching part of her, wishing he would take her in his arms and kiss her just one more time.

Finally, with a muttered oath, he said, 'Very well. I don't want to distress you any further now and you're clearly beyond the reach of reason. So I'll do as you ask and leave. But don't think this is over.'

While she put all her remaining strength into holding herself rigid as she stared out towards the lake, tears blinding her to the cheerful diamond sparkle of its water, she heard him turn and carefully make his way back down the path.

Well, she supposed, after confirming his suspicions about a child, she couldn't have expected him to meekly give up after her first refusal. She need only persevere, until he realised a loving home for the child would be better than the sham of a marriage between them.

Putting her face in her hands, she gave in to the tears and wept.

Chapter Twenty-Two

Cursing the fall that had shocked him into speaking first about the child, instead of immediately declaring his love for Emma, as he'd planned, Theo picked his way back down the trail. With her insecurities about her desirability obviously in full play and her doubts—reinforced by his own unfortunate words—how could he convince her he wasn't just saying what he thought she wanted to hear so she would be coaxed into marriage, preventing his child from being born a bastard?

He hadn't thought it would be easy to persuade her, but neither had he expected so adamant a refusal.

Halfway down, he looked back up to see her still perched on the rock, her gaze on the sky. He wasn't certain, but he thought she was weeping.

One thought sustained his determination not to give in. Emma, ever honest Emma, had not been able to deny that she cared about him. If it had been the truth, she would have flatly denied loving him.

After stopping by Thornton Place to thank Lady Emma once again for her hospitality, but also to inform her he wouldn't stay to dinner, Theo descended the rest of the way to the small village of Bowness-on-Windermere, where he'd rented a room at the village inn. He stopped in the taproom long enough to request that ale, warm food and hot water be brought up, then walked up to his room to begin planning his strategy for wooing Emma Henley.

Knowing that she cared for him, he was almost certain he could convince her of his love and get her to agree to marry him. Eventually. But how to overcome her suspicions and insecurities in the shortest possible time?

He'd never thought much about children—but now he wondered what a child of Emma's might be like. Full of her energy, her tempestuous spirit, her drive to better the world? He smiled, just picturing it.

There was absolutely no way he would allow a child of their love to be given away to another couple, no matter how devoted and deserving.

So—how best to convince her?

He'd always liked Emma—she'd amused and intrigued him from the very beginning. Their far-too-short three trysts had proven the depth of his passion for her. Three weeks of missing her company had shown him how much he'd come to need her in his life. The vastly increased worry and concern he had felt when he returned to London and learned she'd left him without a word just reinforced how completely and passionately he'd grown to love her.

As he sat over dinner in his solitary room, Theo mulled over ways to woo his reluctant Emma. How best to use his famous charm to beguile her into loving him as much as he loved her?

Initially, he'd thought to remain at the inn, perhaps visiting daily to leave bouquets of wild flowers on her doorstep. But since she'd ordered him to leave her alone, considering how stubborn his wilful love could be, remaining nearby might just make her more resistant.

If he couldn't demonstrate love by his presence or convince her with the traditional lover's wooing words, how could he show her how deep and true and sincere his feelings were? Persuade her to give him a second chance and let him love her as she deserved to be loved?

Sighing, he sipped on his ale and pulled out the sketchbook he'd hoped to show Emma after he'd declared his love, gone down on bended knee to ask for her hand and received her joyful acceptance.

He grimaced, recalling just how awry *that* plan had gone.

But as he flipped through the sketchbook, another, better, idea occurred. He'd have to return to London to implement it, but he'd already concluded that remaining in Bowness would be counterproductive anyway.

He would send her letters—but not the usual sort of love letters, filled with affirmations of love and passion like those she'd already rejected. Meanwhile, he'd put all his love and devotion into something beyond words that would show her, with all the skill his artistic soul could muster, just how precious she was to him.

A week later, Emma sat in the pleasant afternoon sunlight of the back parlour at Thornton Place, listlessly trying to read the book her aunt had lent her, when a knock sounded at the door. Lawson entered with a silver tray. 'A letter for you, Miss Henley,' he said, extending the tray to her.

Emma picked up the letter—and caught her breath when she saw her name written on the outside in a bold masculine hand she now recognised.

She held it while Lawson bowed and exited, trying to decide what she would do. Read it—more sweet lying words of love, designed to weaken her resolve and coax her to marry him for the sake of their child. Or throw it into the fire?

In the end, unable to make herself destroy this connection with Theo, no matter how much torment it would mean, she broke the seal and unfolded it. Instead of the sonnet or the flowery expressions of love she'd expected, she read:

> *Dear Miss Henley,*
> *As you may know, a matter of the gravest import is being considered by the governing body of this land. To wit—whether the heart of a good and noble man, a man deserving of honest consideration, shall be rejected and trampled upon without the gentleman being given the benefit of a chance to prove his case to the lady in question.*
>
> *I ask you—is this fair? Is this just? Does this represent the care and concern for one of God's children which all who live in this great country should promote?*

Torn between laughter and tears, Emma read on, smiling at the missive which mimicked so neatly the style of exhortation she and the Ladies' Committee used in the letters they sent to influential men and politicians, hoping to persuade them to support the reform cause.

A clever approach, she had to admit.

Filled with a bittersweet ache, she took the letter to the hearth, intending to toss it in the fire—and found she couldn't. Perhaps she could allow herself to keep this one memento to her love and folly.

But, she was to discover, Theo wasn't content with a single assault. Almost every other day, she received another such missive, all written in the same style, all presenting different aspects of devotion that should convince any person of fairness and discernment that the sentiments expressed by the claimant were honest and true.

By the fourth or fifth letter, her certainty that Theo merely wanted to marry her for the sake of the child began to waver. Did she dare believe that the devotion he kept expressing might be real?

Three weeks after he'd left Thornton Place, the full summer sun lulling her, Emma descended from her walk to the Crescent. With her belly rounding and her breasts enlarging, she was certain now that she was carrying Theo's child. The joy of sheltering that new life within her was tempered by her uncertainty about the child's future.

Could she believe Theo's repeated vows of love?

But if he truly loved her, wouldn't he return to

press his suit in person—even though she'd sent him away and begged him not to return?

As she never answered his letters, it was more likely that eventually, he would give up and stop sending them. She would bear the child, do what was best for him and probably return to London to pick up the life she had once looked forward to with such enthusiasm. Resume her work with the Ladies' Committee and Ellie's school. And if—when—she encountered Lord Theo, she would smile and curtsy, and pretend that everything of life and joy wasn't dead within her.

Entering the hallway, she took off her muddy boots and slipped on the shoes her maid had ready. Handing the girl her pelisse and bonnet, she walked to the back parlour.

Where, to her shock, beside Aunt Emma on the sofa, sat Theo.

'You see,' Aunt Emma said. 'Your London visitor has returned.'

He rose as she entered, his gaze never leaving her face.

'You came back,' she whispered.

'I'll go check on the tea tray,' Aunt Emma said, smiling at Emma and giving Theo's arm a pat as she walked out.

Emma struggled to suppress the joy and wonder of seeing his beloved face again. She wanted so much to go to him, to tangle her fingers in that glossy dark hair and pull his head down for a kiss, no matter how much it was going to hurt when he left again later.

But, of course, she did none of that.

'Won't you sit and talk with me?' he asked, motioning her to the sofa.

'Although I thank you for the clever letters, I'll stay only if you agree not to speak of feelings or ask for my hand again.'

'May I tell you about my work, then?'

That should be safe enough and she did want to know how Arabella was progressing. 'Yes, you can tell me about that.'

And he did, describing the painting he was now doing and his latest project. 'I'm going to find new lodgings with more space, so I can open a studio of my own, where I can invite master painters and draughtsmen to give lessons to promising students like Arabella. I'm also going to establish a fund to support budding artists while they are learning their craft, until they can sell enough of their work to live on their own.'

'You will continue your own work, I hope.'

'Yes. It's too important to me—too central to who I am—to stop now. I won't produce works for sale, of course.'

'Of course not,' she said, smiling.

'But I do intend to do a number of portraits. I find them more compelling than landscapes.' He laughed. 'So all my friends and family had better beware. I did bring one piece with me for you to see. May I show it to you?'

'Of course.'

Theo walked to the corner of the parlour, where a wrapped painting leaned against the wall. Bringing it over, he set it on the sofa beside her.

As he pulled the cloth off the painting, Emma caught her breath. It was a portrait in oil—of her.

The artist had caught her gazing down at a document—closer inspection, she noted with a smile, showed it to be a letter to a Member of Parliament—just like the mock ones he'd written to her.

Every angle of the body, the tilt of the head, the square of the shoulders, vibrated with energy and determination. With one eyebrow quirked upwards, the sitter had focused all her concentration on that page.

And the face… Yes, it *was* her face, a long, pale oval. But if the attitude of the body was energetic, the face was even more so, radiating an intensity and passion that transformed the unremarkable nose and cheekbones.

And the eyes—they were nothing short of magnificent, just as he had once described them.

Large hazel orbs with glowing golden centres that announce this is a woman of courage and purpose, who neither tolerates fools nor allows society's artificial constraints to prevent her from doing the work in which she believes.

A firebrand.

It *was* Emma Henley—but an Emma who looked more passionate and compelling than any reflection she'd ever seen in her glass.

An image, moreover, in which the artist's love for the sitter was evident in every line and hue.

The sensual bow of the lips…the delicate pale cream of the skin…the curve of cheek drawn as if to fit in a lover's caressing hand…those eyes full of fire and purpose.

Overwhelmed, humbled, she sat speechless for some minutes while Theo stood in silence, patiently watching her.

'I'm… I'm not that pretty,' she said at last.

'You are to me. Didn't I tell you never to argue with an artist's eye?'

'It is a magnificent portrait.'

'It's the best work I've ever done. Because it captures the woman who inspired the best in me. Who had the intelligence to see the man who lurked beneath the camouflage of a society dandy and the courage to ignore conventional niceties and challenge him to emerge. A woman who changed me from a man who doubted he could ever be true to one woman, to a man who can't imagine loving anyone else. No one but the woman I love with all my heart, to whom I want to be faithful and devoted for the rest of my life.'

Dropping to one knee before her and taking her hand, he continued, 'Emma darling, if you prefer to live your life alone, devote yourself to the causes that drive you, alone, I will not harangue you further. And I will continue to paint, whether I have you by my side or not. But my life, and my work, would be so much richer, so much better, so much *more*, if you and our child would share it with me. Will you reconsider and agree to be my wife? Allow us to shelter the precious child we have made and pursue together our passion for our work—and for each other?'

Shaking her head in disbelief, she said softly, 'My heart has been yours from the beginning, my body yours for weeks. But today, you have claimed my soul. Yes, my dearest, I will marry you.'

Exhaling a long sigh, Theo bent down to rest his head on the soft swell of her belly. He kissed it and looked up at her, tears glistening in the corners of his eyes.

'Thank you both. I promise I will never let you regret it.'

'I should hope you will not!' she said tartly. 'As someone once told me, I'm a woman of fire and purpose, who does not tolerate fools!' Then, her expression softening, she said. 'A woman who recognises genius, devotion and a pure love when she sees it portrayed in a masterwork. Yes, I will give all of me to all of you, always.'

'Always and for ever, my darling,' he murmured and tipped her face down for his kiss.

Epilogue

Two weeks later, Emma stood impatiently in her London bedchamber while her maid finished pinning up the crown of braids. 'Can't you hurry, Marie? Everyone is downstairs waiting!'

'Everyone can wait for the bride,' Marie replied, still methodically pinning. 'Especially when she looks as pretty as you do!'

She did look as good as was possible for a tall, plain, brown-haired girl, Emma thought. Her gown, fashioned of a green fabric with a sheen of gold that Theo had selected—to match her amazing eyes, he said—truly was becoming.

About to embark on her life with Theo, their child and their work, how could she be less than radiant?

Excitement and nervousness swirling in her stomach, Emma walked down to the large front parlour, which, despite the intimate nature of the ceremony, was filled with friends and family.

Scanning the room, Emma noted her friends Temperance, Olivia and Sara chatting together, her father, her older sister and her husband grouped to their side—and Theo, standing by the hearth with the minister.

Fondly her eye traced him, from the unruly lock of dark hair brushing his forehead, over the handsome face with its noble nose and firm chin, down to the elegantly attired body that radiated masculine appeal. She felt a little thud in her chest, as if her heart itself had kicked up its heels in joy and awe that the Incomparable Lord Theo and the Homely Miss Henley had found each other—and, most improbably, fallen in love.

Theo looked up, saw her and smiled. The warmth and tenderness of his gaze sent a wave of pure love washing through her, filling her with such effervescent happiness she felt she might float to the ceiling rather than walk across the floor.

But walk she did, over to him, her father coming to stand by her side.

As the clergyman opened the prayer book, Theo leaned close to murmur, 'You look beautiful. And no arguing over my opinion.'

'Perhaps I'll let it go just this once. In honour of the occasion.'

Her father frowned at her, the minister cleared his throat—and the service began. Within a very few minutes, they pledged heart, hand, body and future together.

A devilish look on his face, Theo leaned over—and gave her a chaste kiss on the forehead.

'I hope you can do better than that tonight,' Emma muttered as he led her into the next room to sign the register.

'Patience, wench,' he murmured back. 'We have a long drive if we're to reach Dover by tonight. The way you've been feeling lately, you'll probably be too tired for anything but sleep.'

Emma caught herself before she cradled a hand against her belly. Her Aunt Emma knew their secret, but she hadn't confided in anyone else. Mama had been disappointed enough when they insisted on wedding by special licence, at home, rather than waiting for Lady Henley to plan the grand wedding she'd been scheming and hoping to give Emma these last five years.

'Knowing that I can love you openly, with no fear of consequences? I doubt I'll be that tired. Although now that we're married, our intimacy sanctioned by church and society, perhaps it won't have the…zest of our illicit meetings?'

Theo chuckled. 'There's plenty of zest left. I've hardly begun to show you all the ways.'

'Excellent. Perhaps I shall devote the long, dull carriage ride to Dover to thinking of ways to seduce my new husband.'

Theo raised an eyebrow. 'Actually, I already had some plans to enliven that long, dull carriage ride.'

The heat in his gaze made it quite clear what those plans would entail. Emma felt her cheeks warm, even as a spiralling urgency began to curl within.

'How soon can we leave?'

Theo laughed. 'Shouldn't we at least greet our well-wishers first?'

Emma gave a dramatic sigh. 'I suppose I can wait that long…but you must promise me a proper kiss, once we're in the carriage.'

His gaze locked on hers, Theo brushed his free arm against her side. Though to any onlookers, the gesture might have appeared accidental, the subtle caress of his fingers against her hip sent reverberations of delight through her. 'A proper kiss and more.'

The book signed, they rejoined the group, who flocked around to offer their congratulations— Theo's father, the forbidding Marquess, his mother, sister and her husband, Emma's family, Temperance and her Earl, Lady Maggie and Lyndlington, Ellie and her Christopher, and, finally, Olivia with her mother and Sara with her aunt.

While Theo's family claimed him, Emma drew her friends apart. 'Let's steal a few minutes to say a proper goodbye.'

'I can't believe you're leaving us for six months!' Sara said. 'We will miss you so much!'

'And I will miss you,' Emma said, tears coming to her eyes.

Olivia chuckled. 'With your handsome husband to occupy you and all the art treasures of Italy to explore? I rather doubt it!'

'Of course I will miss my dearest friends,' Emma retorted. 'And—I know it's not the way we envisaged ending up…but I hope you can be happy for me.'

'All we ever wanted for each other was to have lives of purpose and fulfilment,' Olivia said. 'Helping Lord Theo in his work—and returning to help us in ours—meets that aim. Where we all live isn't that important.'

'The two of you must go forward with the Judd Street project, though,' Emma said. 'The house is almost completely furnished, waiting for you to claim it as soon as you are ready.'

'At the end of the Season, we shall claim it,' Olivia promised. 'Now, shouldn't you partake of the wedding breakfast to sustain you on that drive to Dover? I doubt that stopping for a meal is on your husband's mind.'

'Or mine either,' Emma said with a wicked grin.

'I do hope that look means what I think it

does,' Theo said, coming back to claim her arm. 'Shall we have a quick bite and be off?'

'Off to the Grand Tour you've always dreamed of?' She pressed his hand. 'I cannot wait.'

* * * * *

COMING SOON!

We really hope you enjoyed reading this book. If you're looking for more romance, be sure to head to the shops when new books are available on

Thursday 31st October

To see which titles are coming soon, please visit

millsandboon.co.uk/nextmonth

MILLS & BOON

Coming next month

MISS LOTTIE'S CHRISTMAS PROTECTOR
Sophia James

'Are you married, sir?'

'I am not.' Jasper tried to keep the relief from his words.

'But would you want to be? Married, I mean? One day?'

She was observing him as if she were a scientist and he was an undiscovered species. One which might be the answer to an age-old question. One from whom she could obtain useful information about the state of Holy Matrimony.

'It would depend on the woman.' He couldn't remember in his life a more unusual conversation. Was she in the market for a groom or was it for someone else she asked?

'But you are not averse to the idea of it?' She blurted this out. 'If she was the right one?'

Lord, was she proposing to him? Was this some wild joke that would be exposed in the next moment or two? Had the Fairclough family fallen down on their luck and she saw his fortune as some sort of a solution? Thoughts spun quickly, one on top of another and suddenly he'd had enough. 'Where the hell is your brother, Miss Fairclough?'

She looked at him blankly. 'Pardon?'

'Silas. Why is he not here with you and seeing to your needs?'

'You know my brother?'

Her eyes were not quite focused on him, he thought then, and wondered momentarily if she could be using some drug to alter perception. But surely not. The Faircloughs were known near and far for their godly works and charitable ways. It was his own appalling past that was colouring such thoughts.

'I do know him. I employed him once in my engineering firm.'

'Oh, my goodness.' She fumbled then for the bag on the floor in front of her, a decent-sized reticule full of belongings. Finally, she extracted some spectacles. He saw they'd been broken, one arm tied on firmly with a piece of string. When she had them in place her eyes widened in shock.

'It is you.'

'I am afraid so.'

'Hell.'

That sounded neither godly nor saintly and everything he believed of Miss Charlotte Fairclough was again turned upside down.

Continue reading
MISS LOTTIE'S CHRISTMAS PROTECTOR
Sophia James

Available next month
www.millsandboon.co.uk

MILLS & BOON

THE HEART OF ROMANCE

A ROMANCE FOR EVERY KIND OF READER

MODERN

Prepare to be swept off your feet by sophisticated, sexy and seductive heroes, in some of the world's most glamourous and romantic locations, where power and passion collide.
8 stories per month.

HISTORICAL

Escape with historical heroes from time gone by. Whether your passion is for wicked Regency Rakes, muscled Vikings or rugged Highlanders, awaken the romance of the past.
6 stories per month.

MEDICAL

Set your pulse racing with dedicated, delectable doctors in the high-pressure world of medicine, where emotions run high and passion, comfort and love are the best medicine.
6 stories per month.

Celebrate true love with tender stories of heartfelt romance, fro the rush of falling in love to the joy a new baby can bring, and a focus on the emotional heart of a relationship.
8 stories per month.

Indulge in secrets and scandal, intense drama and plenty of sizzl hot action with powerful and passionate heroes who have it all: wealth, status, good looks...everything but the right woman.
6 stories per month.

HEROES

Experience all the excitement of a gripping thriller, with an inte romance at its heart. Resourceful, true-to-life women and strong fearless men face danger and desire - a killer combination!
8 stories per month.

DARE

Sensual love stories featuring smart, sassy heroines you'd want as best friend, and compelling intense heroes who are worthy of th
4 stories per month.

To see which titles are coming soon, please visit

millsandboon.co.uk/nextmonth